The Vigil

Marian P. Merritt

The Vigil

COPYRIGHT 2014 by Marian P. Merritt

Contact Information: titleadmin@pelicanbookgroup.com

All scripture quotations, unless otherwise indicated, are taken from the Holy Bible, New International Version(R), NIV(R), Copyright 1973, 1978, 1984, 2011 by Biblica, Inc.™ Used by permission of Zondervan. All rights reserved worldwide. www.zondervan.com

Cover Art by Nicola Martinez

Harbourlight Books, a division of Pelican Ventures, LLC
www.pelicanbookgroup.com PO Box 1738 *Aztec, NM * 87410

Harbourlight Books sail and mast logo is a trademark of Pelican Ventures, LLC

Publishing History
First Harbourlight Edition, 2015
Paperback Edition ISBN 978-1-61116-414-5
Electronic Edition ISBN 978-1-61116-413-8
Published in the United States of America

Dedication

While writing is a solitary endeavor, making a story come to life requires the efforts of many. My thanks to the following for their encouragement and expertise. Your support helped make this book a reality.

To: Gary Zellers, CRT: thank you for sharing your medical knowledge. Any mistakes are my own. Nadine B., your keen eye enhanced this story. LSU's Website and its Cajun Dictionary and Prof. Amanda LeFleur for your diligent dedication to keeping the Cajun language alive. My high school friend, Melanie LeBlanc Acosta, who won the contest on my FB author page for naming the town in this book. The character Aunt Melanie is named for her. My dear friends and prayer partners, Lila C. and Lois R., your prayers hold me up and mean the world to me.

To my daughter, Hope, son, Scotty, and daughter-in-law, Barbara whose encouragement lifts me up and propels me forward especially on the days when the words won't come. My husband, Scott, who always believes in me and has been known to read the roughest of drafts and still have good things to say.

Lastly and mostly, to my Lord and Savior, from whom all blessings flow and for whom I write.

Praise for Southern Fried Christmas

On *Southern Fried Christmas:* A Colorado girl who doesn't cook goes south to write about Cajun cooking. Crawfish and spicy food are foreign to her but the candy cane is a joint heritage. Marian P. Merritt weaves culture (even a gator!), past hurts, a precocious daughter for the hero, and a trusting God into a precious Christmas novella. ~LoRee Peery, author of the *Frivolities Series* and *Creighton's Hideaway.*

Marian P. Merritt's *Southern Fried Christmas* is a charming trip through Cajun country at Christmastime. From traditional food to steamy humidity, I was transported to Louisiana for the holidays by way of this author's descriptive and realistic Deep South Christmas. I rooted for Denny and Kelly all the way and look forward to more from Marian P. Merritt. ~Carla Rossi, author of *Unexpected Wedding.*

With just the right turn of a Cajun phrase and the perfect dash of *laissez les bon temps roule*, Marian P. Merritt's writing takes this bayou girl home to Louisiana every time I open one of her books. ~Kathleen Y'Barbo, author of the award-wining historical series, *The Secret Lives of Will Tucker: Flora's Wish, Millie's Treasure,* and her latest, *Sadie's Secret.*

Marian brings Cajun culture and profound characters alive in her novels. ~Nadine Brandes (Brandes Editorial)

Un

Houston, TX

"Jarrod, stop! You're hurting me."

My boyfriend tightened his grip and twisted the skin on my wrist. "Cheryl, I've told you before about flirting with Barry."

"I wasn't flirting."

Another twist and then a slap to my jaw. My head shook from the force. He'd never hit me before. Bile rose and scorched my throat. Repulsion hit like a tidal wave while the ticking clock on the wall blurred, doubled, then returned to normal. Like the ticking clock, the repulsion remained. He'd hit me. He had actually hit me.

"Don't lie to me." His eyes bored into me like darting lasers. "No girlfriend of mine is going to embarrass me like that and get away with it."

Before I could respond, the second strike followed in the same location along my jaw. My pulse raced. A scream I struggled to contain escaped, fueling his anger.

Something deep within awakened. I'd become the thing I'd detested.

No. He wouldn't do this to me. I wouldn't be that woman. Couldn't be *that* woman.

I kicked his shin with all my strength while yanking my arm out of his grip. "I'm leaving. This is it

Jarrod, we're done." I sprinted toward the front door and freedom.

"Cheryl." His booming voice, edged with alcohol and demand, followed close behind. "Get back here."

Rage boiled under my skin, and the desire to hurt him gripped. A feeling I'd never felt before. I reached for the red ceramic lamp on the foyer table, but before I could wrap my hand around the base, he slammed me into the wall. Thankfully, he stumbled and fell to the floor taking the lamp with him. Its pieces shattered on the unforgiving tile.

With shaking hands, I struggled to turn the front door knob. Just as Jarrod stood behind me, I yanked the door and darted into the hallway. His slurred words spewed from the half-opened door. "You're just like Vivian, you know. Just like your mother."

Jarrod's neighbor, Brent, peered from his door. The knowing look on his face filled me with shame. "Cheryl, are you OK? I've called the police."

~*~

The drive east from Houston to Bijou Bayou, the only place I knew I'd be safe, proved to be the longest four hours of my life. Home. At the prospect, my sweating fingers tightened around the steering wheel. But the larger revolt came when I thought about staying in Houston. I couldn't risk being in the same town, no matter how big, with Jarrod Trumont. I feared for my life. And his.

Yet, the greater question loomed ahead: could I tolerate living in the same town as my mother?

Deux

Bijou Bayou, LA - Two months later

With a wrinkled, liver-spotted hand, my patient, Carlton Perlouix, brushed the strand of gray away from his face. "Need a haircut. Could you?" His gruff voice echoed against the twelve-foot ceilings of the near empty bedroom in the old Acadian style house.

"Yep, I'd say you do."

At seventy-nine, he looked much older. Cancer does that.

I hate cancer.

"Do you have scissors anywhere?" I searched his worn oak nightstand drawer, careful not to disturb the order inside. Patients who've lost control of so much in their life hold on to the little things, like insisting the tissue box remain in the same place, and was why he'd insisted on paying out of pocket for twenty-four hour home care.

"Bathroom. Top drawer." He didn't waste words. Talking required energy. Energy he didn't have.

In the bathroom, a pink-tinged towel hung from a simple iron rack. The top drawer held the aroma of mothballs and a barrage of bathroom items. I grabbed scissors, electric clippers, and a wide toothed comb, and then reached for the hanging bath towel.

"Lean forward a little." He sat up in his rented hospital bed. I slid the towel around his shoulders. "I see you washed something red with this."

He grinned. That Jeremiah-Johnson-man-of-the-wilderness grin. I'd seen it recently from my favorite actor in some newly crafted western. But never on Mr. Perlouix. The tough-guy grin suited him. I liked it.

"Ah, one load," he said.

I smiled.

Deep wrinkles covered his forehead and outlined his soft violet eyes. The lines circling his lips spoke of his long history with cigarettes.

Part of me delighted in helping while a tiny part reconciled that this wasn't included in my nursing job description. Then again the man was dying. I'd do what it took to make him comfortable. The injections into his IV, which struggled to remain in his ever-collapsing veins, didn't seem to be enough. At least not for me.

"Short," he barked.

A smart-aleck retort dissolved in my throat when I saw the lack of hope in eyes bordering frightfully close to death. If giving me orders made him feel better, I could take it. Of course, somehow I believed he liked to banter, and I looked forward to getting to know him better so I could allow him that pleasure. "Short cut or short shaved."

"Shaved. Military style." His lips separated the bare minimum. I'd had to lean in to hear the words.

"Were you in the military?" I knew so little about this man, yet for the past three weeks, I'd watched him wither away. Waited while death slithered a little closer. No family or friends ever came. How could someone live so long and be so alone? And how could I, a stranger, share this important part of his life?

"Korean." His wrinkled hand lay on his lap with

skin so thin I plainly saw the highways of veins and arteries beneath. Vessels that carried a mixture of blood, toxins, and whatever else his body chose to take in. Regardless of technology and amazing inventions, his body had the final say. And there was little else anyone could do. Except, I suppose, pray.

"That must have been tough." *Snip, snip.* Gray strands drifted down to his shoulders and rested there like feathers.

"Umph." He flicked the tobacco-stained fingernail of his index finger with the equally stained nail of his thumb. "Not for me."

My brows tightened. Reining my emotions proved difficult with this patient. "Why so?" I asked.

He shrugged his shoulders and took a deep breath. "Sometimes you're dead..." His eyes, burning with intensity, met mine. Sadness etched the corners. "...before your body says so." A fit of coughing racked him, jerking him right and then left and back and forth in ways his body resisted. The last snippets of hair drifted to the floor and rested on the worn oak planks.

"I suppose that's true." I struggled to keep my expression void of emotion.

I stood bedside, scissors in hand and waited. I knew exactly what he meant. The last few months with Jarrod had killed my spirit more than I realized. The anger I'd experienced with him scared me. Daily I feared he'd find me and finish what he started. One good thing about coming home, Jarrod feared my brother more than he wanted to harm me and would never venture to Bijou Bayou. I was also fairly certain he'd already moved on to another enabling girlfriend. But the lie I'd tendered all my life hung heavy on my soul. I'd thought I was above being in an abusive relationship. Although I hadn't stayed, I'd picked a man who could strike a woman. That crawled deep inside and coiled in my gut making me question my judgment.

Carlton's coughing eased, allowing him to take shallow breaths.

I wanted to know more about this elusive man. Until today he'd asked for and said very little. Asking for a haircut seemed to move me up to a higher level of trust. Yet I shivered to think that he could be a person so cold as to chase away anyone who once loved him. Was I mistaken to think that beneath the crude exterior, a layer of compassion and depth wrapped his heart?

I refitted the prongs of the nasal cannula into his nostrils and wrapped the tubing around his ears. Tightening the adjustment ring beneath his chin, I took extra care to avoid snagging the hanging skin around his neck. A quick glance toward the dial on the concentrator showed his oxygen level at six liters per minute—more than enough to sustain life. But his lungs ruled. In their malfunctioning and diseased state, they resisted what the tubing offered.

I handed him the glass of water from the nightstand and guided the straw to his cracked lips. While he sipped, I collected the shavings of hair and threw them into the small can next to the bed.

I stared at the discarded curls.

"It's true, Sherri, so true. Death can come long before the body quits."

I couldn't believe he had spoken the lengthy sentence. His words, driven by conviction, came from deep within. His violet eyes glistened making my heart swell. What had beaten the cancer cells to kill this man?

I started to remind him, for probably the fiftieth time, that my name was Cheryl, not Sherri, but didn't. It wasn't important. He'd mentioned the name several times during his drug-induced ranting. He seemed to derive some small measure of delight from saying the name, so I didn't press the issue. I didn't understand a lot about him. The sparseness of his home spoke volumes of the simple man, but I suspected there was more to Carlton than simplicity. The grimy dresser tops held no framed photographs. His walls were bare, with the exception of a calendar from a tool vendor, opened to February, three months and two years ago. Was that month and year significant in Mr. Perlouix's life?

Within an hour, I'd buzzed the remaining curls from his head with the clippers, leaving a quarter inch of hair, and then swept the bed and floor. With his shaking hand, he rubbed the top of his head, nodded, and smiled. A huge toothy smile. It warmth me. My time had been well spent.

When Darcy, my high school friend and the night-shift nurse appeared, Carlton had allowed the morphine to carry him to the place he seldom went, deep sleep.

"How'd he do today?" Darcy asked.

"Not bad. He let me give him a haircut."

"Wow, that's an improvement. He looks a little better."

As I gathered my things, Darcy reviewed the chart we kept on Carlton. I stopped on the way out the door and squeezed her shoulder. "Darcy, thanks again for recommending me for this job."

"Hey, that's what old friends do." She gave me a

quick hug. "I'm just glad to have you back in town. Have a good night, hon. I'll see you in the morning."

"You, too." I glanced back toward Carlton. "He should sleep for a while."

Part of me hated I couldn't tell him good night. What if he didn't wake up? But another part was happy he could rest. His mind surely needed a break from his haunting memories as well as the pain tormenting his body. Somehow talking about the war had triggered a change in him. His usual gruffness melted into a deeper melancholy I'd not seen before.

Today held many firsts.

The first time I'd seen him smile, the first time he'd asked me to do something out of the ordinary for him, and the first time he'd said anything about his past.

~*~

I steered my car along the winding road from Carlton's house. Mighty live oaks lined either side of the road. Their moss-filled branches provided shade to the small two-lane road leading to the one-lane bridge crossing the bayou. Its iron and wood moaned under the weight of my car.

What had Carlton's life been like? What had he been like as a younger man? A soldier. Had he been handsome? Brave? I merged into the late afternoon traffic of I-10 west headed home. What would he be like tomorrow? Each night driving home, his mysteries filled my thoughts.

I approached my exit, and switched lanes to accommodate the sharp ramp. I'd only been home two months and the familiar rushed back. My small town had scarcely changed, like so many South Louisiana communities.

Dread had followed me home, but I'd had little choice. I had to come back here to deal with the demons that had driven me away in the first place. Besides, I had to find a safe refuge. This was the place for both.

I liked the opportunity to get a place of my own in the hometown I'd abandoned thirteen years before. But was I coming home to freedom? Time would tell. Of course, it was better than moving in with my mother. We'd never survive living under the same roof. Dwelling in the same town was bad enough. She was my mother and I honored her, but that didn't mean I had to like her or agree with her. Then again, as much as I hated to admit it, I had become the very thing I detested in her.

I crossed the drawbridge, which carried me over Bijou Bayou and into the small community which I now called home again. The purple flowers of the full bloom hyacinths floating on the water danced with the cattails at the water's edge. All the things that made Bijou Bayou unique brought rushing memories of both the good and the bad of my childhood. Guess I couldn't embrace one and escape the other.

While I zipped into the parking lot of Marvin's IGA, I made a mental list of the items I needed for dinner.

Leaning on the grocery cart for support, I scanned the aisles. The day's events had sucked the last vestiges of my energy, more so than I'd realized. Seemed encroaching death had a way of doing that. I craved nothing more than to hurry home to a hot bath.

I picked up a bag of salad and examined the leaves for freshness.

"Cheryl? Is that you?"

That voice. The one that filled my heart during my younger years tickled my ears.

He stood amidst a backdrop of fresh pineapples and mandarins, wearing navy slacks with a light blue oxford shirt, his paisley tie loosened and the first button opened.

A little paunchier than I remembered with his dark hair, shorter and thinner, but the dark electrifying eyes remained. And now, they beamed on me and zapped a hole right through me. Just like before. Just like I remembered. Just like I'd once loved.

"Beau...hello." I kept my hands firmly planted on the plastic bag and prayed he wouldn't extend his. I couldn't touch his skin. Not with my clammy hands. Not ever. Heaven only knew what would happen to me if we touched. "How are you?"

He hesitated as though measuring his words before he spoke. "I-I-I'm good."

Beau, the man I decided at seventeen was the love of my life stood before me, and now thirteen years later, I couldn't think of anything to say to him. He'd stayed in Bijou Bayou, married my friend, Annie Melancon, and last I'd heard, had a son.

"How's your family?" I reverted to the typical Louisiana questions.

He fingered the plastic flap of the cart's seat. "We're managing. You know Mama passed away last year. She and Daddy are finally together. Got a son, Steven, he's ten and growing up into a fine young man. And Annie...is still holding on."

Holding on? What kind of response was that?

I paused. I'm sure confusion painted my face.

"You haven't heard?" He leaned onto the handle

of the shopping cart.

"I don't think so."

"Annie was in a car accident two years ago. She's in a long term care facility in Lafayette." He squeezed his lips together and blinked a few times. "In a coma."

"Oh." I dropped the salad bag into my cart and paused, unable to find words. I ached for him and his son. "I'm so sorry. I didn't know."

"You wouldn't have."

"Any chance...?" I asked.

He shook his head, gazed at me, and then into his cart. The package of crawfish boudin sitting on top became the object of his focus. I hated that my question had initiated such a response. There had been nothing Beau Battice and I hadn't talked about and dreamed about. Now we stood in IGA with enough baggage between us to keep a therapist busy for years. And the worst part, we didn't have anything to say to each other.

I wanted to say the right words to take his pain away, to make up for the pain I'd caused him. He didn't deserve this hand dealt him.

He was a good man—the kind who would be your best friend as well as your husband. A man who'd bring you breakfast in bed and know exactly how to fix your coffee. The kind who would never strike a woman.

He looked up, his eyes drooping at the corners. "I heard you were back in town."

"Yes. Been back a couple of weeks." Seeing him stung like stepping on a box of thumbtacks. Each time our eyes met, a prick shot directly into my heart. His gentle eyes reminded me of the biggest mistake of my life. I couldn't look at him for any length of time for fear that he would see through my eyes and straight into my soul.

His lips twitched into a half smile and a touch of mischief twinkled in his eyes. "How does it feel to be back in...let's see..." He pointed his finger in the air, or was it at the carefully stacked mound of cantaloupes? "...Podunk Bayou Dullsville? I believe that's what you called it."

Ouch, who said words couldn't hurt? Although I knew he was kidding, his words stung like a poison dart into my chest, real enough to take my breath away. I met the compassion in his warm eyes and smiled as best I could through the pain. I deserved this. And more. "Touché."

He grinned—the sweet grin that had melted my heart more times than I could count. Today was no different. "Sorry, *Te'*, I couldn't resist. You look good. I like the shorter haircut."

Double ouch. The nickname I'd not heard since I'd left seared a path through my heart. My lips curled despite the bittersweet emotion. The nickname stirred something long dead and brought back the familiar stirrings of youth, eternal hope, and invincibility. Funny he should comment on my hair. He'd loved my long curly locks.

"You're forgiven."

He shuffled toward the Red Delicious apples. "Well, I guess I'd better get going. Steven has a baseball game tonight. Playing at Toucoin's Park. You should come out sometime."

Dare I ever set foot at Toucoin's Park again? "Maybe."

"It's been good seeing you." He patted my shoulder with an awkward tap.

"Same here." Dare I return his touch? It had been good to see him, more than he would know. But I hoped I wouldn't run into him again. Seeing him brought back a rush of emotions I'd spent years running from. Could he easily capture my heart again if things were different? Who knew? But they weren't. I ran from a past of shame and fear while he was committed to a wife who could never love him or watch her son play baseball at Toucoin's Park. I saw no reason to flirt with the danger that seeing him again would bring. Especially seeing him at Toucoin's Park.

Trois

"Well, hello, Mister Bojangles." My new friend ran circles at my feet. The fifteen-pound Schnauzer barked his delight that I'd returned to bow to his every wish. I led him toward the laundry room and his leash.

I loved coming to my home here in Bijou Bayou. I'd grown to hate going home to the apartment in Houston. There I knew Jarrod would either be calling or coming by soon. At first, I welcomed his presence, but then my blood ran cold at the thought of a visit or call from him. Why had I not seen the selfish, insecure man he was from the very beginning?

"Cheryl, are you home?" My grandma's scratchy voice filtered through the screened door behind me.

"Hello, Mawmaw." I attached the leash to Mister Bojangles and led him through the screened door. "Are you out for your afternoon walk?" I'd rented the shotgun style house two blocks north of Mawmaw's and enjoyed her daily visits.

"I am. It's finally cooled down a bit, and I need all the exercise I can get. These old bones get awfully tired sitting around. Care to come over for suppa? I made stuffed crabs and black eye peas."

My stomach growled in response, but I was determined to shed a few pounds and resigned myself to the salad I'd picked up at the IGA. "I'll pass this time."

"What's wrong?" She cocked her head to the side.

"Is it that no-good ex-boyfriend?"

I shook my head. "No. I haven't heard from him." Mr. Bojangles tugged on the leash.

"Had a bad day with your patient today?"

I led my pooch off the porch and into the front yard. "No, it was better than usual. He actually smiled today."

Mawmaw stood at the porch railing. "Sure wish you'd tell me who he is."

"Sorry, you know the rules. I can't tell."

"I know. I know. Privacy thing and all that malarkey." She flapped her hand in her unique way of dismissing anything she didn't like.

I heard this same thing from my mama a few days ago. Both my mother and grandmother were curious to know the identity of my new patient. I'm still amazed that in such a small town as Bijou Bayou, they hadn't heard. But then again, Mr. Perlouix did live in a neighboring town and from what I gathered from Darcy, he'd only been back a few months. I never imagined thirty miles could help keep his privacy.

My short gray-haired-ball-of-fire grandma walked down the steps toward me. Her face contorted into an overabundance of creases. She placed her soft, wrinkled hand on my arm. "Be strong, Cheryl. Don't let a man lay a hand on you again, OK? Understand? Never." She squeezed my arm.

I nodded and followed her attention to a spot on the yard where the grass was a lighter circle of green, thanks to Mr. Bojangles.

A warm breeze blew through the oaks towering above us sending my hair in crazy directions while my grandmother's words sent my thoughts aflutter. Had my grandfather hurt my grandmother?

"Mawmaw, did PawPaw..." I couldn't bring myself to ask. I had such fond and wonderful memories of PawPaw that I'd be crushed to know he'd been anything but the kind, sensitive man I knew him to be.

She continued to stare at the yard for a moment longer and then shook her head and waved as though the somber exchange had not taken place. "No. No. Your PawPaw was a wonderful man. He never raised his hand or his voice in all the years we were married, he was nothing but good to me and the girls. After the Lord made him, I believe He broke the mold." Her lips spread as she patted my arm once again. "If you change your mind about suppa, come on over."

"Will do." I contemplated her words as she went through the thick St. Augustine grass. Would I ever be in such a long-lasting and committed relationship as Mawmaw?

~*~

"Mornin'." Carlton sat up in bed and smiled as I entered his bedroom.

"Good morning. You seem chipper this morning. How was your night?" I placed my bag at the foot of his bed.

"'Bout the same...restless."

"I'm sorry. I brought some books. Would you like me to read to you?" I held several westerns I'd gathered from the library.

After a while, he nodded and then pointed to an antique dresser in the corner of the room. Bare wood peeked through the edges where the dark stain had worn off. "Top drawer."

I dropped the books onto the chair and walked to the dresser. When I turned back to Carlton, he pointed. "Open it."

I pried the drawer and peered inside. The tender scent of lavender drifted out and captured my senses. Letters filled the space. Bundles of letters. All addressed to him with the return address a post office box in Bijou Bayou.

"You want me to read these to you?" I turned back to face him.

He nodded.

Something new he'd asked for. Another first. I lifted a bundle wrapped by a long strand of twine. A deeper scent of lavender wafted from the letters.

"They're in order." He took a deep breath. "Top right corner."

Faded blue ink marked the number two next to the postmark. A quick search through the drawer produced the number one bundle.

"Would you like anything to eat before we get started?"

He shook his head. "Just water."

I filled his glass and my own. After returning the westerns to my bag, I settled in the chair facing his bed.

With a firm tug, the twine fell apart releasing the letters. Aged paper crinkled as I opened the first envelope and removed the precious letter.

Carlton's eyes darkened and his labored breathing paused, causing a rise in my heartbeat. He stared at my hands. Only when I unfolded the letter did his raspy breathing resume. The words were written in black ink, faded on sepia paper. Broad, elegant strokes filled the entire page. I cleared my throat and began.

Dear Carlton,

It's only been two days since you've left but it feels like years. This bottomless void grows each hour that you're apart from me. I'm not sure I'll survive this tour. I miss you so much it hurts. Mama said it would fade as time went on, but I don't see that happening. Of course, what would she know about true love?

I hope you are well. Maybe you're settled and won't see too much action. I can't bear the thought of something happening to you.

The weather here has been unusually cool. For October that is. If you can imagine we're finally getting some cool weather especially after this summer. I'm holding on to the memory of our day at the water hole. I hope that day was as special to you as it was to me.

I have a candle burning in church for you. Please come back to me. I will be waiting here and praying for you. Write soon.

All my love,
Your Lady S

Carlton's gaze was fixed on the edge of the bed where I'd folded a multi-colored, crocheted afghan.

Was he thinking of the day at the watering hole? I imagined a younger Carlton, handsome and romping through the water with a laughing young girl—one with eyes only for Carlton and his eyes only for her. I folded the letter, careful to duplicate the original creases, slipped it back into the envelope, and returned it to the stack on the nightstand. A quick glance toward the bed revealed an engrossed Carlton still staring at the colorful blanket.

I slipped from the room leaving him alone with his memory. When I stepped onto the peeling paint and raw-wood boards of the front porch, the warm humid air engulfed while guilt riddled through me. A weathered wooden swing hung from chains attached to the rafters. I tested its strength and then sat. A gentle push sent the swing swaying. I glided back and forth and thought about the letter. I didn't belong in the middle of something so personal.

The letter opened a portal to images of Carlton I'd only suspected existed. But now the letter piqued my curiosity. Who was Lady S, and what had happened to their love? Was she Sherri?

I returned to the room to find Carlton asleep, his brows relaxed and his breathing, while still labored, didn't have the same desperate tone as before. I stared at the stack of letters. What answers did those letters contain? I gently tied the envelopes into a tidy bundle and replaced them in the top drawer of the dresser. If Carlton wanted more letters read, then I would happily oblige. Otherwise, his secrets would remain just that—his.

Quatre

I turned into the gravel driveway of my mother's house. The house sat on piers nestled among large oaks, magnolias, and dogwoods. A screened porch circled the front, sides, and back of the house. Maybe it would be cool enough to have dinner on the back porch. The setting sun would be nice this time of day castings its reflection on Bijou Bayou.

I climbed the fifteen steps to the screened door of the porch. A conversation group of brown wicker furniture decorated with lime green and blue flowered cushions filled most of the porch while potted plants crammed the remaining space. Vivian Clement Broussard did have a flare for decorating.

"Mother, I'm here." When I entered her house, the tantalizing aroma of sautéing onions and browning flour sparked the hunger I'd held at bay for most of the day. After reading the letter and seeing Carlton's reaction, I'd skipped lunch. The fragrance sent me back to grade school and coming home to the tantalizing aroma of her Cajun cooking.

"I'm in the kitchen." Vivian's voice drifted down the hallway.

Once I made my way to the large country kitchen, there she stood in all her glory doing what she did best—cooking. Steam from a large iron pot floated toward the exposed beams of her ceiling and curled the small strands of bleached-blonde hair around her temples. Today she wore a purple blouse over dark jeans. Her violet-blue eyes and curling hair reminded me of my brother, Anthony. He'd inherited the blond hair, beautiful-eyed genes, while I had my father's brown eyes and hair.

"Hi, sugah. How was your day?"

"Good." I slid my purse off my shoulder and onto her large antique table. She liked the distressed look. This table looked like it had been beat with an anchor chain and then left in a barn for fifty years. Six chairs, of different form and color surrounded the table. She also liked the eclectic look.

She pointed to the pots on her stove. "I've got all your favorites here."

The woman loved to cook, but mostly she loved to watch people eat the mountains of food she prepared. It was her greatest joy.

She smiled. "I'm so glad you're havin' suppa with us."

The first hour Mama and I spent together usually fared well. After that, neither of us could predict how things would go. Even though we had the same blood, we were like a Southern woman wearing a pastel dress and white shoes after Labor Day. We clashed.

"Thanks for inviting me." I slid onto the bar stool at the center island where the gas stovetop held cast iron pots in bright red, purple, and aqua. Each spouted steam trails toward the twelve-foot ceiling. I curled my hair behind my ears and then leaned over the bar and sniffed. "My favorites, huh?"

"Yes, ma'am. Shrimp okra gumbo and fresh green beans with salt pork." My mother wiped the counter around the stovetop, and then glanced at an index card on the counter.

Wow. I braced myself. She never cooked my favorite dishes unless she wanted something. I knew better than to say anything, yet.

"Thanks."

"I met Beau at the post office yesterday." She peered over the top of her cat-eye reading glasses. "He told me he saw you."

This was why I left Bijou Bayou in the first place. This place was too small to keep my business my own. "Yes."

"Did he tell you about his wife?"

"He did." I leaned back into the barstool.

"Well?"

"Well, what?"

Her fisted hands flew to her hips. "Are you planning to talk to him again?"

"I'm sure if I run into him, we'll have a conversation, but if you're asking if I've made plans to see him again, the answer is no. He's married."

"I know he's married." She huffed and then lifted the heavy cover from the large, bright red pot, the one that held the gumbo, and stirred. She continued to stir, never looking up at me. "I just thought that maybe you two could become friends again. He could use a friend, you know."

"I doubt it. Besides that's not a good idea. There's a lot of water under that bridge."

"What about Jarrod? Are you going to give him another chance? You know he makes good money."

I couldn't believe she asked that question, but then again I somewhat expected it. She allowed her abusive husband, Elray, to drive both my brother and I away when we'd graduated from high school. She'd chosen him over us shortly after our dad died. Hard to understand when you're five and your brother is eight.

"No. There is no second chance for Jarrod. I can't believe I was with him in the first place." I shifted on the stool. At sixty-one, Mama's beauty remained. Her violet-blue eyes with specks of gold reminded me of the sky just before sunset.

"Well, sometimes women have to make certain sacrifices." She tapped the side of the pot with her spoon.

"What? Are you serious?" I slid off the stool ready to have this long overdue conversation. "Not for me. I can take care of myself. I'll not sacrifice my safety for a man to take care of me. Do you really think Elray took care of you? Took care of us?"

Mama lowered her aluminum-stirring spoon onto the spoon rest with a slow, deliberate motion, all the while avoiding my glare. When she finally lifted her eyes to meet mine, anger flashed in them followed by sadness. "I did the best I could at the time. It's time you realize that. You never went without what you needed. Remember that." She flipped the heat off each burner, turned her back to me, and then stormed out of the kitchen. "Spoiled brat." Her last words cut.

Her bedroom door slammed a few moments later. So much for long overdue conversations. While Mama and I had our share of disagreements, she'd never acted that way before. But we never delved that deeply into our past before.

"Hey, sis." Anthony walked into the kitchen. "Where's Mama?"

I nodded toward the bedroom and gave my brother a hug. "She's in her room. We just had words, and she's not at all happy with me right now."

"Words? About what?" His confusion was evident

in his furrowed brow and concerned expression.

"I actually questioned her about Elray." I slid my purse onto my shoulder.

"Really." Anthony lifted his eyebrows. "Let me guess. She refused to discuss it."

"Not quite, she said she did the best she could and then stormed off to her room." I stood on tiptoes and kissed his cheek. "Good night. I think I'll go home. Tell her I'll call her tomorrow."

"I will. That is if she wants to talk to me." He kissed my forehead. "Good night."

I ventured out into the damp evening air and glanced at my phone. I'd been there a little over an hour. Some things never changed.

~*~

Carlton was awake when I entered his room the next day. "How are you today?"

He lifted his hand and vacillated it back and forth. "*Comme ci, comme ça.*" His lips tilted up to the right.

I hadn't heard the Cajun phrase for *so-so* in a long time. "Sorry to hear. Guess that's better than feeling worse."

He laughed. "Yeah, Miss Half-full. It is."

I checked his equipment levels and made sure he'd taken all his medication for the day. "Do you need anything?"

"I'd like to try sitting in my chair for a while." He nodded toward the recliner on the opposite side of his bed.

"Sure." I crossed to the other side of the bed and helped him walk the two steps toward the chair. Once he was comfortable, I draped the colorful, crocheted afghan across his lap. "Do you need anything else?"

"Nope." He pointed to the stack of letters on the nightstand. "Can you read more?"

"Sure." I filled both our glasses with water and angled my chair across from his.

I reached for the stack of letters and unfolded the next one.

Dear Carlton,

I hope this letter finds you well and safe. I got your last letter and have read it at least five to ten times every day. Yes, I am well and trying to keep busy. I miss you so much. Mama keeps pushing me to get out and do things with my friends, but nothing sounds fun without you.

I walked by Mr. Levi's place the other day and thought about the time you and I jumped his fence and his bull nearly pinned us. I was never so scared and excited in my whole life. That's what every moment with you is like— exciting. Everywhere I go in town reminds me of you. Which I guess is good since we have so many wonderful memories together. I can't wait for you to come home so I can be Mrs. Carlton Perlouix. That has a nice sound to it. Of course, if Papa knew that you had proposed to me and I accepted, he would be mighty mad. Even Mama doesn't know that I plan to marry you. I refuse to let a stupid family feud ruin our happy future together. All I want you to concentrate on is staying safe and coming back home to me. I will be praying and waiting.

Love,
Your Lady S

I refolded the paper and slid it back into the lavender scented envelope. When I reached to return it to the stack of letters, he stretched his hand and touched my arm. I gazed into his glistening eyes.

"Thank you," he whispered.

"Sure, Carlton. It's my pleasure." I swallowed back the lump lodged in my throat. Carlton had proposed to Lady S, but he'd never married. I knew that. What could have happened between them?

I patted his hand. His skin held a coolness that sent a chill through me. "Would you like to talk about these?"

He shook his head. "Read more."

"OK." I lifted the next letter in the bundle and read.

Dear Carlton,

Hello! My sweet Carlton, I miss you so very much. I wake up each morning and think of all the fun times we shared. My tantie came in from Arkansas yesterday. She and Mama are making jams and preserves today. So Mama will be occupied until Auntie leaves next Sunday. I saw Mr. Rayburn at the post office yesterday. He said he would hold your job until you got back, but he gave me "the look" like everyone else in town. You know that questioning look we got when we first starting hanging out together. Guess family feuds involve more than just the family. Well, I like being the one who will finally bring our families together. Papa hasn't been as grouchy lately. Guess he figures with you away, I'll forget about you. That will never happen.

I can't wait for you to return. I hope you're doing well and keeping warm and dry. Carlton, please keep dry if you can. I couldn't bear for you to be ill and I wouldn't be there to care for you like a proper wife should. You are always in my thoughts and I pray for your safety daily.

Mr. and Mrs. Badeaux said to tell you hello. They sold the filly you helped deliver. I'm pretty sure they got a real good price. She was a beauty. Just think one day we'll have our own farm and maybe a few horses. I hold on tightly to my dreams, Carlton, because they keep my aching heart warm while you're gone. I can't wait to see your smiling face again. Keep safe and know I am praying for your quick return to me.

Love you always,
Your Lady S

Carlton's lids closed and his steady, raspy breathing indicated he slept. The letter and Lady S consumed me. Who was she? As I returned the letter to the nightstand, Carlton awakened. "Hey," he said.

"Hey, back." I smiled.

He smiled, too. "That was my lady."

Should I dare ask who she was? "Carlton, is your lady still alive?"

He nodded.

"Does she still live in Bijou Bayou?" I sipped from my glass to not appear so eager for his answer.

"Can't say." He closed his eyes again and turned away from me.

I didn't pry any further. Did his answer mean he didn't know if Lady S lived in Bijou Bayou or he couldn't tell me? I helped him return to bed and he slept. He rested easier. It could have been wishful thinking, but I believe his skin had a bit of a rosy glow. Just maybe.

Cinq

"Cheryl, *ma petite,* would you like something to drink?" My Aunt Melanie's strangely mixed accent of Cajun French and the French she'd picked up while living in France, floated from behind the stainless steel refrigerator door. She wasn't the typical Bijou Bayou resident, but that was OK with her. She loved being different.

"Yes, thanks. Diet is fine." I sat on a barstool overlooking her sink filled with the bowls and spatulas she'd used to hand-mix the ingredients for her famous and blue-ribbon-winning red velvet cake. I inhaled the sweet aroma and vowed I'd be gone before she slid that deliciousness out of the oven. Just thinking about her slathering that amazing cream cheese frosting over her moist red cake weakened my knees.

Her flowing chiffon blouse in red, brown, orange, and teal floated around her as she swayed around the kitchen. I'd bet, if she ever sat still long enough, she'd attract hummingbirds. Her bottle-bought auburn curls danced around her neck keeping up with the shirt's fabric flouncing around her hips.

She handed me a glass filled with ice and a can of diet cola. "My sweet, this diet stuff is not so good for you. It's a conspiracy to make you think you're doing something good. I only keep these here because your mama won't drink anything else."

I smirked. "Must be like her."

She tilted her head toward me and knitted her brow. "Don't you even go there. Viv, you are not, but we do have to talk." She stood at the edge of the counter with a whisk and bowl of cream cheese frosting in her hands. "You're mama told me about the little discussion you two had the other night. Honey, I know how you feel about what happened to you during those childhood years, but you've got to remember, people had different ideas about what obligation meant." Aunt Mel stirred the cream cheese frosting a few times. "Your mama always had someone around to do things for her. You should have seen her in high school. If she dropped a book, there were at least four boys waiting and ready to pick it up for her."

"I'd heard about how Daddy pampered her, and I'd surely seen it with Elray." I slid my finger along the rim of the frosting bowl and tasted the creamy goodness she stirred. "And I'm the spoiled brat." My sarcasm didn't have time to register with her.

"When your daddy died, she fell apart. I think she married Elray so soon after because he offered her security, and he had the same last name as your daddy. Guess she figured it made things easier. Besides, I think he really loved her, and in her own way, she loved him." Aunt Mel placed the frosting bowl on the counter and then turned her attention to the sink. She sloshed suds around the bowl with the remains of the cake batter.

Such a waste. I dreamed of licking that red velvet batter. "I try to remember all those things. But I can't understand why she would allow Elray to hurt her the way he did. I would get so mad at him for pushing her around, and then I'd get even madder at her for letting him. Aunt Melanie, I know I have to let this go, but I'm having a hard time with that." I sipped the diet drink, vowing I'd give them up after I finished this one.

"Cheryl, did you ever see him push her around?"

"No, but I'd hear them arguing and see the bruises on her arms the next day."

"You could have come to his funeral, if only for your mama's sake." Aunt Melanie dried the last of the dishes and placed a sparkling china platter in the cupboard.

I hung my head. My absence was another sore spot between my mother and me. She couldn't forgive me for not coming back for Elray's funeral. "I know. I've apologized to her, but it's not enough. That was five years ago."

She slid her damp fingers along the edge of my hand. "I know, honey, sometimes it just takes time. Remember, your mama loves you, and she would do anything for her children. She thought she was doing the right thing. It hurt her when you didn't come."

"I wish I would have, maybe then the rift between us wouldn't be the gaping canyon it's become."

Aunt Melanie smiled. Her brown eyes wrinkled at the corners and glistened. "I have a feeling that being back here in Bijou Bayou will heal many old wounds. Maybe you two can come to church with me on Sunday. You never know what can happen." A ding echoed throughout the spacious kitchen. "My cake is done. Yummy. You'll have a piece with me, right?"

She donned two oversize mitts and then opened the oven door. When she slid the cake onto the counter, the rich aroma spread throughout the kitchen.

"Sure." I reached for the metal spatula. "I'll help you frost it."

~*~

My trips to the post office in Bijou Bayou proved an adventure. Who would I run into today? Someone who knew me when "I was just a little girl." It seemed Mother told everyone she met that her daughter had come back to her. Last week, Mr. Henri, the butcher at Henri's Meat and Greet had commented on my ex-boyfriend in a way that told me he knew more than I wanted him to about my past with Jarrod.

While walking toward the small post office, I rifled through my purse for my mailbox key.

"Whoa, Cheryl."

The deep soothing voice swaddled my heart like a blanket on a cold night. That voice, so familiar, had whispered loving words to me. Long ago.

I met Beau's intense eyes. He wrapped his hands around my arms to keep me from running into him. The subtle crisp scent of clean, woodsy, and manly filled the small space between us, awakening my senses.

"Beau. Hello." Unnerved by our closeness, I took a step back.

"How are things going for you?" he asked.

"Well, I'm trying to adjust to small town living again." Urgh. I wanted to bite my tongue and snatch the words back. Small town living was the reason things had not worked out between us. He loved Bijou Bayou. I couldn't wait to get as far away as possible.

He slipped his hands into the pockets of his blue jeans. "Yeah, I imagine after living in Houston, this place is pretty boring for you."

"I keep busy." I dawdled with the key in my hand.

He stepped aside to allow Mrs. Martin by.

I nodded toward the retreating Elaine Martin. "Now that she's seen us together, the rumor mill will be working overtime. I'd say in about an hour, at the most, the whole town will know we were talking."

He shrugged. "Who cares? People who know me won't care, and it gives the old people something exciting to think about." A grin spread his lips. "Even old people need entertainment. Don't you agree, Cheryl?"

I thought about Carlton and nodded. "Yep, they do. Guess I worry too much about what people think."

"Yes, you do. I'm on my way to Sammy's for a cup of coffee. Come join me. We can catch up."

Should I?

But...

Was I reading too much into the invitation? Catching up with Beau did sound inviting, and I wanted to know how his life had been. One cup. That would be all. Just one cup. "OK. I'll pick up my mail and meet you there."

With my mail in the deep pockets of my scrub top, I walked the block and a half to Sammy's Diner. As I slid into the booth across from Beau, the coolness of the red vinyl felt good through the thin cotton of my scrub pants. Especially after coming in from the stifling heat. A steaming cup of coffee awaited me. Its bold aroma and creamy color teased as I sat across from Beau. He had already put the sweetener and creamer in.

"Hope you still like your coffee with two sweeteners and two teaspoons of cream."

He still remembered.

I nodded and took the first sip, savoring the creamy richness. The first sip of a fresh cup of coffee — one of the few simple pleasures in life I held dear.

Determined to maintain the 'just friends' atmosphere, I thanked him and moved on to the catching up part. "I saw something with a Battice Medical Supply sticker on it and wondered if your family still owned the company."

"When Dad passed away, I took over running the place. All my brothers moved away, so I was the only one left. I bought them out a couple of years ago. So now, it's mine. I'm hoping Steven will be interested in staying here and running it one day. How about you, Cheryl? What are you doing?"

"I'm a hospice nurse. I'm doing a private duty job right now." I peered at the opening door.

His attention followed mine to the door and then tracked back to me. "Cheryl, relax. We're not doing anything wrong. I have coffee with old friends all the time. It's not a crime."

"I'm sorry. It's just that I remember our time together so long ago..." I ran my finger along the edge of the cup.

He smiled or maybe grimaced. I wasn't sure, but I saw a brief flash of pain cross his face. "That was a long time ago. My heart has healed, and I realized you needed to leave this town. This place held unpleasant memories for you. I just hoped we would make new ones that would be grander and better than the bad ones. Guess God had other plans."

I nodded. "Yeah, he did. But I believe I took that whole free will thing to the extreme. Lord, knows I'm paying for many of my poor choices."

His dark eyes seemed to melt at the outer corners. As the sunlight streamed in from the window, his eyes reflected the soft glow. "Not unlike your mother."

Wow, I couldn't believe he'd said that. I shrugged.

"Not unlike my mother. As hard as that is to admit, I finally realize I'm a bit like her."

He arched his right eyebrow, grinned, and then leaned in a little closer across the table. His clean-shaven skin glistened around the cleft in his chin. "Just a little?"

I refused to acknowledge his question. Admitting I was a little like my mother took more than he would know or understand. There was no way I would go any further.

I took another sip of the aromatic coffee and placed the cup on the table. OK, it was now, or I'd never have the nerve to do what I should've done years ago. I drew in a deep breath. "Beau, I'm sorry for the way I ended things with us. I never wanted to hurt you. You were the best thing in my life at the time, and truthfully, I didn't think I deserved you."

"Cheryl, quit apologizing. It's OK. Really. I'm over it. Annie and I had a great life together. Steven is a great kid, and together we're working through the rough road we're on. Although, I miss Annie terribly, we've come to grips with our situation, and we're doing OK."

"I'm glad things were good for you with Annie. I always liked her. I'm not sure why we quit being friends. We were inseparable until tenth grade." Although, a twitch of sadness and jealousy stabbed, I was happy for him. It had been my choice that we weren't together, and I'd let my friendship with Annie wither. "Tell me more about Steven."

Beau's smile stretched the width of his face and his eyes twinkled. His proud papa persona shone through as he told me about his son's extraordinary talent for baseball. "I try to keep things as normal as possible for him and try to spend time with Annie, but between work, trying to attend Steven's games, and the drive to Lafayette, I'm spread thin. I do feel blessed to have a few friends who help. While life hasn't been quite as I expected, things could be far worse."

I nodded. "Yeah, I get caught up in my little pity parties and then realize things are not so bad. Hey, Beau if you need someone to sit with Annie, maybe I can help on my days off. Do you think she'd be upset if I sat with her?"

Beau's lips curled into a smile, and his eyes creased at the corners. "Cheryl, that's the nicest offer I've had in a long time. At first, people came often, but as time went by, she kinda got forgotten. I believe she would love your company. She liked you, too, and never let our past bother her. That's the kind lady Annie was."

I jotted down my schedule on the back of one of the junk mail envelopes I pulled from my pocket. "Here's my schedule. When is a good time for me to drop by?"

He glanced at the scribbles. "Saturdays are good. That's when Steven has baseball games. I always feel torn on those days."

"It's settled. I'll visit her on Saturday afternoons."

He swallowed. "This means a lot to me, and I'm sure to Annie."

I became lost in his voice and enthusiasm. By eleven o'clock, I'd traveled back to a time when things were much simpler, although, I hadn't believed that back then. The uneasiness I'd felt earlier vanished, and in its place, comfort emerged.

A warm, safe feeling stirred—one I hadn't experienced in a very long time. Thirteen years, actually. I gathered my purse. "Beau, thanks for the coffee and the conversation. Both warmed my heart. I hate to run, but I have to be at work at noon."

"I'm glad you came. This was long overdue with us. We can do it again sometime if you'd like." He lifted the check the waitress placed on the table.

I paused and examined my conscience. I had enjoyed our time and saw no reason we couldn't continue this way. As friends. He had been clear about his intent to remain faithful to his wife, so I saw no reason not to meet him again. "Yes, I'd like that."

"Very well. Do you go in at noon every Wednesday?"

I nodded.

"Maybe sometime we can meet on Wednesday before school. I'd like you to meet Steven. It'll be my treat."

I hadn't expected him to want me to meet his son. "Sure, call me and I'll be here. I would like to meet Steven. He sounds like a wonderful kid."

As we parted from the diner in opposite directions and I meandered to my car, a twinge of doubt pierced. Would Steven like me? And would *I* be OK with just being friends with Beau Battice?

Six

Carlton sat in the recliner next to his bed and chewed a bite of Salisbury steak. Although, his skin sported a sallow tone, his eyes shone brighter today. More alive. My heart leapt. It was good to see him eating and looking better, even though I knew his prognosis remained poor.

He wiped the corner of his mouth and dropped the napkin into his tray. "'Bout time you get here."

"'Bout time you started eating."

He grinned and the corner of his left eye creased. I'd been right about him liking to banter. I lifted the tray from his lap and brought it into the kitchen. The aroma of pine and antiseptic filtered through the house.

"Well?" he asked when I returned to the bedroom.

"Well, what?"

"Where you been?" He took a few deep breaths. "Got readin' to do."

"Remember, I don't start work until noon on Wednesdays. Your housekeeper is here with you after Darcy leaves."

"Uh. I guess."

"Don't you let Darcy read the letters to you at night?"

He furrowed his brow. "Nope." He pointed his bony index finger at me and then at himself. "That's all."

"OK." My heart stirred knowing he trusted me with his precious letters. I performed my letter-reading routine—filling my cup and his before I retrieved the letters. The afternoon sunshine filtered in through the gauzy sheers. Its warmth, along with the steady hum of the concentrator and the air-conditioning, set the atmosphere for our reading session.

Dear Carlton,

I know it's been a few days since I've written, and I do apologize, but my sister broke her leg after a motorcycle accident. She took off to Lafayette with Terry Thibodeaux and they wrecked on the way. It could have been a lot worse. Terry had a few broken ribs. I've had to pick up all my sister's work and do mom's job while she's been in the hospital with her. Anyway they're home now and I still have to pick up extra, but I slipped away to write this note to you. We're getting ready for the holidays. I was so looking forward to spending our first Christmas together. Guess that wasn't meant to be. I hope you are doing well. Your last letter made me so happy. I was glad to hear that you haven't seen too much activity yet and that you are dry. Please keep your spirits up. I want to see your smiling face soon. I already see it nightly in my dreams.

All my love and praying always,
Your Lady S

Carlton's lids fluttered. "Tell my Lady..." His voice quivered making him pause longer than normal. Had he fallen asleep? "I'm dry."

I slid my hand over his and gave him a tender squeeze. "I'll tell her."

A heavy silence clung in the air broken only by the

concentrator's steady drone. His words hung like the morning fog. I tipped the recliner back so he could sleep comfortably.

Who was this mysterious Lady S? The content of the last two letters drifted in and out of my thoughts. Lady S had an aunt from Arkansas. Maybe my grandmother would know who Lady S could be. She would have been about the same age so maybe she'd remember someone in the community with a broken leg.

For several minutes, I watched the rise and fall of Carlton's chest as he slipped into a deep sleep. I ventured to the kitchen and washed the few bowls and cups lying in the sink and piled a few crackers and blocks of cheese on a plate as a small snack when he awoke. Just as I sealed the plate with cellophane wrapping, the distinct belts of an accordion from "Jolie Blonde," a familiar Cajun song, played in response to a call on my cellphone. Mother. What could she want?

"Hello," I answered.

"Cheryl." The way she placed more emphasis on the first part of my name made me flinch. Something was wrong. "It's your grandmother. She's had a stroke. They've just rushed her to St. Martin's General. I'm headed there now."

"Oh, no. Is she all right?" Not Mawmaw.

"They haven't told me much."

"I'm so sorry. I'll call the night nurse and see if she can come earlier, and I'll meet you there as soon as I can."

"OK. Please..." Her words were blurred with emotion. "...as soon as you can."

I swallowed and pushed away the grip of guilt and sadness. My poor Mawmaw. I needed to be there.

For Mawmaw and for my mother. "Hang in there. Have you called Aunt Mel?"

"Not yet. You were the first person I thought of."

Another stab of guilt. "I'll call her and Anthony. Please be careful and try not to be afraid."

"OK." The word escaped as nothing more than a whisper proving she struggled to keep her emotions in check. I hoped she would be OK for the thirty-minute drive to St. Martin's.

"Mom..." before I could say anymore she hung up.

I quickly made the calls I'd promised to make. Darcy agreed to be here in thirty minutes. I tidied up Carlton's kitchen and bedroom, checked his medications, and prepared the evening dosages for Darcy. As I stood at the foot of the bed, his eyes flew open, and he took in a deep breath.

Fear gripped me. "Carlton?"

His stare remained transfixed on me, but he seemed to be somewhere else. Was he dreaming? I came around to the front of his chair and with a gentle hand touched his arm. "Carlton, it's me Cheryl."

He turned toward me. His violet eyes sharp and clear. "My Lady, my Lady S needs to know I'm dry. Tell her I'm dry."

"Carlton, honey, wake up. It's OK. She knows. I'm sure she knows."

His grip tightened around my wrist. A memory and a flicker of panic blazed through me. Reflexively, I tugged against the pressure and freed my hand.

Carlton's brows furrowed and his lips pressed together. Tears dimmed the brightness of his eyes. "I'm so...so...sorry. So sorry. I didn't mean to...my Lady, please...please." His sobs and his struggle for breaths created a guttural noise that lifted the hair on my arms.

I quickly removed the nasal cannula and replaced it with an oxygen facemask.

I bent low and whispered in his ear. "Carlton, she's OK. Calm down and take deep breaths." I softened my voice. "Breathe in through your nose. Take a deep breath, slow and deep. It's OK. She's OK."

After a few agonizing minutes, his chest rose and fell in a sustained rhythm. Throughout the whole ordeal his eyes had been opened, but I didn't think he was awake. As he relaxed, the parchment-paper lids closed over his eyes, pressing moisture out onto his cheeks.

~*~

I rushed into the emergency room of St. Martin Hospital scanning each chair in the waiting room, searching for my mother. Anthony was offshore so he couldn't be here, and Aunt Melanie was out of town.

I spied Mother sitting in the back corner, her lively eyes dimmed to an ashen lilac. Streaks of mascara stained the outer corners of her face, and her ruddy cheeks puffed beneath the rims of her eyes. She stood as I approached.

"They're not telling me much." Fresh tears spilled onto her swollen cheeks.

I placed my hands on her elbows and met her eyes. "Mom, they're taking good care of her, I'm sure. Can I get you anything? Something to drink?"

She shook her head and rested it on my shoulder. I paused. What was I to do? I lifted the anvils that were now my arms and placed them around her. "She'll be OK."

"Mrs. Broussard." We both turned toward the

sound. A nurse stood at the double doors of the emergency room entrance.

Sept

My mother pulled away and darted toward the nurse, I followed close behind.

"What is it?" she asked.

"Your mama is stable," the nurse replied.

"Can we see her?" I asked.

"Immediate family only."

"This is my daughter. Show us where she is." My mom locked her arm through mine.

We followed the nurse through double doors and passed drawn curtains with swooshing and beeping noises following us down the hall. She stopped next to a single glass door and pointed to the bed. "She's in there with Dr. Sanders." She patted my mom's shoulder and walked away.

Mawmaw lay on the bed with hoses and cords coming from what seemed every portal of her body. The thin veil of her eyelids covered her eyes. The doctor stood at her bedside and reviewed the monitors.

While Mom usually roared into every situation with horns blaring and little regard for others, this time she acted differently. Her eyes met mine, and I nodded. With slow deliberate steps, we entered the room. Our arms still linked together.

The doctor looked up as we approached. "Hello." He extended a long-fingered hand. "I'm Dr. Sanders."

I grasped his hand when it became evident my mother hadn't noticed his offer. "I'm Cheryl Broussard, her granddaughter, and this is her daughter, Vivian Broussard."

He proceeded to explain that my grandmother suffered a mild stroke. She was being monitored closely. He also stated she had difficulty with her speech and some slight weakness on the right side of her body. "Fortunately, she received medical attention very soon. She's resting comfortably right now. We'll continue to monitor her for another few hours and then move her upstairs. Do you have any questions for me?"

No words escaped my mother's mouth. She simply stared at my grandmother.

Again I stepped in. "Prognosis?"

"It's too soon to really say for sure, but all indications are good for some degree of recovery. Can't say to what extent."

My mother's chest heaved as she sighed. "Thank God."

"Any more questions for me?"

"Not right now, I'm sure as time progresses we'll have several." I shook the doctor's hand once more.

As he left, he nodded toward Mama.

I nudged her toward the bed. "Mama. Come talk to Mawmaw."

She shuffled forward. "You never call me Mama anymore."

She was right. I hadn't in a long time. Why now? I couldn't say.

When we reached the bed, she rested her hand on my grandmother's swollen hand. "Mama," she whispered.

Seeing my feisty ball-of-fire grandmother lying helpless splintered my heart. What would happen to my mother if something happened to my grandmother? Mama relied so much on Mawmaw who was the strong force in our family—a true matriarch.

I slid my arm around my mother's waist. "Mawmaw, it's Cheryl. Mama and I are here."

Her lids fluttered slightly, and she half-opened her eyes. A moan filled the room when she tried to speak and then, as though she decided the effort was too great, she closed her eyes and drifted back to sleep.

The nurse came back into the room to add medication to her IV. "Mrs. Broussard, would you like to sit with her for a while?"

My mother nodded, and I guided her to a chair in the corner. "Mama, do you need anything?"

She shook her head.

I was at a loss for what to do next. So I sat next to Mama and slipped my hand into hers. We sat in silence except for the sounds that sustained my grandmother while she slept. I hoped she would return to her old self. And sometime in the hour we sat there, my simple hope turned into a prayer for both my Mawmaw and my Mama.

When the medical staff team came to move Mawmaw into an upstairs room, Mama and I ventured to the cafeteria for a cup of coffee. I flipped on my phone and scanned through the many messages I'd received.

"Did you get in touch with Melanie and Anthony?" Mama asked.

"I did. Anthony's shift change is today, so he'll be flying in tomorrow morning and will be here as soon as he gets in. Aunt Melanie was in Lake Charles; she'll be here soon. She texted me about twenty minutes ago saying she would be here in about half an hour. She said to tell you to hang on."

Mama nodded and sipped from the steaming cup. "Cheryl, your grandmother is a rock. I've never seen her ill or hurting. I wish I had been more like her." She stared out the window at an enormous live oak in the adjacent lot. Its large branches grazed the ground several yards away from its base.

I wanted to ask why she hadn't been more like Mawmaw, the woman who'd raised her. But Mama had been pampered, and I never understood why. Aunt Melanie's character traits and personality were more like Mawmaw's. Her fiercely independent nature contrasted sharply to Mama's constant dependence on someone. We sat in silence as the sun beamed through the branches of the large tree and into the window of the cafeteria.

My phone buzzed. "Aunt Melanie is here." I texted, telling her where to find us.

Mama sighed, and I wasn't sure if it was a sigh of relief or frustration. With her, it was hard to tell.

Moments later, from across the cafeteria, a kaleidoscope of colors captured my attention. Aunt Melanie darted toward us in a dress of vibrant colors. "How is she?" Her cheeks, reddened from her sprint, matched the shade of red in her dress. Her disheveled auburn curls stuck out in odd angles around her temples. Panting, she came around the table and sat next to me across from Mama.

My mother's intense laser-like gaze bored into my aunt. "Where were you?" She spat the words. Unbridled venom laced her voice.

I shot a glance at Mama. Had she spoken to Aunt Melanie or me? Her eyes were on my aunt. Shock rendered me speechless as I gulped in surprise. Where had that come from? My mother had never spoken to my aunt that way. She usually saved those outbursts for me.

Aunt Melanie slid her hand across the table and with a gentle touch, took Mama's hand. "Viv, I was in Lake Charles." While she was slightly out of breath, her soft voice carried no hint of irritation.

My mother placed her other hand over Aunt Melanie's. "Oh, Mel. I'm so glad you're here. I was so scared. Here alone with Mama. I didn't know what to do."

The skin on my scalp prickled at her words. Did she not realize I had been here the whole time?

"Viv, Cheryl has been right here. It's OK."

When my mom turned toward me, her eyes widened as though seeing me for the first time, or was it that she realized what she'd said? I wasn't sure and it didn't matter. Anger and hurt heated my face, but I was determined not to say anything to her. I would not engage.

"Oh, Cheryl. I didn't mean anything. I just meant that...that I was alone when I got the call, her only child here when this happened."

I couldn't understand the difference and why it was so important to my mother. But it did fit into her "poor me" persona and how she always got people to bow to her wishes. To feel sorry for her.

Rising from the chair, I addressed both my aunt and mother. "I'm going upstairs to see if they've got Mawmaw settled in."

Before either one could respond, I headed for the door. Why did I continue to allow her careless words to inflict so much pain? To slice open healed-over wounds and pour chunks of rock salt into them?

My grandmother lay settled in her new bed with a myriad of medical equipment attached to some part of her body.

The rules for ICU allowed only two family members to visit during specific hours, so I stood next to her bed and slipped her hand into mine. The coldness of her fingers sent shivers through me. "Hang in there, Mawmaw. Please." I slid my hand free, draped the covers over every part of her, and then headed for the door.

My mother and aunt exited the elevator onto the floor. "Is she settled?" My mother asked as though nothing had happened.

"Yes, she's sleeping. Y'all can go in to see her. Is there anything you need done at home?"

"I left a pot of soup on the stove. The heat's off, but it needs to be put into the fridge. Also, would you bring my medicine and a change of clothes? I want to spend the night here with her." She explained where to find her bag of daily medications and what clothes she wanted.

I didn't try to talk my mom out of spending the night. "Sure. I'll take care of it. Anything else?"

"No," she said.

As I turned to leave, she called after me. "Cheryl, thank you for being here with me. It meant a lot, and I know you're worried about her, too."

I paused. She sounded sincere, but I couldn't help feeling that her words were merely to make up for her earlier comment. My feet became logs sunken into swamp mud. I couldn't go forward nor turn back toward her. This was indicative of life with Mama—a revolving door of emotions that left me paralyzed. Why couldn't I just let things go?

Support her. A tiny voice echoed through my head. The invisible bindings that kept my legs from moving loosened, and I turned toward her. The few feet that separated us seemed like thousands. I wanted to be her rock, but each time I tried, my own selfish nature whispered: *she'll drain you, and who'll be your rock?*

Crossing those few feet took a lifetime. When I reached her, I gazed into her misty violet-blue eyes then gently put my arms around her. "I am worried about her." I whispered into her ear. "I'm also worried about you. I'll be back in a bit."

She buried her head into my shoulder and sobbed—deep gut-wrenching sobs that replaced my hard feelings with the desire to make things right. I imagined this is what being a mother felt like. Only our roles were reversed.

"It's OK, Mama. It's OK." With each gentle pat on her back, her sobs began to subside. She lifted her head and our eyes connected.

"I'm so glad you're here. It's nice having you back home." When she tried to smile, her lips quivered and tears spilled from her swollen eyes.

I offered a weak smile, which was all I could venture without becoming captive to the army of invading emotions. "It's good to be back." I kissed her forehead. "I'll grab your stuff and check on Mr. Bojangles, and then I'll be back."

I kissed my Aunt Melanie's cheek.

She squeezed my hand. "Honey, thank you for being here. I know your Mama needed you. Come back and sit with us." She smiled. "We'll be right here waiting."

I nodded and then headed toward the elevator while struggling to make sense of my emotions. My heart was swollen for my mama, and it felt nice in a bittersweet sort of way. As I walked toward my car, a voice sailed through the air from the far side of the parking lot.

"Cheryl, wait." Beau Battice jogged toward me.

Huit

Beau approached, his face flushed from the heat. "Cheryl, I just heard. How is she?"

Unlike with my mother, I resisted the pressing urge to run into his arms and melt against the support of his strong chest.

If only...

I shook my head to erase the plaguing thoughts. "She's holding her own. The doctor said she got medical care soon, so it's not as bad as it could have been. We still don't know the extent of the damage yet. Mama and Aunt Melanie are in the waiting room."

"Thank the Lord. I thought she...I thought it was worse." His warm chocolate eyes met mine, naturally easing the tension. It was Beau's gift. "I'll go up and check on them." He reached out and placed his hands on my arms. "If y'all need anything, anything at all, don't hesitate to call me. Ya hear." The tender squeeze conveyed his sincerity.

"I will. I'm going home to get some of Mama's things. Oh and Beau, thanks. Mama and Aunt Melanie will appreciate seeing you."

He smiled, nodded, then guided me to my car and opened the door for me. After I settled into the driver's seat, he leaned in. "I'm serious. If you need anything, please call me."

I nodded. Emotions attacked like a tornado— spiraling feelings that threatened to consume. I breathed deep and stared straight ahead. The huge oak I'd seen earlier from the cafeteria window began to blur. Not able to trust my voice, I simply nodded again.

~*~

Mr. Bojangles danced at my feet when I entered my house. The typical long, slender shotgun style home had each room flowing into the next and had been tastefully remodeled. The butter yellow paint in the kitchen and Mr. Bojangles yapping his delight usually lifted my spirits, but today, neither brightened my mood.

"Hello, sweetie." I opened the back door. He hesitated, walked back toward my foot, and then licked my ankle before darting through the opened door.

My smile spread despite my melancholy mood.

After changing clothes and spending a few moments playing with my pooch, I headed to my mother's house to gather her things and confront my conflicting thoughts.

I entered Mama's house, and the enticing aroma of vegetable soup surrounded me. My stomach growled. I hadn't eaten all day, except the cup of coffee in the cafeteria and the cups this morning with Beau at Sammy's. A cake plate filled with miniature pecan pies sat on the counter. No doubt Aunt Mel's handiwork. I'd recognize her baking anywhere. She placed a chocolate kiss on top of each one, as though the sugar and cane syrup weren't sweet enough.

I searched the cupboards for a soup bowl and the medications Mama said would be in the kitchen. The bowls were stacked where they'd always been—next to the coffee cups and glasses. Some things never changed. I guess that offered a certain degree of comfort, although, most times it didn't.

I dished several ladles of the soup into the bowl and popped it into the microwave. While the soup heated, I searched the other cupboards for the small red bag of medications Mama had described. The bag I found was red but not small. When had my mother started taking so many drugs?

I lifted the bag by the handle causing the unzipped flap to open. Multicolored bottles clanked against the tile, rolled around the kitchen, and then under the table. I dropped to my knees to corral the runaway medicine. As I gathered each, I noticed several were typically prescribed to patients with high blood pressure and a couple I recognized as drugs given for personality disorders. Crawling on all fours under the table, I gathered the last of the elusive bottles. As I slid from under the table, my cellphone rang.

It took me a few minutes to get to my phone and when I did, the caller ID showed my nurse supervisor's name on the screen. I slid the bar to answer her call. "Hello, Jane."

"Cheryl, how's your grandmother?"

I relayed the details. "We're waiting to see. I'm sorry I haven't called. It's been a crazy day."

"No, I understand. Darcy let me know what happened. Are you planning to be at work tomorrow?"

Work. I hadn't even thought about work. I was so focused on everything going on in my life, I'd completely forgotten about poor Carlton. "Jane, I'm headed back to the hospital in a few minutes. Can I call you when I get there? I need to talk to Mama. I should be able to come in, but I'll know more later."

"Cheryl, if you need to be with your family, I can get someone to cover for you."

"Thanks Jane. I appreciate that. Would it be possible to get someone to cover for tomorrow so I can be with my mother until Anthony comes in?"

"Yes, I think so."

"Thanks. I'll call you later. Oh, Jane, hold on." I read the name from a prescription bottle. "Who is Dr. Byron Dickerson?"

"He's the psychiatrist on staff at St. Martin's."

"Thanks, Jane."

After I hung up, I scanned each of the labels of Mama's medications. Based on the type and dosage, she must have serious problems. Maybe this would explain so much about the past.

My growling stomach reminded me of the bowl of soup in the microwave. After a few bites of the hot soup, I began to relax. Mama had not lost her talent for cooking. The subtle spice with big chunks of vegetables took me back to my childhood days. Cajun aromas greeted us at the door when we'd return from school. A snack waited for Anthony and me to hold us up until suppertime. Too bad Elray had been part of that picture. Had Mama been taking these drugs then?

I gathered her things, placed the pecan pies in a portable storage container, and headed back to the hospital. Was this condition something she'd battled all her life or just since Elray died?

When I got back to the hospital Aunt Melanie and Mama sat in the waiting room, deep in conversation. I handed Mama her things and placed the sweet treats on the table between her and Aunt Mel. I remained silent.

Our eyes met.

She smiled and then took the bag. "Thank you, Cheryl. I think I'll go down the hall and freshen up."

I nodded. After she left, I sat next to Aunt Melanie.

She reached for my hand. "You saw the meds, didn't you?"

Was I the only one who didn't know about my mother's illness? "Yes. How long?"

"All her life. But things spiraled into the deep end when your dad died."

The erratic behavior, her neediness, all the hushed whispers after explosive episodes, made sense now for the first time. "That's why she was so pampered."

"It took a while for an accurate schizophrenic diagnosis." Aunt Melanie laced her fingers through mine. "If it's any consolation, Mawmaw and I felt that you and Anthony should know. Your mom insisted you not know." She shrugged her shoulders. "So we respected her wishes."

"Why did she have me pick up her meds? She could have asked you."

"I think she wanted you to know but couldn't tell you. You'd recognize the prescriptions."

I turned sideways in my seat. "Was she that sure I'd look at the labels?"

Melanie shrugged. "I can't speak for your mother or explain her way of thinking."

I backed off. I'm sure over the years my aunt had been put in this same position and had learned the hard way to stay neutral.

There were some things I couldn't let go. "What's the big deal? I could have understood this more than her unwillingness to get out of a bad situation."

"I can't answer for your mom, but I do know she

did the best she could. Her determination to keep you and Anthony together as a family drove her to make some hard decisions. She wouldn't move back in with Mama. I offered to come back from France, but she wouldn't hear of it. So she married Elray."

"But with her men...her medical issues, couldn't Mawmaw have intervened?"

"Cheryl, as dependent as your mother is, she can be fiercely independent about certain things. She guarded her family and her decision-making like an alligator guarding her eggs. She made her own decision and dared anyone to question her. Another thing, I suspect after this morning's episode, that she's stopped taking those meds. Having you pick them up is an indication that she's going back on them. It's been a vicious and dangerous cycle."

"That is dangerous. Those are not the type of drugs you just stop taking. Have they been able to find a dosage that works for her?"

"It's been hit and miss. But when she starts to feel better, she stops taking them. Or something else makes her stop. I'm not sure. As close as we are, it's one area that she doesn't talk much about." Aunt Mel placed her hand on my arm. "Try to understand."

I battled with understanding. It was hard to forget the past and its pain. I stared at the tapestry of dull grays, greens, and blues of the institutional carpeting in the waiting room. Its design seemed to mimic my life at this point—random with no clear pattern.

My mother's loud whisper broke the silence. "She's awake, Cheryl. Do you want to come in to see her?"

My mother, a beautiful woman despite the smudged mascara, stood with shoulders erect, gleaming blonde hair with arresting violet eyes. The epitome of self-confidence, even in this unlikely place. For a brief moment, I doubted the meds I picked up today belonged to her.

~*~

The next few days, our family took turns keeping watch over Mawmaw. Her steady progress gave us hope she would return to her normal self soon. The stroke had not been as severe as her doctor first thought, which brought a collective sense of gratefulness to the whole family. Especially Mama.

I visited the hospital in the evenings after my shift ended with Carlton. Unlike my Mawmaw, his condition worsened, and his medications did not offer the same level of relief as in the beginning. His increased dosages cast him into long hours of fitful sleep. I performed the nursing tasks required and then sat and watched him sleep. The letters from Lady S sat on the nightstand like a patient lover, waiting to be embraced.

After a week of watching him sleep, I wondered if this was the beginning of the end for Carlton. Would he ever be lucid again, and would I ever get to know the real Carlton? Know the identity of Lady S? Had I read the last of her letters to Carlton?

I finished lunch and settled in next to his bed to work on the knitting project I'd started yesterday—a winter hat with a matching scarf. It seemed like a simple project and one I could actually complete. Although, in Bijou Bayou with its mild winters, I'd probably never wear it.

"Where you been?" Carlton's raspy voice echoed

through the quiet bedroom.

I lowered my yarn and needles into the basket on the floor and leaned toward him. His gaze locked onto mine. Did he know how happy I was to see those eyes again?

"Right here next to you," I answered. "How ya feeling?"

"Like I been hit by a wrecking ball. Twice."

I placed my hand on his arm. "I'm sorry. Can I get you anything?"

"Water."

I lifted the head of his bed. He followed my movements with a tender smile and kind eyes. I reached for the full glass and guided the straw toward him. Surprisingly, he didn't try to take the glass from me as he'd done in the past but let me place the straw between his dry lips. After he'd taken all he wanted, I wiped his lips with a moistened towel and applied lip balm.

He nodded when I'd finished and then pointed to the stack of letters on the nightstand. "I miss my Lady."

I'd missed her, too. "Would you like me to read to you?"

"Please."

I smiled when he said the word. "Be careful being so polite. I might mistake you for a nice guy."

He smiled and then his lips bent downward and a crease formed between his brows. He pursed his lips and shook his head. "Won't happen. I'm not...a nice..." He leaned his head back onto the pillow and closed his eyes.

Troubled by his response, I searched for what to say. After a few moments, he looked at the stack of letters and pointed.

I unfolded the next letter and began to read.

Dear Carlton,

I loved getting your letter the other day. It was so nice to hear about the other men in your regiment. Things are getting busier here at home as we get closer to Christmas. I really wish we had married before you left. At least if I couldn't be with you, I could celebrate Christmas as Mrs. Carlton Perlouix. Papa got really mad the other day at your Papa. Seems one of your family's horses broke the fence to our pasture, and several of Papa's precious cows got free. He had to chase them down the road about a mile before he could corral them. I wonder if they'll ever give up arguing over such mundane things. Maybe when we announce our engagement, we'll shake up their long-suffering, silly feud. I can't wait. Of course, they'll probably argue about me being too young to get married. I don't think seventeen is too young. Do you? I've been thinking. If you come home by next May, we could have a June wedding. I'll be almost eighteen by then. Do you think that may be a possibility? I hope so. I would love to be a June bride. When we go to town, I sneak down to the Woolworths and look through the patterns of wedding dresses. I'm looking forward to walking down the aisle and seeing you waiting there for me. I know you will be so handsome. Well, my love. I hear Mama calling. Stay warm and dry. Remember, I am praying for your safe return and waiting for you.

All my love,
Your Lady S

Carlton rested on his pillow, his thin lids covered his eyes and a tender smile graced his face. Not wanting to disturb his memories, I returned the letter to the envelope making as little noise as possible. The Carlton of these letters must have been a good guy. What had changed if his assessment of himself faired true?

I walked to the kitchen with a heavy heart. Would I ever feel for someone the way Lady S had for Carlton? Regardless of what had happened between them, they had loved one another. At thirty years old, I had yet to find that kind of love. Or had I? Could Beau and I have been that couple if I'd let things follow their natural course? If I had not run away?

I gazed out the window above the sink at the open field next to Carlton's house. The howling wind of a brewing thunderstorm blew the tall grass toward the east and rattled through the wind chimes left over from a happier time. Had Carlton put the chimes up? Or were they forgotten by the people who lived here before he did? The melody increased in intensity as the wind ravaged the chimes from different directions. The harsh notes and anguished tune grated against my nerves, reflecting the myriad of emotions eating away at my peace.

Was this just a case of self-pity?

~*~

Mawmaw improved daily. Conversations with Mama consisted of updates. She and Aunt Melanie made sure Mawmaw got the best care possible. They prepared Mama's house for her homecoming. There hadn't been any disagreements in quite some time.

Carlton's condition stabilized. He wasn't getting better, but the last few days he'd not gotten worse. The letters calmed him and gave him a reason to hold on.

What would happen when I read the last letter?

Carlton said Lady S still lived. What if he could see her before he died? I glanced out the window and into my own reflection. I'd allowed fear to control so many of my choices and had missed countless opportunities because I'd done so. So many regrets haunted me. I couldn't let Carlton die without seeing his precious Lady S one last time, could I?

There were many things I couldn't let go.

I hadn't heard from Beau about Wednesday breakfast. Had he decided it was best not to pursue our friendship? I'd still plan to visit Annie Saturday.

I couldn't accept Mama's illness. Why? I'd treated many patients with the same diagnosis. Was my deep-rooted anger keeping me from accepting the truth? How different—better would I be had my childhood been different?

One thing was certain—I didn't want another regret on my conscious. "I'm going to find out who Lady S is."

The words floated through the empty kitchen and when they came back to me as a whisper, I knew it would happen. I would find her.

Neuf

I navigated my car between hedges of purple azaleas running along Beau's grandmother's driveway. Before my shift ended, he'd called to see if I was OK after he'd seen a car like mine overturned in a ditch a few miles from his house. One thing led to another and before I knew it, I'd agreed to have dinner with Beau, his son, and his grandmother.

His grandmother would be the right age. Maybe she'd know who Lady S could be. I'd have to be careful with how I asked. But maybe, just maybe, she'd know. It was worth the effort.

Now that I'd decided to find Lady S, I plowed forward like a bulldozer. If the letters calmed Carlton, then maybe her presence would do much more. And maybe he could leave this earth with a clear conscience. Not that I knew he didn't—have a clear conscience, that is—but judging from his actions and words, I suspected something deep within him needed to release. And that something had everything to do with Lady S.

When I reached the top of the driveway, I saw Beau's black Chevy pickup parked next to the garage. Beau, in faded jeans and a green polo shirt, stood waiting at the front door. "Hello, I'm glad you could come." His smiled widened. "Shrimp boulettes with white beans and rice."

"Sounds great." My willpower skills for eating in

moderation would have to kick into overdrive tonight. "Thanks for inviting me."

His grandmother approached. She was dressed in a flowered silk dress, tall and elegant even at eighty. The scent of fried seafood and gardenias accompanied her. "Cheryl, Cheryl Broussard. I didn't know you came back home. I don't get around town as much as I used to." Her slender arms wrapped around my shoulders. She pulled me close, and her red lips kissed the air next to my cheek. "I'm glad you could have suppa with us tonight." She strolled toward the kitchen. "Food is ready when y'all are."

Beau leaned into the adjoining living room. "Steven, turn the TV off and get in here."

I followed Mrs. Mouton into the kitchen and waited by the table. Beau walked in moments later led by a lanky kid with the same chocolate brown eyes and thick, coffee colored hair.

He placed his hands on Steven's shoulders. "Cheryl, I'd like you to meet my son, Steven. Miss Cheryl and I went to school together. She's been a friend for a long time."

The lingering sent of fried shrimp boulettes hung in the air like our past. Steven's likeness to Beau took me back to our younger years. I extended my hand. "Hello, Steven. It's very nice to meet you. I've known your dad since he was about your age."

He shook my hand with a firm grip.

"And he looked just like you."

Steven turned to Beau. "Really? You looked like me?"

"It's more like you look like I did. C'mon. Let's get our food. Nana's ready to eat."

Steven reached for a plate and handed it to me.

"Here ya go, Miss Cheryl. You can tell me more about dad while we eat."

"Sure thing."

We served our plates at the stove and met at the dining room table. The white molding on the charcoal walls gave the room a regal look, not unlike its owner. Mrs. Mouton's silver bun gathered at the nape of her neck showcased her dangling pearl and diamond earrings. She sat at the head of the table, posture upright, and her head level above her shoulders with her sharp green eyes settled on Beau. "How is Annie today?" she asked.

Had she asked the question to remind me Beau was married? Beau remained Beau and didn't let her rouse him. "I called before I came here. She's the same. No change."

I hung my head. Maybe this had not been a good idea. "Are you still involved in the Junior League?" I asked remembering she'd headed up their cookbook committee for many years.

She shook her head. "No. Gave that up about a year ago. Don't like driving to Lafayette."

Steven snickered. "Especially, since you backed into the garage door. Remember that, Nana?"

She turned to him and smiled. "I remember." Then she turned back to me.

I racked my brain in search of other things she'd been involved in when we were in high school, but I couldn't remember anything. I squirmed under her intense gaze.

If she knew anything, now would be the time to ask. I'd told Beau I searched for information about a couple in the fifties, but I had not said much else. "Mrs. Mouton, I'm trying to find a couple from Bijou Bayou who were seeing each other around 1950."

The green of her eyes lit up and her pupils dilated. "Really. How interesting." She leaned forward. "Do you have any names?"

I paused. I hadn't said anything about one member of the couple being a patient, but I didn't want Beau to make the connection. "The man would have gone off to war. Korean War."

Her eyes flashed toward Beau and then back to me. She straightened her shoulders and aligned her spoon next to her bowl. "Hmm." She furrowed her brow. "The Perlouix family had a couple of boys go off to war, Carlton and Rusty. They were pretty popular back in our younger days for being rabble-rousers. They lived down the street from my childhood home, but *we* were never close. Then there was Troy Anderson and Billy Comeaux who lived in town. Those were the only veterans from our small town. Billy never came home." She shrugged her shoulders.

"Did either of them date a girl from town?"

She took a bite of her shrimp boulette and chewed for much longer than necessary. Once she finally swallowed, she patted each side of her red lips, placed her napkin back onto her lap, and then asked, "How's your grandmother?"

The abrupt change of subject threw me. I scrambled to understand why she would ignore my question. I turned to Beau. Had he noticed the brush off?

He smiled.

"She's doing well. We anticipate she'll be able to go home soon."

"Have you asked her about this couple? Did you know her family used to live close to ours out on

Highway 62?"

I hadn't known my family had lived out in the country. "No, I haven't asked her. Not yet. And I didn't know you used to be neighbors."

"We were best friends growing up." She sipped her sweet tea. Her gaze met mine head on. "It's a good idea to wait. She probably doesn't know any more than I do. Most good people kept their distance from the Perlouix family." Her forced grin made me regret accepting Beau's invitation.

"Well." Beau lowered his fork and crossed his arms on the edge of the table. "Steven is doing great in baseball. They haven't lost a game yet. Isn't that right, buddy?"

"Yeah, if we win all our games we get to go to state. Isn't that cool?" Steven shoved a whole shrimp boulette into his mouth.

Grateful for Beau's rescue, I nodded and thought of excuses to leave before dessert. The hammering pain growing in my temples should do it.

For the next half-hour, Beau and Steven volleyed for control of the conversation with exploits from Steven's ball games. I suspected the diversion from his grandmother was intentional.

I struggled through dessert, bread pudding with bourbon sauce, and Mrs. Mouton's fake smiles.

Out in the driveway, Beau opened my car door. "I'm sorry about my grandmother's behavior. I'm not sure what that was about."

"It's OK. Not your fault." I slid into the driver's seat.

Steven ran out before Beau could close my car door. "Miss Cheryl, it was nice meeting you. Can you come out to one of my games? I'm playing tomorrow afternoon."

What could I say? His big brown eyes were looking at me as though his very happiness depended on me attending his ballgame. With Beau's brothers living out of town and his parents gone, Beau was the only family attending Steven's games. "How about a rain check. I promised I'd sit with your mom this Saturday."

"You know my mom?"

"We used to be friends a long time ago."

"Cool. Maybe you can come out next week."

"Maybe." I smiled. "I'd like to see you slam those home runs you keep talking about."

Beau shuffled on the asphalt driveway. "Cheryl, if you're busy it's OK. You don't have to come out."

"Dad, she said she wants to see me play."

"Tell me what time next week, and I'll be there." I could do both, this one time.

Steven smiled and his eyes twinkled as he relayed the time and place.

The throbbing pain in my head ramped up its beat, and I knew I needed to get home. "I'll see you then. Good night."

"OK. Drive safely." Beau closed the car door.

As I drove away, he and Steven waved.

On the way home, with my headache in full-attack mode, I tried to rationalize why I'd accepted Steven's invitation but could only come up with one reason: I liked the kid, and he wanted someone other than his dad to watch him do what he loved and was good at. Saturday after next, when I went to Toucoin's Park, I'd know for sure whether I'd made a mistake or not.

I recalled Beau's grandmother's words and body language. The two did not match. Was she Lady S? I scanned every inch of my hurting brain to remember her first name but couldn't. I'd only known her as Mrs. Mouton.

Once home and neck-deep in bath bubbles, the tension in my muscles eased. Accepting Beau's supper invitation proved to be one of my biggest mistakes lately. When would I learn? Although meeting Steven had been the more pleasant part of the evening. But...had my curiosity about Lady S skewed my better judgment? The simple question about Beau's wife from his grandmother triggered a spasm of guilt that I'm sure manifested into my inferno headache. Maybe I deserved it. Maybe I should mind my own business and quit asking questions. Or had my questions hit a nerve that could reveal the truth about Lady S?

~*~

I spent Saturday morning cleaning house and playing with my poor neglected pooch. So much had happened in the last few weeks I'd been taking care of his primary needs only. Today I braved the heat and humidity and took him to a small dog park near my house. I sat on one of the park benches around a small pond waiting for Anthony, who'd promised to meet us there.

Mr. Bojangles ran wild after being cooped up for too long.

Anthony approached wearing blue jean shorts and a Festival Acadiens T-shirt. He carried two snow-cones, one in each hand. The gentle wind blew through his sandy-blond hair. So handsome and considerate. Why hadn't he been snatched up yet? "Hey, *Te*."

"Tante Lulu's snoballs. You remembered!"

"The best snoballs in South Louisiana." He handed me the dark red one.

"Anisette, my favorite." I sucked from the straw and was rewarded with sweet syrupy goodness.

He kissed my cheek and then sat on the bench next to me. "Couldn't pass by her snoball stand without stopping. Especially on a hot day like today."

"Thank you. These are as good as I remembered." I turned sideways on the bench. "What's going on at the Broussard palace?"

He laughed. "You got that right. It's like Mama is trying to turn Mawmaw into a queen. She's doing her best to pamper her. So you can imagine what happens when the pampered tries to pamper and vice versa. Not pleasant." He chuckled.

I laughed with him. "I bet it would rival the best reality shows."

"Yep. Mawmaw is ready for her own house and keeps bugging Mama to take her home."

Mr. Bojangles dropped his ragged tennis ball at my feet. I picked it up and threw it toward the woods. "I bet she is. She's not one to be taken care of. She likes to be the one in charge. Do you think she's ready?"

"I don't know. She doesn't seem to remember things as well as she did before. I'm a little worried about her being alone just yet." He used the straw-spoon combination to shovel bits of blue bubble-gum flavored ice into his mouth. The edges of his lips sported a shade of electric blue. "Are you going over today? Maybe you can talk some sense into her."

"Me?" I pointed to my chest. "Yeah, right. Like I could make Clarice Clement do anything she doesn't want to do."

"She is pretty stubborn." Anthony lifted the ball

Mr. Bojangles dropped at his feet. He stood and flung it across the park. We both watched in horror as it sailed toward the pond. I held my breath hoping it wouldn't go in. My crazy dog would jump right in after it. Nothing like a gray and white dog in muddy pond water.

Anthony handed me his snoball and darted toward the pond.

I placed the tips of our snoball between the slants of the bench and raced after him.

His broad shoulders and athletic frame moved like lightning toward my dog. As fast as Anthony beamed forward, he missed by seconds.

The ball made a huge splash followed by a bigger one made by Mr. Bojangles.

Anthony turned back to me as I sailed after them. He shrugged his shoulders, kicked off his shoes, and tromped into the muddy water after my soaked dog.

He lifted my dripping Schnauzer from the pond and onto the bank and even went in after the floating ball that Mr. Bojangles had missed. Anthony threw the ball back toward the bench, and we both laughed as mud and water flew out from the once clean gray fur attached to the overexcited dog.

I grabbed Anthony's shoes and headed back to the bench. Anthony caught up to me as Mr. Bojangles, covered in muck and mud, met us with the ball firmly planted between his teeth.

"He's like a robot. Does he ever get tired of fetching?"

"Yes, in about thirty minutes."

Anthony flung the ball away from the pond and then plopped next to me. Our icy treats slumped over as the hot sun melted them. We gathered what was left

Marian P. Merritt

and slurped the slushy mix while Mr. Bojangles fetched his favorite toy.

I loved Anthony's patience and gentle spirit. He was three years older than me and had not yet married. I wondered if he had some of the same hang ups I did. I slid my knee onto the bench and turned toward him. "Anthony, do you ever wonder why we aren't married yet?"

He snickered or sighed. I couldn't tell which. "Yeah, I wonder, and then I quickly erase the thought." His eyes twinkled and tiny lines creased in the corners when he smiled.

"Seriously. Do you?"

He grabbed my hand. "*Te.* Yeah, I do wonder. I want a wife and kids. The whole thing, but then I think of Mama's marriage and the pain it caused all of us. I'm not sure I could do it. Besides working seven-and-seven is hard on a marriage. I see those men with families. They're miserable when they're offshore. Of course, those are the ones who still care. Some of the men have empty-shell marriages so they're happy offshore and dread going home. And then there are the ones who are crazy jealous and fear their wives are cheating on them when they're gone. Sad thing is, some of them are right."

"You know we had it good when Daddy was alive. I don't remember too much but enough to know that Mama was happy and Daddy was a good man."

He nodded. "He was. They were happy together. Mama didn't act all weird with him."

"I know we didn't have a good role model for a happy marriage after Daddy died, but we both know that. So why haven't we been able to commit?"

He shrugged his shoulders. "I haven't found the

right girl. I know that. The truth is, I'm not going to find her unless I leave here."

"Well, a lot of good it did me to leave. I didn't find Mr. Right. And Houston is a big city. What about Angelle? Y'all dated for a while."

"That was twelve years ago. She wanted a ring. I didn't want to be married then. So she went off to college. Last I heard, she graduated from med school and was doing her residency at Children's Hospital in New Orleans. I often wonder if she was "the one" I let get away." He patted Mr. Bojangles on the head and tossed his ball again.

"Is she married?" I asked.

He shook his head. "I don't know."

A smile tugged at the corner of my lips. "We could find out."

"What do you mean?"

"Duh, the Internet has everything. Especially if she's a doctor. We could find out real quick."

The corners of his eyes squinted as he contemplated what I suggested. "It would be nice to know. Not that I'll go find her or anything."

I laughed. "Why not go find her? Or at least send an e-mail or call. What would be the harm in that?"

"Cheryl, you don't know what you're asking." He wiped off the perspiration dripping from his temple with the sleeve of his T-shirt.

"What do you mean by that?"

"If I called her, I'd be opening a can of worms I'm not sure I can deal with."

A panting Mr. Bojangles perched at my feet.

"Let's go back to my house and see if she's married. If not, you can think about what to do next. No pressure. 'K?" The word was one we used as kids when we wanted to reassure each other we were fine.

"'K." He smiled revealing a line of blue along his lips and on his teeth.

I laughed and stuck my tongue out at him knowing mine was a deep dark red. Just like when we were kids.

~*~

"Look." I pointed to the picture of Dr. Angelle Guidry on the St. Theresa's Children's Clinic homepage. "Same last name. My bet is, she's still single."

The corners of Anthony's lips spread into a slow smile.

Angelle's golden-brown hair reflected the light and her butterscotch eyes stared back from a professional photograph on the staff page. Her embroidered lab coat boasted her name. The website listed her as a pediatrician.

I'm sure her patients adored her.

Not unlike my older brother, judging from the way his eyes never left the screen. "Wow," he finally said. "She hasn't changed much.

"Oh, I bet she's changed a lot." I clicked on the *contact us* tab and jotted down the address and phone number to the clinic. I pressed the sticky note into Anthony's hand. "Here you go, bro. It's up to you. My bet is she would love to hear from you, and you know she's less than two hours away."

He slipped the note into his pocket. "I must be crazy for letting you talk me into this. I was better off not knowing."

"Really?" I arched my brow. "Really?"

He squinted and glared. "Yes. Really."

I shook my head. "I don't think so. You should call her."

"I'll think about it." He turned away.

"Anthony." I placed my hand on his arm. "I let Beau get away and look where we are now. He's married but doesn't have his wife. It's an impossible situation for us. But maybe for you and Angelle, it's not too late. Promise me you'll give it some serious thought."

He kissed my forehead the way he used to when we were teenagers. "I love you, sis, and I promise I'll think about it."

After he left, I gave Mr. Bojangles a well-needed bath. He went to his cozy bed in the living room and fell asleep. I envied him. I took forever to fall asleep.

I glanced toward the clock. Just enough time to grab a bite for lunch and drive to Lafayette.

A quick phone call to Mama confirmed what Anthony said.

"She's driving me crazy, Cheryl," Mama whispered. An interesting choice of words coming from her, but I let it pass. We had not discussed the pills, and I hoped my visit later this afternoon would present the opportunity. "Can you come over and talk to her? You're a nurse. She might listen to you."

This was big coming from her. That she thought I could accomplish something she couldn't was a first. "I'll be over later. But first, I'm going to see Annie Battice."

Her silence spoke volumes.

I smiled and then hung up.

Dix

The familiar scent of pine and ammonia mingled through the halls of the long-term care facility. In the shiny floor, I saw the reflection of an elderly lady walking toward me. She smiled as she passed by. The nurses had been pleasant at the front desk, and when they'd discovered Beau had left my name as a visitor today, they gave me a visitor's badge and directions to Annie's room.

As I entered her room, the familiar, yet foreign greeted me. I'd treated patients in comas before, but never one who'd been in a coma for so long. Her thin body lay tilted slightly toward the right where the nurses had turned her for pressure relief. Her thin arms seemed about the same size they were when we were teens. Annie's skin glistened from a freshly applied layer of lotion. The lingering floral scent hung in the air next to her bed. As I gazed into her pale face and lips, I was surprised to see peace settled there. And relieved to see her small button nose, long elegant eyelashes, and high defined cheekbones remained. Her long, dark hair had been cut into a short, layered style perfectly framing her heart-shaped face.

A well-worn recliner sat next to her bed. I lowered both my purse and the small bag I brought to the floor and sat next to her. Once her hand lay cradled in my own, I began, "Annie, hi, it's Cheryl Broussard. Bet you never expected to hear from me." I laughed, the nervous laugh of someone uncertain of what to say next because truth was I didn't know what to say and, at that moment, wondered why I'd come.

I cleared my throat. "Let's try this again. I came to say hello and also to apologize for losing touch all those years ago. We had a lot of fun times as kids." Thousands of memories flooded and as they came to mind, I shared them with her. If she heard me, I know she'd remember them, too, and was laughing inside. The thought made me smile.

The words flowed along with the easy laughter that came with our childhood antics. I reached down and retrieved the bottle of nail polish I'd brought. It was her favorite shade of pink. We'd spent long summer afternoons during our pre-teen years painting each other's nails—fingers and toes.

The promise we'd made that hot August afternoon so many years ago came to me as though Annie herself had whispered the memory into the room. "No respectful Bijou Bayou woman will ever spend a summer in flip-flops unless her nails are painted," she'd said. "Pinky promise." She'd lifted her pinky, and I'd hooked mine with hers. "We'll never wear flip-flops without nail polish. Ever."

As the memory washed over me, I longed for that kind of friendship again. I craved it more than I had realized. With a gentle touch, I slid the polish-filled brush along her nails, one after the other until each fingernail glistened pink and shiny.

"Annie Melancon Battice, you sly girl. I never knew you were sweet on Beau. Of course, with all my ranting on about him and how I was going to marry him, I never really gave you a chance, did I?" I paused. "Annie, I'm glad you married Beau and that you were happy together. Honest."

Next, I moved to her toes all the while telling her this incredible love story about this couple from Bijou Bayou who were in love during the Korean War.

Once each toe was as shiny as her fingers, I blew tenderly over her feet. After a while, I returned to the comfortable chair, leaned back, closed my eyes, and absorbed the silence. Somehow being with my childhood friend had made me feel better. And for a short while, I'd forgotten that she was Beau Battice's wife.

~*~

The minute I shifted my car into park, Mama appeared at my window. Strands of hair curled around her face and neck. Her skin lacked the usual even tone of perfectly applied makeup. When I rolled down the window she said, "Oh, Cheryl, it's about time you got here. She's packing her suitcase, and I can't stop her."

"OK, I'll talk to her."

I followed a scrambling Mama up the sidewalk. She kept turning around to list the things Mawmaw had done this morning. Once inside the house, Mama's heels clicked on the hardwood floors as she scurried to the guestroom where Mawmaw stayed.

I had little choice but to follow.

The guest room sported lavender walls, ruffled comforter, and frilly curtains—so not my grandmother. She was the solid-color-no-frills kind of gal and must have hated staying in this room. She stood next to the white four-poster bed, tossing items into her suitcase.

I knocked on the doorframe. "Can I come in?"

She turned toward me, shot a simple smile, and

then resumed her task. "Only if you gonna help."

She'd made up her mind.

"I hear you're going back home."

"Yep."

"Do you think that's a good idea? It's only been a couple weeks since you left the hospital." I folded a white cotton nightgown and handed it to her.

"The doctors said I'm fine. The stroke was very mild. Look." She wiggled her fingers and then did a little jig next to the bed. "I'm as good as new. Nothing is wrong with me."

"Anthony said you were having trouble remembering some things."

She flapped her hand. "Phffff. That's malarkey. I'm almost eighty. It's natural to have trouble remembering things." She continued layering clothes in her suitcase.

I couldn't argue with her. "Mawmaw, Mama's worried about you being home alone. She's concerned that something will happen."

Mawmaw stopped packing and turned to me. Her sharp blue eyes lasered into me. "Something will happen if I stay here. Your mama means well, but she's driving me crazy. She treats me like an invalid." She stomped her foot. "And I'm not."

"OK. OK." I placed my hand on her elbow and guided her to the chair next to the bed. I sat on the bed facing her. "What if I talked to her, told her to back off some? She's only trying to help you. And--" I touched her hand and stared into her eyes. "--you have to admit, she's never been taught how to take care of anyone. Everyone has always taken care of her. Even when we were little, you took care of us more than she did."

My grandmother pursed her lips and stared back. At first I thought I had really infuriated her, but finally she spoke. "Honey, you're right. But I'm not changing my mind. I'm going home."

"OK, I'll support your decision. But you have to agree to a few things before I'll back you."

She turned her head toward the side and narrowed her right eye. "And if I don't?"

"I won't tell Mama I think you're ready to be home alone."

"That's blackmail." She folded her arms and jutted her chin. Her eyes sparked.

"Call it what you like. Don't you want to hear what you have to agree to?"

She sighed. "OK."

"No cooking. Mama cooks your meals and brings them to you or freezes them for you to microwave later. No housework. None. That includes laundry. I'll send the lady that does my housekeeping to your house twice a week. No walks until I get home from work. We'll go for afternoon walks together. And if you feel the slightest, tiniest bit dizzy or have a headache, you call Mama or Aunt Melanie immediately. Oh, and one more thing, I'm getting one of those alert buttons that you can press and it contacts emergency services. You have to wear one." I tried to think of what else she might attempt but couldn't come up with anything. "And whatever else we catch you doing that can harm you; we have the right to limit, too."

Her eyes widened at the last item on my list. "What? An open-ended agreement? Ya think that's fair?"

I shrugged and smiled. "Take it or leave it." I

patted the flowered bedspread and exaggerated a glance around the room. "You could be sleeping in your own bed tonight. No flowered frilly anywhere."

"I'll take it."

"I'll talk to Mama."

Now the real fun would begin. When I left the room, I caught a glimpse of my mother's back rounding the corner. Eavesdropping? My mother? She looked up from the pot she was stirring. "Well, did you talk some sense into her?"

I sighed. This would be much harder than I thought. I shook my head. "Mama, she's determined, and you know how she is when she's determined."

"I know. But—"

"But I made her promise to let you cook her meals and bring them to her. Are you OK with that?"

"Well, I guess, but who'll stay with her? I'm not staying in that tiny cottage with her. There's only one bedroom."

"I think she'd be OK at home if she doesn't have to cook or clean. I'll send my cleaning lady to help a few times a week."

Mama put the spoon down and returned the lid to the pot. She walked around the bar to where I stood. "Cheryl, if anything happens to her, I'll never forgive myself for letting her go."

I grabbed my mother's hand and tenderly brushed the top of her thumb. "Mama, something could happen to her here just as easy. And she's not happy here. She wants to be in her own home. Surely, you can understand how she feels."

She took a deep breath. "You'll check in on her when you get back from work?" Tears glistened in my mother's eyes.

"Yes. I promised I would walk with her in the afternoons. She had to agree to never walk alone and to not go out in the heat of the middle of the day."

"What about her medicines? She'll forget to take them."

"We'll get her one of those pill boxes and you can call her every day or make sure she takes them when you bring her breakfast."

"Will she let me do that?" she asked.

"I think she will. But you can't hover, OK? No hovering. She needs her space. You know how independent she is."

"OK, I'll go help her finish packing."

"Err...Mama, I don't think that's necessary."

Mawmaw appeared, suitcase in tow.

~*~

Once Mawmaw was settled in her house and Mama gone, I sat at her kitchen table with a cup of my favorite dark roast coffee.

She steeped the coffee into an aluminum pot through a handmade filter made from an old flour sack. Her coffee rivaled the most popular expensive brands and came with special memories. When she walked into the kitchen, the setting sun beaming through the window reflected off her face, emphasizing the lines around her eyes and mouth.

For the first time, I realized she was getting old.

She filled so many of my childhood memories in her larger-than-life way. Her take-charge nature and can-do attitude gave me so much. I'd refused to recognize her aging body, but today the wrinkles gathered around her tired eyes did it.

"I'm a little pooped from all that drama today," she said.

I poured the dark liquid into her delicate demitasse as she sat next to me. "Ah, you know you loved every bit of it. Besides that wasn't drama. It could have been much worse. I believe Mama gave in pretty easily. Maybe you were driving her a bit crazy, too." I winked.

She rubbed her hands together and giggled. "Maybe my plan worked."

"Mawmaw!" I gave her my best wide-eyed and surprised look.

She flipped her wrist and grinned. "I'm only kidding."

I nodded, but a niggling doubt made me wonder.

While we sipped from rose-patterned cups, Mrs. Mouton's words invaded my thoughts. "Tell me something. Did your family have a farm on Highway 62 outside of town?"

She placed her cup on the table. "We did. Daddy raised cattle, and we had some chickens, too. We were pretty happy out there. Lived next to my best friend, Sylvia Mouton. But later, after we'd all gotten married, it was too much for just Papa and Mama. When Papa died, Mama sold the whole place to Mr. Dugas." The wrinkles around her eyes softened.

Had I heard her correctly? Beau's grandmother, Sylvia Mouton? Her first name was Sylvia. Could she be Lady S? "Mr. Dugas's place used to belong to our family?" I couldn't believe the large farm used to be my grandparents' place.

"Not quite. He bought our place and several of the neighbor's places as they got too old to care for them."

I took a sip of my sweetened coffee. "Did the

Perlouixs live close by?"

The blue in her eyes seemed to lighten for a split second. "Why do you ask? Do you know the Perlouixs?"

Great. I'd backed myself into this corner. If I told her, I'm pretty sure she would deduce he was my patient. "I had dinner with Beau's grandmother, and she mentioned the Perlouixs lived on Highway 62, also. She said two of the boys went off to war."

"Yep, they did." She furrowed her brows and tilted her head toward me. "Why is this important to you?"

"I'm curious about a love affair that happened back in 1950 between one of the Perlouix boys and a young lady from Bijou Bayou."

"How did you hear about that?"

"From some old letters." I took the last sip from my cup.

"Really? Where did you come across these letters?"

Her rapid-fire questions darted like bullets, and she hadn't really answered any of mine. I repeated my question. "Did the Perlouixs live close to you?"

"Yes. Down the street."

"Do you know if one of the Perlouix boys was in love before he went off to war?"

She avoided my question by glancing at her watch. "Oh, honey. Look at the time. It's getting late, and I haven't been sleeping well at your mama's house. So I think I'll go to bed early tonight. If that's OK."

I bit my lower lip. Why wouldn't she answer my question? Guilt swallowed my desire to press her. Here I was interrogating her when she'd had a busy day and needed rest. "OK."

Her wrinkles had deepened in the last few minutes. I stood, grabbed our cups, and rinsed them at the sink.

She disappeared from the kitchen.

I locked all the doors and windows and then gathered and set up the pot and filter for coffee in the morning. When I walked to her room, she'd changed and was climbing into bed.

"I can sleep on the couch if you want."

"No. Not necessary. I'm fine. Just a little tired. Need my rest you know." She snuggled into her bed. "It feels so good to be back home."

"I bet it does. I'll come by and have coffee with you before I leave for work in morning. About six."

She nodded.

I bent over and kissed her cheek. "Good night, Mawmaw. Call me if you need anything. OK?"

"OK."

As I walked to my car in the moist air of that June night, I breathed in the heady scent of jasmine and honeysuckle. Mawmaw's reaction weighed heavy on my mind.

The lamplight on the street buzzed and a swarm of flies danced around its subtle glow. Avoiding my questions as she'd done could mean a number of things. Her fatigue proved too great to keep her focused. Or she protected her best friend, Sylvia. Or she had a greater secret to keep—could Mawmaw be Lady S?

The radiance of my porch light ushered me home, and I looked forward to the welcome of my favorite pooch. Instead, the persistent *beep, beep, beep* of my answering machine greeted me. After settling Mr. Bojangles with a dog treat, I listened to the messages.

"Hey, Sis, I contacted, Angelle. We're going to meet this weekend. I'll talk to you tomorrow." Anthony's rushed and excited voice made me smile.

"Way to go, Anthony."

My over exuberant pup came barreling around the corner and yipped his excitement. He searched around the kitchen. I'd deducted that his excitement and searching meant he thought his favorite Uncle Tony was here. I picked him up and let him lick my chin. "Down you go." He slid from my hands onto the floor. I grabbed another treat from the box and let him retrieve it from my fingertips. I pushed the button for the next message.

"Cheryl, it's Debra Hebert, used to be Debra Sanders. Remember me? We worked on the high school yearbook together. I heard you were back in town and got your number from a friend. We're planning the July 4th *fais do do* and wondered if you'd like to help. I remembered we worked on it together when we were in high school. Call me." She left her number.

I was amazed to hear from her. We had been good friends in high school. Another friendship I'd let lapse because when I left I wanted to put as much distance as possible between Bijou Bayou and me.

Debra had moved to Bijou Bayou in sixth grade and became the most popular girl in our school. She'd kept that title later as homecoming queen and our valedictorian. She still lived here. Surprising. With the last name of Hebert, she must have married someone from here. Had she gone to college and come back?

My curiosity grew as well as my guilt. Some friend I'd been. Another lost opportunity. Was this my chance to make up for ignoring her all these years?

Onze

I returned Debra's call and agreed to help with the *fais do do*. Our conversation lasted over an hour as we caught up with each other's lives. She'd married the local bad boy and seemed happy.

I left out why I'd left Jarrod. Maybe later, but not in this first conversation. Our first planning committee meeting was scheduled for tomorrow night, and I looked forward to it.

Once in bed, I tossed and fought a no-win battle with my sheets. Carlton and Lady S consumed my thoughts. I couldn't imagine Beau's grandmother writing those letters. They were written by someone passionate and loving. Sylvia Mouton did not fit that image. But then again, a broken heart can change a person. What had happened to Carlton and his Lady S?

~*~

Carlton sat up against his headboard and rasped out his greeting. "Missed you this weekend."

"Well, look at you. Sitting up. That's got to feel pretty good." I checked his water cup and the new medication schedule.

Darcy had left everything in great order as usual.

He nodded. "Feelin' a lil bit...better today."

I figured the change in his medications had been responsible. "Good for you." I smiled and tried to ignore the sadness in his smile. "More reading today?"

"You bet." He pointed toward the stack of letters.

Dare I ask him about Lady S? Would today be a good day since he was feeling better or would my question set him back? I sat in my usual seat, reached for the letters, and opened the next one. A quick glance toward Carlton rewarded me with a wink. I smiled and began to read.

Dear Carlton,

Today's been unusually hot for this time of year. Christmas is just around the corner, and Mama is getting a little anxious because the whole family is coming here for Christmas dinner. Our aunts from Arkansas will be here and their children. The house will be full. I'm looking forward to spending time with all my cousins. Sure wish you were here. It would be so nice to tell everyone about our engagement at Christmas dinner. I know Papa would be mad, but I believe once he got to know the real you, he would support us. Maybe we can get him to sell us that piece of the farm that borders the bayou and we can build our own house there. Wouldn't that be nice? We'd be close to both our families. Then again, I'm not sure that would be a good idea.

Mrs. Guillot at the dress shop said she might have a job for me after Christmas. She said I could work from nine to five Tuesday through Saturdays. I'm so excited. She has catalogs with wedding dresses! Wouldn't that be fun to scour the pages for the perfect wedding dress? Oh, Carlton, I do miss you so much. I hope you're being careful. I was a little concerned when it took so long for you to write back to me. But I understand your troops are moving so much. It's a wonder any of these letters get delivered. I'm so glad the memory of our day at the watering hole keeps you happy. Hold on to that memory. When you get back, we'll spend another afternoon there.

I saw your mama at the meat market the other day. She looked very sad. She avoided me, and I guess that's a good thing. I'm sure she didn't want to get the rumor mill going again about us. Are you writing to her, too? I'm sure she's worried about you like I am. And with your brother at war, too, it must be hard for her.

Well, Mama needs me to help get the Christmas decorations from the barn. Remember, I love you and miss you. I'm praying for your safety.

Your Lady S

Carlton stared at the letter in my hands. His breaths came in short shallow gasps. He gazed into my eyes. "She...was...special," he said.

"She seems to be. Was she your first love?"

He blinked a few times and then nodded. "First and only."

Could now be when he would tell me who she was? "Does she still live in Bijou Bayou?" I held my breath. Would he answer me?

He paused, and I wondered if he'd heard me. His eyes never left mine, and the intensity sent tiny chills through me. "Yep...she does."

Dare I ask her name? "Carlton, would you like me to contact her so you can see her?"

Fear, anger, or regret—I'm not sure which— flashed, but his expression shifted to a glare, and the lines around his eyes deepened. "Don't." His lips set into a tight line. "Never...tell...her...never—" he labored to take each breath "—about me...here."

I stood and took in a deep breath. Why the response? I'd never seen this emotion from him. I leaned over his bed. "Carlton, I don't know who she is.

I won't tell. I promise." I patted his arm and leaned closer to him. "Carlton?" His emotions took him to a place far away. I suspected an unpleasant place from his furrowed brow and frown.

He struggled for air. I replaced his nasal cannula with an air mask. After a few minutes, he calmed, and his breathing, while still labored, settled.

Why couldn't I just share this time with him and quit worrying about who Lady S was? I'd upset him and felt like a heathen. "Carlton, I'm sorry," I whispered. "I won't tell. I promise." I repeated the phrase until he drifted to sleep.

When he awoke three hours later, he seemed calm and didn't mention the earlier episode.

We had lunch and played a few games of rummy in the afternoon. He usually beat me, but today I won three of the four games we played.

After the fourth game, I asked, "Do you want me to read more letters to you?"

He shook his head. "Nope, not today."

My heart sank. Had I ruined his enjoyment of our time reading the letters? I hoped not. It was the only joy he had, and I wanted to give him as much as I could in his remaining days, however many there were.

"Do you...believe...in God?" Carlton asked. Had he spoken to me?

I wasn't sure because he stared out the window across the room. How to answer his question? My life had surely not been an example of someone who followed God. I'd fallen short in that department. But did I believe? I sat straighter in my chair and stared out the same window.

The leaves of a large sycamore tree near the corner

of the house fluttered in the afternoon breeze.

"Yes, I do. But I haven't been very good at living like I do. Do you believe?" I glanced his way.

"I used to." He turned from the window and closed his eyes.

Was this the sadness of everyone who bordered so close to death or a man who had loved so deeply and lost? Or of someone filled with much regret.

"Maybe we can find Him again. Together."

"He...doesn't...want me." His lips separated the bare minimum.

My chest expanded with grief for this man. What could he have done to make him feel God had abandoned him? I patted his arm. "I bet he does." I instantly regretted the simple and weak response. As I revisited the words, their lameness battered me. Was that all I could come up with at such a crucial moment?

He shrugged his shoulders, closed his eyes, and turned his head away. His breathing slowed and before long, the raspy, steady breaths of sleep took over.

As I gathered my things to go home, Carlton's question rubbed me and left a pounding dissonance. Did he think about God because death seemed so close? And what about my life? Where was God there?

~*~

Later that evening, I sat next to Debra and awaited the arrival of the other *fais do do* committee members.

"Cheryl, thanks so much for helping with this." Debra squeezed my shoulder. "We'll have to meet for coffee sometime and catch up."

"I'd like that. And thanks for asking me to help.

It'll be nice to be involved in something fun." Fun had been lacking in my life for the past year it seemed.

"Well, this *fais do do* has grown quite a bit since our high school days. Close to a thousand or so people come each year."

"Wow, it has grown. Who are the other committee members?"

Just as Debra pulled her list of names, several people entered the room.

At the sight of Beau Battice, my hand flew to my throat and my breath caught. Great. Spending this much time with him was not what I wanted, but I'd already volunteered. I couldn't back out now.

He sat next to me—the brown in his eyes intensified by the bright fluorescent bulbs in the town hall. "Hi, Cheryl. I didn't know you were on this committee."

I smiled. "Just volunteered last night." I shot Debra a we've-got-to-talk look. She simply smiled and began to call roll.

~*~

Beau milled about in the corner of the room with a few of the members after the meeting ended.

"Cheryl, wait." His voice rendered my every muscle useless. He walked along as I headed toward the parking lot. "It's good to see you on this committee, getting involved in the community. Maybe you'll want to stay."

I slowed. "It feels good to get involved." I turned toward him. "I had a good visit with Annie."

"Did you? Were you the one who painted her nails?"

I nodded, and he laughed. "I knew it. She told me about that silly promise you gals made in Junior High."

We stood at my car, Beau smiling as he shared his wife's memory with me. I smiled too. "I'm glad I went to see her."

He opened my car door. "I'm glad you did, too. I know she enjoyed it. Why had I never thought about painting her nails?" He tapped the top of his head.

I slid into my car seat. "Sorry, Beau. It's a girl thing. Besides, it's not like you haven't had a million other things on your mind."

"Yeah, I guess so. I'm grateful for you. Thanks, again."

"No need to thank me. I think it did me more good than Annie."

He smiled. "My sweet Annie. She has a way of doing that, doesn't she?"

"That she does." I pulled the door, but before I could close it, Beau pulled it back.

"Say, have you unraveled the mystery of your couple from the past? It sounds intriguing. I wish I had the whole story."

I hadn't told him all the details about Carlton. Only enough, it seemed to pique his interest. "I wish I had the whole story, too. I'm still working on it. I'll let you know if I learn more."

"Good night, Cheryl." He gently closed my car door.

Good night, Beau," I whispered in the car as I watched him walk away. I wiped the perspiration from my palms onto my jeans and started the engine. As I drove out the parking lot, I glimpsed Beau getting into his car. Still handsome after all these years. Should I include Beau in my hunt for Lady S? A tiny voice in my head answered. *No.*

Douze

"Good morning, Carlton." I stood at the foot of his bed and hoped he had forgotten yesterday's episode or at least forgiven my prying.

"Hey...I'm sorry 'bout yester...day," he said. He hadn't forgotten.

I sensed a change in him today. Carlton wasn't the type to apologize, so I tugged on his big toe. "No problem." I should give up trying to find Lady S.

I reviewed the night shift's notes and took care of his needs before settling in the chair next to his bed. "Would you like me to read the letters today?"

He nodded. As I reached for the letters, he grabbed my hand. His blue eyes pierced. "She can't know I'm here." The intensity from yesterday flashed in his eyes.

Fear snaked through me. I didn't want to upset him. "Carlton, is it better if we don't read the letters?"

He shook his head and released his grip. "No. I need them."

"OK. Your secret is safe with me." I stood and leaned over his bed. "You know that don't you?"

He nodded. "Yep."

The question about God continued to nag at me. Should I call a priest or pastor to minister to him?

I returned to my seat, grabbed the letters from the nightstand, and pulled the next one out of the string-tied bundle. "Carlton, before I read, I have a question for you. Just answer yes or no. OK?"

He nodded.

"Would you like for me to call a priest or pastor to come visit you?"

"Why?"

"You asked about God yesterday, and they'd be able to answer your questions better than I can."

"Devil's...got me."

I paused. Had I heard him correctly?

"Really? Why would you think that?" No sooner had the words escaped my lips, my stomach pitted. I had no right to ask that question, but the more he revealed the more of a mystery he became.

I didn't give him time to answer. "It's not too late."

"It is for me."

"You never answered my question about calling someone."

He shrugged his shoulders but didn't say anything.

"I'll take that as a yes."

"Can...we read?"

I slid the letter from the envelope and thought about his response. He hadn't said no, so I could ask around for a priest or pastor who could minister to Carlton. Maybe Aunt Melanie's pastor. It was the least I could do. And what if he died before he could repent of whatever sin had been eating away at him more feverishly than the cancer cells? Could I ever forgive myself for not trying?

He gazed at the letter in my hands. He cleared his throat, lifted his eyebrows, and pointed toward the letter.

"OK, OK." I smiled. "I'm ready, already. Don't get your panties in a wad."

He smiled back—an unexpected response. "Don't wear...panties. Boxers."

I laughed, shook my head, and began reading the sixth letter.

My dearest Carlton,

Merry Christmas! It breaks my heart wondering where you are tonight. Are you safe? Are you warm? My biggest wish this Christmas is that you return safely to me. I would give up a lifetime of Christmas presents just to have that one.

The family is here, my Aunt and her girls made the trip from Arkansas. It has been so nice to see everyone again and be with family. My heart still has this big empty spot because you are not here. Any word on getting leave? I have been saving my money, and maybe I could fly somewhere so we could see each other?

I pray you are safe and will continue to pray for you every day until you are in my arms. Then I will pray for our life together.

All my love,
Your Lady S.

I glanced toward Carlton. His attention was fixed on the letter in my hand and a single tear streamed down his cheek. He was engrossed in his world, and I imagined Lady S there with him. I reached for the tissue box next to his bed. As gently as possible, I wiped the moisture from his cheek careful not to disturb his reverie. Typical of our past readings, he didn't speak or acknowledge my presence.

I returned the letter to the nightstand and slipped out of his room. From the kitchen window, I watched the field grass blow in the slight breeze until the sight blurred from my tears. Had Carlton's questions about God sparked something long dead in me? *Oh Lord, what can I do?*

The day flew by. I didn't offer to read any more letters, and Carlton didn't ask. He stayed longer in his world after each reading, and I felt guilty for being the one to put him there. Although, I sensed a deep regret in him and suspected the memories tormented him, the letters seemed to bring temporary peace. What could have happened between him and Lady S to cause this much anguish and pain? Had he hurt her in some way? Had she hurt him? I knew she was still alive. He'd said so. Did he really not want to see her? Maybe, just maybe, if he could apologize, he could die in peace?

"Quit, Cheryl." I chastised myself. Once again I was trying to do exactly what Carlton didn't want. Why couldn't I leave things alone?

~*~

Notes for the upcoming *fais do do* lay strewn on my dining room table amid the take-out shrimp salad I'd picked up.

Debra sat next to me, reviewing each idea. "We could call the *fais do do*, The Revolution," she said.

"That sounds a little too revolting."

She wrinkled her nose. "No pun intended, of course."

I laughed. It felt good to laugh and forget all the heavy things occupying my mind. "Totally intended."

"It has to be something in tune with Independence Day but also something that reflects our life here in South Louisiana."

I nodded. "How about a costume *fais do do* that reflects the importance of community? Have people dress as their favorite person. It could be a friend, relative, shop owner, public official, or even just their neighbor. Make it a hometown *fais do do*."

"Oh, that sounds fun. I like it. We can present it to the committee members at our next meeting," she said.

"Good." Glad that our meeting time had been somewhat productive, I gathered all the notes from the table. "Deb, would you like another cup of coffee?"

"Yes, I would. Besides I hope you don't mind if I stay a little longer. There's something I wanted to talk about."

I filled her cup and my own, wondering what could elicit the seriousness of her look. "Let's sit on the couch. It's much more comfortable."

We settled on my thick couch with Mr. Bojangles nestled on the rug at my feet. I tucked my leg under me and turned to face her. "What's up?"

"It's about Beau."

"What about Beau?" I tried to keep my face from showing the emotion that crept in at the mention of his name.

She sighed. "Cheryl, this is hard. I know we've not been in contact for a while, but I feel that since you've returned, we've picked up where we left off. I love having my good friend back, and I hope you feel the same."

I tapped her knee. "Are you kidding? I'm lovin' this. Do you know how long it's been since I've had coffee with a girlfriend I could trust?"

She squeezed her lips together. "I'm glad. It's just that there are rumors around town that you and Beau are an item." She lifted her hands. "Don't worry. I put a stop to it—a few carefully placed words to the right person."

I shook my head. "Wow, that didn't take long. We had coffee at Sammy's Diner once. Do *you* think there's something going on?"

"I don't...the Cheryl I knew wouldn't have an affair with a married man. I believe that's the Cheryl I still know. I remember how much you loved him at one time. And his situation..."

I stared at her for a while, unable to identify the emotions brewing in me. My heart stirred when I thought of Beau, but it also became as heavy as an anvil when I thought of his wife.

"Deb, nothing is going on between me and Beau. He's married. Period."

"I believe you. I wish things were different for you." She grasped my hand. "It's good to see the two of you as friends. I'm glad the past hasn't stopped you from being his friend."

Tears stung my eyes. For a second I debated telling the truth. Her wide eyes and compassionate touch propelled. I so needed to have a friend I could trust. "Deb?

"Yes."

"I want to be his friend, but I do struggle with seeing him as more. He's so kind and considerate. I question if I let Mr. Right get away."

"Oh, honey." She curled her fingers around mine. "I'm so sorry."

"It's my fault. I thought he was a young girl's crush. I had to see what was out there for me." I fought the rush of tears. "No way could I ever settle for a small town boy who was content to stay there. What a fool, I've been. There's been no one *out there* who's come close to him. Sad part is I didn't realize that until I saw him again."

"He is a good man. Too good to have to go through what he's going through."

"I know. He wants to be friends. And so do I. But there's a part that wonders if I can be happy just being his friend. Would I want more? And what about Annie? Would being friends with Beau disrespect her?"

"That's tough. I can't answer your questions. Examine your heart." Her eyes held compassion and understanding. She slid her hands around mine. "Can I pray for you?"

The question seemed strange until I realized she meant right then. No one had ever prayed out loud for me. No one had ever asked to. Not wanting to hurt her feelings, I simply nodded.

She closed her eyes and bowed her head.

I followed her lead.

"Dear Lord, I lift Cheryl up to you today. Father, we know You have her life in Your hands, and You want the best for her. Guide Cheryl in this situation with Beau. Keep them in Your hands and keep them from falling away from You. You know the end of this story, and I ask that You give Cheryl peace that You will bring her to where she is meant to be. Let her have faith that You will use her to show Your character to everyone she encounters. She's Your child, and You love her. Let her see You in everything. We ask this through the name of Your son, Jesus. Amen."

I kept my eyes closed and head bowed. I hid the moisture collecting in my eyes. Her prayer stirred my heart. I felt special. Loved. It had been a long time since I'd felt those emotions. My thoughts darted to Carlton.

After a moment, when I felt confident I could speak without stammering or fighting a ball of emotion in my throat, I gazed at Debra. "Thank you." The words seemed lame compared to my heart-filled gratitude.

Her smiling face greeted me. "It's good to have you back, Cheryl. I've missed you."

I smiled back and gave her a quick hug. "I've missed you, too."

Would she know someone I could ask to speak to Carlton? I told her about the situation with Carlton without divulging his name or any of his information, especially the part about Lady S. "Would your pastor be willing to talk to him?" I asked.

"Oh, yes, I know he would."

"How can you be so sure?" I asked.

"Because I'm married to him."

I gaped. "Married to him? Chuck, a pastor?"

She smiled, a Cheshire cat grin. "Yep. Can you believe it? He's the pastor of Grace Community Church."

"Wow, I would have never guessed."

Would Carlton be upset if I brought him to his bedside? After all, he'd not said no when I'd asked if he wanted to see someone. There was only one way to find out—bring Pastor Hebert to see him.

Treize

"Carlton, this is Pastor Hebert." I pulled the chair from next to Carlton's bed and placed it facing him. "He wanted to visit with you for a while. Is that OK?"

Carlton's blank look gave no indication of his thoughts. He simply nodded.

"I'll leave you two to visit."

"Thank you, Cheryl." Chuck Hebert sat in the chair next to Carlton's bed.

I never would have thought the rabble-rouser, Chuckie, would have become a pastor. Debra had mentioned she married Chuck when we'd spoken that first night, but she didn't say anything about him being a pastor. Especially one at such a large church as Grace Community. The church sat on ten acres off of the interstate between Bijou Bayou and Point Duson where Carlton lived. I passed by it every day on my way to and from work. I'd only given it a passing glance.

It was hard to forget the first time I'd seen Chuck. Debra and I had been driving home from a friend's house late one night and found him walking down the lonely winding road, dressed only in his underwear. His friends had dropped him off as some sort of weird initiation into their motorcycle group. I guessed he'd changed since those days. At least, I hoped so. He had agreed to see Carlton when Debra had mentioned it to him that night. I couldn't think of one more suited to minister to my patient.

The sound of laughter drifted into the kitchen. Carlton's laughter. The sound mingling with Chuck's deep resonating mirth comforted my soul.

Thank you, Lord. The prayer surprised me, but when I examined my heart, I found gratitude filled it.

Maybe Chuck can help Carlton to forgive and perhaps die in peace. But what if Carlton needed forgiveness from Lady S? What then?

Should I attempt to find her?

~*~

I edged the door open into Mawmaw's house and peeked in. "It's me. Cheryl."

"Hey, *sha.* Come in. I'm in the bedroom." She poked her head around the doorframe. "Coffee's hot. Fix us a cup."

I poured the steaming dark brew. I'd regret this. The tantalizing aroma was hard to resist. As I stirred the cream into my cup, I made a mental list of things I would do later tonight when sleep eluded.

Mawmaw approached with a slight limp to her gait, but overall she'd made an excellent recovery. "Missed you last night." She sat in the chair next to me. "How did your committee meeting go?"

"Very well. We're doing a hometown theme for the Fourth of July *fais do do.* We've expanded it to include people in the present and in the past. So that should be interesting. We've had a few famous people from here. Wonder how many will dress like Troy Williams? A simple costume: cowboy boots and hat with a guitar."

She giggled.

Her giggle made me smile. It was the first time I'd

heard her do so since her stroke.

"I like him. You know that's Boots McArthur's grandson. We grew up together. His family lived down the road from us." She stared into her cup. A dreamy faraway look with a sweet smile wrinkled the corners of her eyes.

I set the cup on the table and nudged her arm gently. "Did you and this Boots have something going on you're not telling me about?"

The lines on her cheeks reddened. "No way. He was too hard-nosed for me. We were just friends."

"Just friends, huh? I detect you were a little more than that by how red your cheeks became."

She turned to me with a twinkle in her eyes. The look reminded me of a schoolgirl in love. And I could see her as a younger version. I bet she was beautiful.

"Well, if you have to know." She leaned toward me as though she would be telling me the greatest secret of her life. "He was sweet on me, but my heart was already taken."

"Was Pawpaw jealous?" I smiled at the vision of my grandparents in their teens.

She swirled her coffee and took a slow sip. When she returned the cup to the table her mood had changed. She no longer looked like the schoolgirl in love. She simply shook her head and asked, "Who you gonna dress up as?"

And that's when it hit me. I'd been debating on a costume. Seeing my grandmother's earlier look helped me decide. I would be a younger version of her. "You, of course," I told her.

"You don't want to be me. Goodness, girl, with all the choices." She giggled again.

And the sound made my heart flutter.

I loved that sound.

I loved her.

"Do you have any clothes from when you were younger?"

Her expression became pensive. "I do. They're in the attic at your mama's house. Dresses I served in friend's weddings, gowns from dances, and my wedding dress."

"Really? That is so cool. I can't believe you kept all those." Excited by the prospect, I leaned in closer.

She nodded. "I did. They're in the trunks we moved to your mama's after the last hurricane. You're welcome to go through them to find something for the *fais do do*."

I hugged her. "Thank you. This should be fun."

"Maybe your mama can help you."

My heart sank. There went the fun, but I regretted the thought.

Maybe Mama could go as an older version of Mawmaw and Mawmaw could go as herself. That might be fun.

I finished the coffee and reached for Mawmaw's cup. "I need to get going. It's getting late, and you need your beauty sleep."

She laughed out loud. "No way I can sleep that long."

I washed the cups and returned them to the cupboard. Just as I headed for the door, I remembered a question I'd wanted to ask her. "Mawmaw, you said you and Sylvia Mouton were friends when you were younger. Right?"

"Yep. We were best friends."

"Did she date any of the Perlouix boys?"

Again, she became pensive and reverted to her

thoughts. "I think she did for a short while."

"Do you remember which one?"

She gazed away from me and toward the clock. "Can't say that I do. There was a bunch of dem."

"Did she date one before he left for the war?"

She paused. "I don't remember."

I saw her reluctance to answer, but I needed to know. "What about the feud with the Perlouixs? What families were involved?"

"Cheryl, how do you know about that?"

This time I would be the one to avoid answering. "Were the Moutons in the feud?"

She nodded. "Just about every family on our street. Mr. Perlouix did not have a neighborly disposition. Are you on that romance thing again?"

I nodded.

She yawned and shifted in her chair. "It's getting late. Sometimes the past should stay there." Her eyes bored into me.

Maybe dropping the subject for tonight was best.

I kissed her cheek. "G'night. Call me if you need anything."

"G'night, Cheryl. And, honey, don't go worrying yourself about the past. The present and the future have enough to keep you real busy."

Thoughts about Sylvia Mouton and Carlton Perlouix filled my head during the walk home. Had Mrs. Mouton dated Carlton? And why had she said she didn't know the Perlouix family? Was Mrs. Mouton Lady S? Perhaps I would have coffee with Beau tomorrow morning. Who cared what the town thought?

~*~

Steven stuffed the last few bites of pancakes into his mouth. "Hmmm."

"Hey, Slugger, manners."

He swallowed. "Sorry, Miss Cheryl. I want to get to school early and study with my group for a history test."

I laughed and enjoyed seeing a kid with a hearty appetite for breakfast and eagerness to do well. "Then you best get over there."

He stood next to the booth and lifted his backpack onto his shoulders. "Dad, thanks for breakfast and Miss Cheryl, thanks for meeting us here."

"You are welcome. It was my pleasure. Do well on your test."

He grunted. "I hope to."

"See you this afternoon. Don't worry, Stevie. You got this in the bag. You're ready." Beau stood and walked him to the door.

Beau returned and slid into the booth. "Guess I gotta let loose sometime. It's only two blocks to school, and I'm silly nervous."

"It's only natural for you to feel a little possessive."

"Yeah, I guess." He met my gaze and smiled. "I don't want to scare him away."

"You won't." I finished the last of my oatmeal.

He fingered the handle of his coffee cup. "I was surprised to hear from you. Glad you finally decided that it's not worth worrying about what the gossipmongers say." He laughed. "I don't."

"That's true. Annie would have been right here with us had she been able to. And I have questions about your grandmother."

His dark eyes widened, and he leaned in closer. "This sounds intriguing. Like what?"

"Remember the other night when we discussed the Perlouix family?"

"Yeah, she said she heard of them but didn't know them personally."

I sipped the hot coffee and let the warmth comfort my tongue. "Well, when I spoke to Mawmaw, she remembers your grandma dating one of the Perlouix boys. But she couldn't remember which one."

He shook his head and wrapped his hands together. "The plot thickens. Why would my grandma lie about that?"

"I don't know. Seems the Perlouix boys were not well respected in Bijou Bayou for some reason." I lowered my voice. "Maybe, it was a secret romance."

"Maybe." He grinned. "You're taking this seriously, aren't you?"

I nodded. "Yep."

"Do you think my grandmother might be the lady in the couple from the '50s?"

"I honestly don't know. She could be."

He took a long sip. "How did you learn about this couple?"

The waitress, a young redhead with a small butterfly tattoo on her forearm, topped off our coffee cups and removed our plates. I thanked her and watched her walk away. She had another tattoo on her ankle, but I couldn't see it well enough to identify it.

I emptied another packet of sweetener into my cup. "From some old letters."

"Can you ask the person who sent the letters? Received them?"

"Yes and no. Yes, I could ask, but no it wouldn't

do any good. The recipient doesn't want their identity revealed. Seems they were going to get married and something happened to change their plans. There's a lot of guilt, and they may carry it to their graves."

"That's tough. So you think if you got these two together you could alleviate this guilt?"

"That's the idea."

"Cheryl, I'm a little confused. If neither wants this brought to light, why are you pursuing this? You know this could backfire." He placed both hands around his cup and stared directly at me, his expression one of gentle concern.

In a moment of enormous strength, I met his gaze straight on. "Maybe. But Beau, I've got to try. I owe it to one of this couple. If you only knew the torment, you'd do the same thing."

"Digging up the past can cause more pain sometimes."

A memory of Beau and me at Toucoin's Park flashed. Guilt gripped my heart. He was right. "I know. I'll handle it respectfully."

"I'm sure you would, but these situations have a way of taking a path of their own. You may not have control over the outcome." He sighed.

"I know, but it's really important to me."

The lines around his eyes deepened. He shifted his position, lowered his shoulders, and then pursed his lips. "How can I help?"

Had I heard correctly? Had he volunteered to help? I lowered my eyes away from the intensity of his gaze. "See if you can find out anything about when your grandma lived on Highway 62. It seems Mawmaw, your grandma, someone named Boots McArthur, and the Perlouixs all lived in the same general area."

"I'll ask grandma. She may know something." He lifted his hand to cut me off. "I'll be discreet."

"Thanks. In the meantime, I'll keep trying to get information from Mawmaw. But she doesn't like to talk much about it."

"Sounds like my grandma is no different. Maybe something did happen, and they're protecting each other."

A distinct possibility. The past seemed locked in a vault with all the players owning a small piece of the combination. Would the truth come to light before Carlton died?

We changed the subject and discussed Steven's future games and his science project. I volunteered to help him after work on Thursday. As we finished our breakfast, several of the town gossips entered the diner. I spied a few disapproving looks as they settled in their booth. They sat huddled over the table sharing hushed conversation.

"I thought you said you wouldn't worry about what the townspeople thought."

"I know. It's hard."

"Don't."

I knew he was right. "Right." I nodded at Beau and didn't let my eyes settle too long in the warmth of his gaze. I thanked him for breakfast and stood to leave.

He stood, also. "I'll find out what I can and keep you posted," he said.

"Thanks, Beau. I appreciate it." As I left the diner, I turned toward the matriarchs of the group, smiled, and waved.

Quatorze

Anger bubbled as I headed to my car. I'd let those women get to me. Why couldn't I just be like Beau and not worry about what people thought?

Mawmaw had known them in high school and said they were the same back then. Perhaps drama queens remain just that.

Guilt stabbed like a splinter to my heart. Maybe they wouldn't bother me so much, if I didn't feel so good about spending time with Beau. His heart was pure; perhaps mine wasn't. I'd have to make an honest assessment of my heart.

I had some time before I had to get to work so I headed to my mama's house to see if she thought the *fais do do* plan was as great an idea as me and Mawmaw did.

Interesting how whenever guilt entered my heart, I thought of Mama.

~*~

"Are you kiddin' me? You want me to dress up in moldy old clothes from the attic?" Mama's brows arched in disbelief.

I should have expected this, but after the way she'd acted when Mawmaw had her stroke, I thought she'd be willing. Guess I was wrong.

"We'll clean them, of course. I just thought it

would be a great way for us to honor her. Especially after her..." I let the words linger in hopes that she'd change her mind. A sliver of self-reproach pricked. What a heathen I was trying to guilt her into doing this. I searched her face for any signs of defeat.

None.

She just stared at me with that I-am-Vivian-Broussard-the-queen look that sent most people scampering to give her what she wanted. The look quit working on me in tenth grade when she'd tried to guilt me into not going to the Sadie Hawkins dance with Thomas Chambeau. She'd had a row with his mother when we were in third grade and not forgiven her yet. There was no way her daughter would be asking *that* boy to a dance.

I did. And sneaked out to meet him at the junior high school gym.

She blew a gasket.

I was grounded for weeks.

"OK," I said. "Suit yourself."

Her stoic face melted and a questioning expression replaced the entitled glare. "Cheryl, it's a great idea. Only, well, I..."

I waited for her to finish her thought, but she just shook her head.

"...let me think about it. OK?"

That was more than I expected. But I suspected there was more to her response. "Sure. Will you help me find a dress?"

"Yes. You want to do it now?"

I glanced at the kitchen clock. Ten thirty. "I don't have much time. How about this weekend?"

She smiled. "Maybe Melanie can help, too." Her eyes lit up. "She may want to be Mawmaw at her age.

Wouldn't that work for you?"

Mama had missed the point. This would be a grandmother-mother-daughter thing. Not a grandmother-aunt-niece thing.

"I've already made other plans for the *fais do do*." She lowered her eyes refusing to meet mine.

"Yeah? Anything special?"

She kept her head tilted toward her coffee cup. "Oh, just a weekend away."

"Care to share?"

She shook her head. "It's nothing."

I knew not to press her further; she wasn't going to tell me more.

"Mama?" I wrapped both hands around my cup and leaned in closer.

"Yes."

"Why didn't you tell me about the schizophrenia?"

She ran her finger along the rim of her coffee for what seemed an eternity. Just when I'd given up hope that she'd answer me, she lifted her head and met my gaze. The glint of her eyes dimmed from the glistening moisture. She expelled a long breath that brushed the tips of my fingers. Her lips twitched into a quasi-smile. "Guess this conversation is long overdue."

I nodded.

She took in a deep breath and exhaled slowly.

"When your father died, things really escalated. The symptoms became worse. Mawmaw helped as much as she could. But your grandfather was sick and dying. There wasn't much money. I was also embarrassed. I had two children to raise alone. I didn't want you or Anthony to think less of me—to think your Mama couldn't take care of you. I never wanted you to feel like you couldn't trust me, but I was drowning, and I didn't know where to turn. Then Elray came along."

"But he hurt you."

She shook her head. "No, he didn't."

I thought this conversation would be a breakthrough. But, once again, she chose to deny the abuse she'd suffered from her husband, because she'd been too spoiled to leave him.

"Mama, how could you say he didn't hurt you? I saw the bruises on your arms. Do you really think that was OK?"

"Did you ever go without?" she asked, ignoring my question.

"No." Elray had a good job. He'd provided us with all we needed and many times what we wanted. I didn't see how that was more important than withstanding the abuse he'd inflicted.

"He never hurt you or Anthony, did he?"

I shook my head. "No, just you."

"Cheryl." She leaned closer and met my eyes with searing intensity. "I hurt me."

Once again, she justified his actions. "Mama, don't you see —"

She lifted both hands, palms facing me. "Cheryl, listen. My...condition had worsened. I hadn't been fully diagnosed at that time." She paused and looked off toward the kitchen window. A single tear slid along the side of her face. She turned back toward me — her eyes pools of water.

"I attacked him. He never hit me. It was me." She jabbed her index finger into her chest. "The bruises you saw were from me striking him. And him trying to defend himself from my blows. I was out of control."

She paused again. Her tears flowed freely and produced streaks where carefully applied makeup had been. She lowered her lashes causing a fresh flow of moisture. "But, most importantly, he protected you and Anthony."

Her words slammed into me like a wrecking ball. Their enormity settled into my gut with the weight of an anvil. I'd blamed Elray all those years. I hadn't even gone to his funeral. To find out he'd protected us from Mama's abuse was almost more than I could bear.

The image of him sitting at the kitchen table reading his Bible flashed. I'd thought him a hypocrite. No words seemed appropriate to fully capture the tornado of emotions whirling through me. I slid into the giant sinkhole opening beneath me and was swallowed along with everything I'd ever known. Spiraling down, down, down—drowning in all my misshapen memories and truths.

I looked at this woman who was Mama and realized that I truly saw her for the first time in my life.

I saw her sacrifice and shame.

I saw her love and strength.

And finally, I saw the burden she'd carried and understood so much. For the first time in my life, love for Elray spread through me. He'd taken care of her and *us*.

I stood and hugged her and then whispered in her ear, "Mama, I'm so sorry." The words seemed lame in light of what I'd just learned, but I knew no other words could effectively convey the bevy of emotions reeling through me.

She wrapped her arms around my shoulders and held on with intense ferocity. "I'm so sorry, honey. I'm so sorry. Please forgive me."

My vision blurred. How could I have not known this? Guilt wrapped its cruel talons around my heart and squeezed. I pulled away and looked into her tear-streaked face. "Oh, Mama, I was so hateful to Elray. I can't imagine what he thought of my ungrateful attitude."

Her lips parted into a slow smile while her eyes glistened with tears. "Honey, he knew. We decided you and Anthony would not know. So he was OK with taking the blame. He was a very special man."

I couldn't speak. Raw emotion bubbled through me and speaking would unleash a torrent I could not control.

~*~

Carlton, sat wide-eyed and alert when I walked into his room carrying the lunch the housekeeper prepared.

I tried to process the bomb Mama dropped earlier. As I hurried to arrange things on his tray, I dropped a bowl. Thankfully, the plastic just bounced off the floor. "Sheesh," I pushed through gritted teeth.

"What's got your...goat t'day?" he asked as I walked into the bedroom.

I shook my head. How could he have heard me? I tried to smile. "Oh, it's nothing."

"Mus' be some...tin'. Not like you...to..." He let the words linger and took in a deep breath. "...mope and cuss."

"I'm not moping. Or cussing. Just have something on my mind is all." I laid the bed tray over his lap.

He shook his head. "You're mopin'."

I stood next to his bed and propped my fisted

hands on my hips. "And what makes you so sure?"

He jutted out his bottom lip like a grade school kid. "Jus' know." He shrugged his shoulders. "Wanna talk?"

Would this man never cease to amaze me? He had sat clammed up for the past few weeks, and now he wanted to talk about my issues. "Wouldn't you rather I read to you?"

"Not...in your bad mood." He lifted the spoonful of soup to his mouth.

I let out an audible sigh. "I'm not in a bad mood."

He arched his brows. "Really?" A smile spread his cracked lips. The effort made me cringe. It must be painful, but Carlton's eyes matched the sentiment. "Your turn...to share."

I plopped into the chair next to him. "OK, but not until you eat all your lunch."

He smiled again—a devilish child-like grin—which made me laugh out loud. He seemed good today. Like maybe there was hope he'd pulled through. The doctors had said six to eight months before...

But that was six months ago.

And the only reason he stayed in bed or in the chair next to his bed was because walking was so taxing.

I glanced toward him. This man I'd grown to love like a grandfather. It crushed my heart that he didn't have any family, people who loved him, to be at his bedside. His last dollars were spent on the extra care Darcy and I provided, not handed down to love ones.

He slurped his soup and crunched on the crackers a bit more hurried today. Could he want to hear *my* story? He'd never showed interest in anything but the letters from Lady S. He'd never asked any personal questions when I came to work here. He'd simply accepted my help at times and refused it at other times.

"Slow down, Sergeant. You'll choke on those crackers."

He gulped the rest of his milk. "Ah, love milk." He swiped the napkin across his crusted lips and then dropped it into the tray.

I handed him a tube of lip balm.

Sharing Mama's story with Carlton seemed a daunting task. Would opening up to him change our professional relationship too much? Or would it deepen the trust between us?

Once I'd gathered his tray and returned from the kitchen, he sat straighter against the headboard with pillows under each arm propping his elbows. His alert gaze followed me as I approached his bed. Then he pointed to the recliner next to his bed.

Hopeful, I asked, "Would you like to sit in the recliner?"

He shook his head and pointed at me. "Pull it closer."

I did as he asked and sat in the cushioned chair on the left side of his bed near his feet. "You look different from this angle."

He grinned, jutted his chin and turned his head slightly. "This...my good side."

"Yeah, handsome for sure." I tucked one leg beneath me and leaned back. Our banter and his snarky mood chased away the haunting dissonance sitting like a bowl of ball bearings in my gut. Mama's story came rushing back. So did the weight.

I glanced toward Carlton who sat in his bed looking like a five-year-old on library day anxiously awaiting a story.

"Spit...it out." He cupped his left ear. "My good ear." The significance of his words wasn't lost.

I swallowed the wedge of emotion lodged in my throat.

He cared.

Quinze

I turned away from Carlton and cleared my throat. With my gaze fixed on the hanging branches of the willow tree at the corner of his front yard, I told him my story beginning with Jarrod and my exodus from Houston, and then about Vivian and her startling revelation. I didn't give him names, just the facts, and shared with him about the guilt entrapping my heart.

"How could I not know?" I turned toward him.

Compassion from his soft eyes enveloped me like a roaring fire on a cold winter night. He smiled for a while, but the quiver of his lips took over. He stared. After a few deep breaths and a pause that lasted an eternity he spoke. "We...see what we want." He sucked in more air and continued. "Hard to...swallow when...the truth...is not what we think."

We locked gazes. It seemed he was trying to tell me something more. Was it the breathing that stopped him? Or something else? I waited for him to continue.

"Your pastor...friend."

"Chuck?" I asked.

He nodded. "He knows. Ask him 'bout forgive...ness."

"Is that what the two of you talked about?"

He nodded. After a deep inhale, he adjusted the prongs of his tubing into his nostrils. "Hardest to for...give." He pointed to his chest. "Yourself."

I nodded.

Neither of us spoke.

The hum of the concentrator pumping oxygen to Carlton's lungs dominated the room. The steady drone accompanied the thoughts circling through my brain. My whole life I couldn't forgive Mama. It was easy to blame her for all the hardness in my heart and for any poor choices I'd made as a result. But what now? The truth had set Vivian free. I no longer blamed her. But now I hated myself for how I'd acted and what I'd thought toward her. Toward Elray. The truth had not set me free.

I'm not sure how much time passed, but late afternoon shadows played on the worn oak flooring of Carlton's bedroom. I expected him to be asleep, but when I glanced toward him, his eyes met mine.

He lifted the index finger of his left hand. "And...'nother thing. No man--" He punched the air with his finger and pursed his lips. "--No man...hits you." He took several labored breaths. "...or anything else." His glare bored into me. "Hear?"

I nodded. "Those days are over, Carlton."

"Good." He exhaled long and slow, and then slid down into the bed. I helped him rearrange his pillows. The exchange had exhausted him.

And me. I clicked the bedside lamp and a soft glow replaced the shadows. "Need anything?"

He shook his head and then pointed toward me. "Talk to pastor."

"Did he answer your questions about God?" I asked.

He nodded. "Said...you can't have both."

Just as I was about to ask him what he meant, he spoke again. "God...and no forgiveness."

"Yoo-hoo, it's me," Darcy whispered as she

entered the room. "Cheryl, can you help me unload the groceries?"

"Sure." I glanced toward Carlton and then at my watch. The afternoon had flown by. A quick glance back to Carlton revealed arched eyebrows and a questioning look.

Once the groceries were put up and I'd given Darcy Carlton's updates, I gathered my belongings and went into his room.

"Just wanted to say good night and thanks for listening today."

He smiled. "Thank you...for sharing." His eyebrows arched. "Too late for me...not for you. Talk to pastor."

"OK, I will. But only if you quit thinking it's too late for you."

He shook his head. "Don't give up...do ya?"

I tugged on his foot. "Nope. See ya tomorrow."

"I'll be here." He adjusted his blanket. "I hope."

"G'night, Carlton."

"Night, Cheryl."

I walked out the door. My chest tightened when I realized that was the first time he'd called me by my name.

~*~

As morning beckoned, the day's first sunbeams peeked through the pine trees standing guard along the edge of the bayou that ran next to Oak Grove Cemetery.

"I know this pales in comparison to what you did for me." I fitted the bouquet of fresh daisies into the vase attached to Elray's tombstone. "Also, I'm sorry.

Sorry for everything. The way I treated you, the things I said about you, and for how I blamed you for the abuse. You were a better man than I gave you credit for, and I missed out on so much for not ever really knowing you."

I sat on the edge of his granite tomb and placed my elbows on my knees. "Most of all, thank you for being there for Mama and for me and Anthony. I didn't deserve what you did for me."

The words etched into the granite blurred as my heart filled with gratitude. How could he have loved us so much to do what he did? The question burned a path through me, provoking another more important one. Could I ever love anyone enough to do the same?

While I wasn't the type to visit cemeteries, the words I shared with Elray seemed to ease some of the pain Mama's revelation had created. I hoped he heard my words from heaven. Surely, after what he'd put up with here on earth, there had to be a special place in heaven for him. Maybe his morning Bible time had given him the strength and courage to be the man he'd been. He tried to share God with me. Another spear of regret jabbed.

My words to him came back to slap causing my body to shiver as the scene played in my mind. *You hypocrite. How can you preach to me? I want nothing to do with your God.* Now I knew how he'd had such peace. Now I wanted his God to be my God. I wanted that kind of peace.

My cellphone jangled as I reached my car. A quick peek to the LED showed my brother's smiling face. Had Anthony known? I swiped the screen. "Hello, my handsome brother."

"Well, hello to you, too." I heard the smile in his

voice.

"Where are you?"

"I'm driving in from the dock, and I'm on vacation for the next twenty-one days. Woohoo."

"Nice. Did you get in touch with Angelle?"

"Yes, didn't you get my message?"

I slid into the driver's seat and glanced back at Elray's tombstone. "I did, and I'm sorry I didn't call back. Things have been a bit...unusual."

"Really. Start talking."

I checked my makeup in the visor mirror. Streaks ran down my cheeks. "Can't. I'm headed to work and don't want to be late. Have dinner with me Friday night. You can tell me all about Angelle, and I'll share my news."

"OK. Only if you let me buy. How about Nonc Nubs Seafood Hut?

"Sounds great. About seven?"

"See you then."

After I hung up, I called Mama. She answered after the second ring. "Cheryl, is everything all right?"

"Yes, and good morning. I have a quick question. Does Anthony know about Elray?"

"No."

"I'm meeting him Friday night for dinner, would you like to join us so you can tell him?"

Her heavy sigh floated through the phone. "Do you think he'd be mad if you told him?"

"I think he has a right to know, and it would be better coming from you."

"I'd rather not in public. Why don't I cook, and you two come here for dinner?"

"That sounds great. I'll let him know. We'll see you Friday."

I called Anthony. When he didn't answer, I left a message telling him about our change of plans. My next call proved not as easy, but I needed to make the effort. I dialed the number to Grace Community Church and set up an appointment to meet with Chuck. If I had to choose between God and no forgiveness, I wanted to choose God but wasn't quite sure how.

The next two days were uneventful.

Carlton quit bugging me to talk to Chuck when I'd told him I'd scheduled a meeting over the weekend. With much insistence on my part, Carlton agreed to see him again.

Something serious had happened between Carlton and Lady S. My heart broke when I thought of Carlton carrying a heavy burden to his grave. If he wouldn't talk with me about it, maybe he could share with Chuck.

I'd read two letters to Carlton and still wasn't any closer to figuring out who Lady S could be. My bet lay heavy on Beau's grandmother, but a part of me didn't want it to be her. She seemed so cold and unloving. There would be no way I could bring her to Carlton and expect a forgiving outcome. The thought left me feeling hopeless. If Mrs. Mouton was Lady S, how could someone so loving and passionate become so cold? And what happened to make that drastic change, in both her and Carlton?

~*~

Anthony and I sat next to one another at Mama's rectangular table while she sat across from us. The ceiling fans on the back porch whirled the warm air around us. Its gentle breeze brushed across my forearms.

Bijou Bayou snaked lazily through the back end of her property. The setting sun sparkled on the water like a million gemstones. Evidence of how Bijou Bayou had gotten its name. A batch of hyacinth covered a portion of its width. Their purple flowers in full bloom emitted their sweet fragrance into the night. I caught an occasional whiff when the wind picked up.

Anthony interlaced his fingers and leaned forward onto his elbows. "OK, I know something's going on. Spit it out."

Mama squirmed a bit in her seat, but finally relayed the same truth to Anthony she shared with me. After she'd finished, he sat silent for several minutes.

"She told you this a few days ago?" he said.

I nodded.

He turned back toward Mama. "Mama, I'm really sorry you had to deal with everything." He paused and took in a deep breath. "But I think this is a glaring example of why it's important to always be honest. If we had known this growing up..." He pointed to me and then back to himself. "We wouldn't have such harsh feelings about our childhood."

He raised his hand when Mama tried to defend herself. "I'm not blaming. I know you and Elray did what you thought was best. And that's all anybody can do. But for the future, can we try to be more honest and open? I wasted a lot of time hating a man who didn't deserve it. And to be honest, it makes me feel like dirt for having done so."

I nodded.

Anthony had covered the topic dead on.

It was exactly how I'd felt.

And we both felt cheated out of getting to know a wonderful man.

Mama stared at Anthony, and then glanced in my direction. Tears formed in her eyes. "I know. And if it makes you feel any better. I hated the way we handled things. I've regretted it more than you could ever know."

Anthony reached across the table and grasped Mama's hand. "Thank you for telling me." Then he turned to me. "You, too, sis. I feel so much better knowing Elray wasn't a wife beater."

I agreed.

We ate the wonderful shrimp jambalaya and white beans Mama prepared. Maybe it was just my imagination, but the atmosphere seemed more relaxed and loving. I guessed it had to do with finally letting go of long held secrets and hatred. The twinkling lights from the multitude of citronella candles added to the scene.

"Oh, by the way..." Anthony lingered on the last word while a sassy smirk covered his face. "Y'all are looking at a man who has a date tomorrow night with the one and only Dr. Angelle Guidry."

"Yay! I knew it. I knew it." I could barely contain my delight. I reached over and gave him a nudge on the shoulder. "You do still like her. I'm so happy."

Mama clapped her hands together like a cheerleader. "That's wonderful, son. I really liked that girl."

"Me, too," I said.

Anthony smiled. His eyes twinkled like diamonds in the soft candle glow. "Me, too."

Anthony's news had added an additional layer of comfort to the evening. We finished our meal with relaxed conversation and sharing of our week. For the first time, sharing a meal with Mama hadn't been a stressful event. So much between us had been let go and it felt good. It was dusk and the last embers of light bathed the bayou in soft hues of yellow and red. The moss hanging on the extended branches of the huge live oak swayed in the gentle breeze.

Darkness soon enveloped our setting and all that remained were the shadows cast by the flickering candles.

Anthony and I took kitchen duty while Mama cleared the table. I glanced toward the outdoor clock. I'd been here over three hours. I smiled.

As I was leaving, I remembered something I wanted to ask Mama. I stopped on the front porch amidst her potted plants. Crickets and frogs sang to us. "Mama, do you know if Beau's grandmother, Mrs. Mouton, had any family who lived in Arkansas?"

She furrowed her brow slightly. "No, not that I know of. I believe the whole family is from here, and I don't think any of them left. Her mother and father's family is from here. They were a pretty small family, and I'm sure none of them left here. I don't know a whole lot about that generation. I do know she only has the one sister, Mrs. Chandler, and one brother, Arvin Gerard. Why do you ask?"

"Oh, just something I was curious about. Is Mrs. Chandler older than she is?"

"Yes. I believe she is."

I walked to the door, and from the steps, I leaned in and gave Mama a hug. "G'night Mama. And thanks for a great evening." I yelled toward the kitchen. "Good night, Anthony."

He poked his head around the doorframe. "Hey,

no need to yell. I'm right here. Do you think I'd let you leave without a hug?"

I hugged my brother. When I reached the bottom of the steps, Mama called out. "You do know Mawmaw had a couple of aunts from Arkansas."

I turned toward Mama and let the information percolate. "Oh, OK. Thanks."

Her words grabbed hold of my heart and twisted it just a little.

Lady S…Mawmaw?

I drove home with the thought swirling through my mind. I could see Mawmaw's spirit in those letters before I could see Mrs. Mouton's. And what if Mawmaw was Lady S? Would she come to see Carlton before he died? Although, those questions were important, the most important question was how to find the true identity of Lady S when the two people who knew the truth weren't speaking.

Seize

"Cheryl, it's nice to see you. Thanks for setting up the appointment with Carlton. He's an interesting gentleman." Pastor Chuck sat on a leather chair across from my matching one. A small wood and wrought-iron table stood between our chairs.

"Interesting is a good word to describe him." I smiled. "I suspect there's more to him than he's willing to share right now."

"I think you're right." He leaned back and crossed one leg over the other. "How can I help you?"

I leaned back also and picked at an imaginary lint ball on my black slacks. "Actually, Carlton suggested I see you. It has to do with belief in God, but most importantly, I'm struggling with forgiveness issues."

"I see. Tell me."

It took a few moments to gather my courage. After all, I'd not seen Chuck since that night when Debra and I had rescued him. A quick shake of my head helped clear the mental image.

He leaned toward me. "We can just sit here and not say a thing if you want. Or I can pray for you if it's too difficult."

His kindness warmed me, and if I didn't tell him the truth now, I wouldn't ever be able to. Once I opened my mouth, the words flowed. I told him about Mama and Elray. I shared feelings about the past and described my current level of faith. The story took about thirty minutes. I sighed. I'd summed up a lifetime of discontent in half an hour. There seemed to be something inherently wrong with that.

"Cheryl, I could tell you not to be so hard on yourself and forgive yourself, but you and I both know that's not what works. You've known me way before Christ claimed by heart, and you know the reputation I had. Can you imagine what it's been like to be a preacher here in the same location where I committed the majority of my sins?" His left eyebrow shot up. "Been like the valley of the shadow of death, but you know what? It's been the best thing that could have happened. God's omnipotence and perfect timing made sure it did. All I had to do was surrender to His prompting."

I hadn't considered Chuck's position before. "I imagine it's been tough."

"In some ways, yes, but in others, it's been great. What better way to showcase God's almighty ability to use anyone as His vessel? Including a cracked one like me. But there's no way I could have been receptive and open to teach had I not let go of the guilt. Have you ever stopped to think maybe God wants to use you to minister to Carlton?"

"Me? No. How could God use me? There are days I'm not sure I believe He exists."

"He can reflect His character through your compassion, strength, loving kindness, and gentle caring hands to Carlton."

"I never thought of those things as reflecting God's character."

"Yes, those things are all God's character. Harboring unnecessary guilt, hatred, or withholding forgiveness can act as a filter to keep those good things from coming or going from us. It hinders us in ways we don't realize. Sometimes forgiveness takes time, whether it's ourselves we have to forgive or someone else."

He leaned back in his chair. "I can tell you from experience, if you have a receptive heart and pray, amazing things can happen." He chuckled and then spread his arms out wide. His jacket opened to reveal the lilac shirt underneath. "Look at me. I look in the mirror every day and wonder what God saw in me, but I thank Him every day for seeing it. I often tell my congregation that me becoming a preacher is proof positive that God really does have a sense of humor."

I smiled. A flash of his walk on the old road came to mind, and I quickly dismissed it. I could not—would not go there.

Chuck scribbled a few notes on the yellow legal pad lying on the table. "Here are a few Bible verses to read and study. Also, remember to pray before you read these. Ask God to open your heart and mind to what He wants you to receive from these verses."

He tore the sheet and folded it in half. "Do you have a Bible?"

I did a mental scan of my bookshelf and couldn't remember ever having a Bible. Maybe as a child I'd had one. "No, I don't think I do. I can stop by the bookstore on my way home and buy one. What do you recommend?"

He reached around to the shelves behind him and lifted a Bible and a pamphlet off the top shelf. He opened the cover, slid the pamphlet inside, wrote something on the first page, and then lowered the cover. "Here." He handed me the Bible. "A gift from Grace Community Church."

Tears gathered in my eyes, turning the Bible in my hand into a fuzzy blue blob. A 'thank you' in a voice I hardly recognized eked out my quivering lips.

Chuck smiled. "The pamphlet is for our next Bible study class if you're interested."

Not able to trust my voice, I nodded.

He stood and I followed. "Cheryl, would you like to meet again?"

"Can I think about it before making another appointment?" I didn't want to take up his time until I'd processed all he said.

"That's fine. Just call my secretary if you decide you'd like to. I'm here for you." He squeezed my shoulder. "You're also welcome to come to our services tomorrow. Debra and I would love to have you worship with us."

"Thanks, Chu....er...Pastor Chuck."

His cheeks reddened as he laughed out loud and shook his head. "For heaven's sake, Cheryl, you've seen me in my underwear. I think you can call me Chuck."

Laughter bellowed from my gut. The heaviness I'd lived with for so long disappeared. I loved being free from the trappings of my emotions.

~*~

Driving to Lafayette, windows down, warm air blowing through my hair, gave me time to think about what Chuck had said. He'd gotten over the bindings of his past and allowed God to work through his life. Maybe it was time I did the same.

What would Annie be like today? Did she even know I'd stood at her bedside, painted her nails? Guess it didn't really matter if she knew or not. I did. And being with her had freed me from some of the crazy guilt twinges that plagued me for losing touch with her. Seeing her pale face with the angular lines helped remind me that she was real. A breathing person. One still married to Beau.

The shrill chirp of my cellphone rang as I navigated the car into an open spot near the front door.

A quick glance at my screen confirmed an unknown number. "Hello."

"Miss Cheryl, hello, this is Steven. Are you coming to my game this afternoon?"

Drats, I'd forgotten about Steven's game and my promise to consider going. "What time does it start?"

"Well, today's a double-header. The first one is getting ready to start in about twenty minutes. The next one should be in about two hours, tops."

"Sorry, buddy, I won't be able to make the first one. I'm at Bayou Pines visiting your mama."

I waited for his response, and when I didn't get one as expected, I wondered if he'd heard me. "Steven, you still there?"

"Yes, ma'am." His voice was thick with emotion. "Tell Mama I said hi, and I'll see her after the games."

"Will do. I should be at the park in time for your next game. So I'll see you then."

He hurried through the directions on what diamond he'd be playing on and hung up before I could ask if his father was there.

When I entered Annie's room, the coolness of the blowing air conditioner brushed along my bare arms. With a gentle stroke along Annie's arm, I let her know I stood next to her. "Annie, hello, honey. It's Cheryl. How's it going today?"

Oxygen tubing ran around her face and into her nostrils. Had she had difficulty breathing?

I sat next to her bed and told her what Steven had said. "You have a fine boy there, Annie. You and Beau have done a good job with him. He's playing a double-header today at the park. Would it be OK with you if I watched his game? It's just that Beau doesn't have much family left in town, and it's too far for your family to drive from Lake Charles to come to his games every Saturday. So I thought I'd go cheer him on. I'll yell a few times for you. How's that?

Annie remained with the same peaceful expression she'd worn last week. Only this week the tubing interrupted the smooth lines of her porcelain skin. Was she aware of my presence? If so, what was she thinking? Was I trespassing on her life?

I wanted to be her friend again. I wanted to believe she could hear me. I pulled the *Southern Living* magazine I'd bought this morning and began reading the articles to her, describing the elegant table settings, and lush summer gardens. After an hour, no detail had been overlooked. I'd shared the entire magazine with her. I gave her a good-bye kiss on her forehead and told her I'd be back next week.

As I stood to leave, her door opened. The shadow of a man entered the room and as the light bathed his face, I recognized him. "Gerald?"

Annie's brother stepped further into the room and stared. "Cheryl? Cheryl, is it still Broussard?"

I extended my hand. "It is."

Instead of taking my hand, he pulled me into his arms and gave me a bear-hug squeeze. "It's so good to see you again. What...are you doing here? I thought you left town."

"I did. I'm back."

"I see." He walked to Annie's bedside and brushed a few strands of hair away from her face. "The nurses said she's developed some fluid on her lungs. They've added the oxygen and are giving her breathing treatments."

"I'm sorry to hear that. I wondered." I walked toward the door. "I was just leaving, Gerald. It's good to see you again."

"Hey, let me walk you to your car, and then I'll come back and sit with Annie."

"Sure." He followed me to the door and out into the hallway. Gerald was four years older than Annie and had been our protector when we were in grade school. He'd made sure no one gave us a hard time.

"Still looking out for Annie, aren't you?"

He slid his hands into his pockets and walked with his head lowered. "Yeah, guess I am. I moved to Shreveport a few years ago, so I don't get here as much as I'd like, but I come when I can. "

I paused and turned toward him. "I'm sure she appreciates your visits."

"I wish I knew if she knows I'm even here. But if she does, I know she appreciates your visits, too. It's nice of you to come see her. Ya know, Cheryl, she tried to contact you when she and Beau started seeing each other."

"She did?"

"Yep, she wanted to know if it was OK with you. She valued your friendship and hated that you two drifted apart. She knew how crazy you'd been about Beau."

I sighed. "That was Annie. So considerate." I swallowed the rising lump. "It's not fair. She's too good for this to happen to her."

"She didn't deserve this. Neither did Beau and Steven." Emotion slurred his words. Moisture glistening in his eyes reflected in the afternoon sun.

"Gerald, do you think she'd be OK with me going to Steven's game this afternoon?"

He laid his hand on my shoulder. "She would love for you to be at Steven's game. If she couldn't go, I can't think of anyone else she'd rather have there."

I stared at the crack in the sidewalk and waited until the emotion rising in my throat settled. When I finally found the courage to look at Gerald, his smile warmed me. "Thanks. I needed to hear that. Now go sit with your amazing sister." I nudged him on the arm.

He chuckled. "I will."

~*~

I drove through Toucoin's Park negotiating the curves to the back of the park to the Little League fields. I swore the last time I was here, I'd never return. Yet here I was. Another never-say-never lesson learned.

So many spots throughout the park brought back a cadre of memories. Did Beau remember the last time we were at this park together? The memory so vivid, my gut tightened thinking about that day, our last day of high school, and I'd met Beau here. He waited for me next to one of the picnic tables near the lake so handsome in his navy and gold football jersey, the number seventeen emblazoned on his back and sleeves. His dark hair feathered back in smooth layers, framed the unbridled joy on his face when he saw me approach. The tenderness of his brown eyes enveloped me, and I have never felt such acceptance and love since.

On that day, I'd turned down his marriage proposal. The rejection tangled in the warmth of those brown eyes continued to haunt me.

I drove around the lake and passed *the* picnic table. The tree next to it drew me, so much so that I had to stop. As I walked toward the mighty oak, I tried to imagine how different my life would have been had I said yes all those years ago.

Looking up at the large trunk, I found what I'd come for. *B & C* carved into the hefty bark. Beau's twinkling eyes after he'd finished the task filled my thoughts. So proud. *There, future generations will know all about our love.* He'd said those words with such confidence that we'd be together forever.

Regret seemed such a useless emotion especially as I've realized things are the way they are and our stories have made us who we are. I'm not sure Beau and I would still be married had I said yes at eighteen.

Certain things were becoming very clear.

I needed to leave here.

He needed to stay and marry Annie. Plain and simple.

It had not been our time. I ran my fingers over the rough bark and the carved letters and then turned away from the towering tree and walked back to my car feeling more confident than I had in years.

The parking lot at the last baseball diamond in the park held a throng of cars, SUVs, and trucks of every make and model. I parked my car and headed to the stands.

Beau wasn't hard to spot. He was the dad at the

end of the row cheering with whoops and hollers rivaling any rapid, die-hard Saints fan. After all, Saints and LSU fans are the icons of Louisiana sports loyalty. If Louisiana had a pro-baseball team, I'm sure they'd get the same devotion.

"C'mon, Steven, take it home!"

I slid onto the bench next to him and glanced at the scoreboard. "Tied. Are you kidding me?"

"Nope. It's the bottom of the ninth. Bases are loaded. Two outs and Steven is at bat. You've got good timing, girl."

I smiled. Timing had nothing to do with it. If he'd only known where I'd stopped before coming here. "Glad I made it in time."

We watched as Steven swung at the first ball the pitcher fired his way and missed.

"Strike one!" The umpire yelled.

"C'mon, buddy. You can do this." I barely heard Beau's words as he stopped yelling and focused on the drama unfolding below us. Even though he remained seated, his knee bounced up and down. "C'mon. C'mon."

"Strike two."

A collective *ahh* spread throughout the stands.

Steven, looking so much like his father, wiped his hands on his uniform pants and then tightened his grip on the bat.

"C'mon, buddy. C'mon." Beau spoke into his clasped hands.

Whack. The ball connected with the bat and sailed past the right fielder's head to the far end of the field.

Beau and I jumped from our seats. "Run! Run!" we yelled in unison.

Everyone in the stands cheered and the noise

melted in one shout for Steven to run.

When he zipped around third base and headed for home the outfielder retrieved the ball and threw to the cutoff man. Steven closed in on home as the ball flew toward the plate. The catcher, in his perfect catcher pose, awaited the ball. As though the action happened in slow motion, Steven lay back and let his feet slide forward in front of him while the ball dashed passed him. The ball stopped inside the catcher's mitt seconds after Steven's feet crossed the plate.

"Safe!" the umpire yelled.

The crowd's volume tripled, something I didn't think possible.

Beau jumped up and down. "He did it. He did it."

I jumped up and down.

We laughed loud. We laughed from deep places that had forgotten the pure joy of laughing, and over something as simple as a child's baseball game.

But to Steven this was *the* world and something he sorely needed after the last few months—well, years—of his life.

"C'mon. Let's go down closer to the field." Beau guided me off the stands.

Steven's teammates lifted him onto their shoulders and pranced him around the field.

Beau watched with a grin. A prouder papa could not be found.

When the boys came back toward the team dugout, Steven spied his father and me. "Dad, I did it!"

"Yes, you did, son. Good job."

"Miz Cheryl, you came! Did you see my homerun?"

"I did. You were remarkable."

Several parents of Steven's team members

congratulated Steven. Many patted Beau on the back and asked about Annie. I stepped back and watched the scene. Beau had amazing community support, but with work, trips to sit with Annie, and trying to keep Steven's life as normal as possible for a ten-year-old, he'd not had time to keep close friends. Like me, the friends he'd had in school had either left town or were busy with their own lives. So the community was what he had, and they'd rallied around him as best they could.

The short time Beau had with Annie seemed filled with more of the things that mattered. I was thankful he'd had those years and the memories. A part of me battled the pangs of jealousy. I wanted those things, too. But I realized with blinding clarity that I'd passed that opportunity with Beau many years ago.

I was grateful for the second chance I'd been given with Mama and accepted the contentment that I could be Beau's and Steven's friend during their time of need. Those things had been more than I imagined possible. *Thank you, Lord.*

Dix-Sept

Later that afternoon, after Steven's game I gathered Mr. Bojangles and walked the few blocks to Mawmaw's house. He ran circles around my feet during the entire walk. Was he excited about being outdoors or getting the treat he knew Mawmaw had waiting for him?

"Hello." I walked into the back door. "Mawmaw?" Silence quickened my pulse. I ventured further into the house. "Mawmaw?" I raised my voice.

"Cheryl, in here." Her muted voice drifted from her bedroom.

As I peered around the doorframe, my heart did a two-step. "Mawmaw, what are you doing?"

She stood on the top rung of her stepladder, leaning over to adjust the curtains over the window above her bed. "Just can't get the curtains closed. Every morning a slit of sunshine hits me right smack dab in the eyes. I'm tired of it."

"OK." I held the ladder to keep it from tipping over. "Why don't you come down and let me do that for you?"

She stretched a little more. "Almost got it."

I held my breath. *Please Lord, don't let her fall.*

Even Mr. Bojangles seemed to have stopped breathing. With his leash on the floor beside him, he waited at the door with his dark eyes fixed on Mawmaw.

"There." She leaned back toward the center. "I think that'll do it."

I placed my hands on her sides and guided her off the ladder.

"Please don't ever do that again." I placed my hand on my heart. "You about scared me to death."

"Oh, Cheryl, I've told you a million times not to exaggerate." She flashed her mischievous smile toward me and then giggled.

"Mawmaw, you could have fallen and broken a bone. Then where would you be? Living with Mama, for sure."

"Oh, thanks for painting that picture. C'mon, pooch, I've got your treat ready." She walked toward the door and a bouncing Mr. Bojangles.

I followed behind, ladder in hand. "Please wait for one of us to do those things for you."

She held up her hands. "OK, I give. Are we still going for our afternoon walk, or will you keep lecturing me?"

"Yes, our walk and no more lectures."

"Good." She fed the treat to my now impatient dog.

With Mr. Bojangles on my left side and Mawmaw on my right, we strolled our small neighborhood. Giant live oaks lined our street, their large out-reaching branches forming a canopy over our heads.

I wanted desperately to broach the subject of Carlton but didn't feel the time was right. When would it be?

"Hear your brother's gonna take that Guidry girl out again. 'Bout time he gets off his keister and connects wit' that girl. They were a good match." Her walking cane tapped against the asphalt.

"Yep. I hope things work out for them. I liked her."

"What about you, Cheryl? When you gonna find someone to spend your life wit'?"

"I don't know. Evidently Mr. Right hasn't made his presence known."

Mr. Bojangles tugged on his leash and pulled my arm forward as a squirrel ferried up the bark of one of the large trees.

"Are you sure he hasn't made his presence known?"

I stopped and turned toward her. "What do you mean?"

"Seems I remember you were pretty sweet on Beau Battice there in high school."

"Mawmaw, you know he's married. But I find myself wondering if he was my Mr. Right, and I let him get away."

"I know he's married, and I'm certainly not saying you should be involved with a married man, but you could do a lot worse than hooking up wit' someone like him. There are a lot of guys like him around here."

After quieting Mr. Bojangles and untangling his leash from around my ankles, I resumed our forward progression. "I'm too busy to think about starting a relationship with anyone right now. The timing is wrong, and there really isn't anyone I've met who fits the bill."

"Well, there is a lot to be said for timing. The right man will come along when you're receptive to the idea. The good Lord will send you someone when he knows you're ready."

That was the second time today I'd been reminded that good things happen when my heart is open and receptive. Maybe I should listen.

We walked a few more blocks in silence and then turned around just as the sun was sinking low on the horizon. Its rays cast a soft glow through the branches of the oaks.

Mawmaw stopped walking for a moment. "You know, I hear Beau's wife is not doing real well. She got pneumonia or something and has taken a turn for the worse. That poor woman, she's had a hard time, not to mention how tough this whole thing has been on Beau and Steven. Just breaks my heart for dem."

"I know. I can't imagine how difficult it's been for everyone." I removed Mr. Bojangles' leash and scratched his belly.

We climbed the steps onto Mawmaw's porch and sat on the hanging swing. She turned to me with a distant look in her eyes. "Cheryl, I know what it feels like to think you've lost Mr. Right. That one person who could, how do you young people say it, rock your world. The person who made you feel so alive the very thought of life without dem tears your heart into shreds."

Was Mawmaw talking about Carlton? Dare I ask? I tapped my fingers on my thighs while gathering the nerve to ask. "Mawmaw—"

A flash of white bolted past me and off the porch. Mr. Bojangles darted through the yard, toward the street in full chase of a squirrel.

I gasped and dashed after him.

The headlights of an oncoming car illuminated the squirrel's path.

"Oh, no. Mr. Bojangles, stop!" I waved my arms to get the driver's attention. The car approached.

I huffed and puffed—reminded of how out of

shape I'd become. "C'mon." I waved again and just as I turned to face the oncoming car, it turned into Mawmaw's driveway. Anthony. "Thank you, Jesus."

I trotted across the street to gather my dog. He'd scared me half to death. When I bent over to pick him up, he hopped into my arms and licked my face—his tactic to deflect my anger. It worked. His big dark eyes and bushy eyebrows had a way of melting me like wax in the midday sun. I carried him back to the porch, at a slower pace. "No... running off...again." His scolding came between gasps.

"Sis, I haven't seen you run that fast since we were in high school and Mr. Avery's bull got loose from his pasture." Anthony walked up and lifted Mr. Bojangles from my arms. "Come with nice Uncle Tony."

"Angelle." I gasped again but began to catch my breath.

She nodded. "Hello, Cheryl. It's been awhile."

"Oh, my, yes it has. Probably since the year I ran from Mr. Avery's bull." I chuckled.

She laughed softly and nodded. "You're right."

I linked my arm with hers and guided her up the stairs to where Mawmaw waited on the porch.

Anthony followed with Mr. Bojangles.

We sat on the porch for a couple of hours drinking iced tea with citronella candles burning and the ceiling fan whirling. Our smooth, easy conversation mingled well with the symphony of cicadas and the flashes of light from the lightning bugs. It felt right having her around again.

I loved seeing the pure joy and contentment on my brother's face. Happiness for him filled my heart. It was nice to feel good for a change.

~*~

Sunday morning I awoke at 4:00 AM. Wide awake. No more coffee for me after 5:00 PM.

I'd been invited by Chuck and Debra to attend worship service at their church. The thought of going to church left me unsettled. The services I'd attended in the past were staunch and ritualistic. I'd left feeling relieved to be out in fresh air. I *should* not feel this way when leaving church. So I'd abandon all ties to religion and just lived my life. I guess the problem was, I'd lived it without God. Could God really make that much of a difference? Enough to change a bad boy like Chuck into a pastor? I had to admit that was quite a transformation.

I punched my pillow and rolled over in an attempt to return to sleep. Thoughts of Anthony and Angelle, Mama and Elray, Mawmaw and Carlton, Beau and Annie, and Steven whizzed through my mind jostling to see which one claimed the coveted forefront position. I couldn't calm my brain. After wrestling for an hour, I threw the covers back and marched into the kitchen.

The steady hum of the air conditioner provided a backdrop to the quietness of the morning.

Mr. Bojangles slept soundly in his bed in the laundry room.

I rustled into the kitchen and fixed my black gold—coffee. I carried my cup into the living room and settled into the corner of the couch ready to tackle my mail from the past few days.

Beau weighed heavy on my mind and my heart. I could only imagine what he was going through. I'd started to call when I got home from Mawmaw's last night and then realized it was past ten, and I didn't want to bother him that late. I loved being his friend, but something kept pulling me back. I didn't want Beau to get the wrong impression. Or was it Beau I was really worried about? I wrestled with my true feelings. Was I concerned more about what others thought? Did I battle with some of the old feelings I'd had for him?

He was married. I pushed thoughts of Annie, so close to death, away. I didn't want to think about her for fear I may have thoughts I couldn't be proud of. I didn't want her to die. But I also didn't want Beau to suffer the way he'd suffered. The situation was all so confusing and unsettling.

I turned to the mail stack on my lap—credit card applications, subscription requests for magazines months from expiration, and bills. On the table next to the couch, sat the Bible Chuck had given me. I opened the cover to the short note he'd scribbled on the inside.

Cheryl, Thanks so much for coming to see me and trusting me. Remember God can use any one of us at any time to serve His purposes. Love in Christ, Chuck.

Below his signature he had written in very neat print, *Jeremiah 29:11-13.*

I flipped pages to Jeremiah and read the verse Chuck had quoted. "For I know the plans I have for you," declares the Lord, "plans to prosper you and not to harm you, plans to give you hope and a future."

God had plans for me? Plans to prosper me and not harm me. I guess prosper can mean different things to different people in different circumstances. I didn't particularly feel like I had prospered, but I wasn't destitute, either.

I thought about the time Jarrod had struck me. He could have seriously injured me. Had God been watching out for me back then? Had He done the same when Mama brought Elray into our lives? To give me hope and a future. Was coming home to discover the truth, hope for my future?

While reading the next lines, my heart stirred.

"Then you will call on Me and come and pray to Me, and I will listen to you. You will seek Me and find Me when you seek Me with all your heart."

I remembered praying to God when Mr. Bojangles ran into the street, when Mawmaw had her stroke, when she had climbed on the ladder and I thought she'd fall, and when I felt helpless in how to care for Carlton. Some of those things were minor and some were major, but one thing struck me: I hadn't consciously thought about those prayers. They'd come automatically. And I'm pretty sure God had heard me.

I volleyed the idea of whether or not to go to church for a moment. Then I downed the last sip of my coffee, cared for Mr. Bojangles, and headed to my room to change. I'd go today. *Lord, show me what You want me to be.*

~*~

Monday morning, the sweet aroma of pancakes enveloped me as I walked into Carlton's house. Darcy walked into the kitchen, a dishtowel draped over her right shoulder and her long brown ponytail swinging back and forth. "Mornin' Cheryl. How are you?"

"Doing well. You?"

"I'm OK. Ready to get home to bed."

"Did Carlton have a bad night?"

"He woke up a couple of times last night crying about Sherri. I don't know who this gal is, but I'd like to meet her to give her a piece of my mind. She sure broke his heart but good."

I nodded. "I'd like to meet her, too."

I helped Darcy clean the kitchen.

She filled me in on what Carlton needed before she headed out the door.

When I entered Carlton's room, his raspy breathing and snoring filled the air. I tiptoed out and headed for the kitchen table wishing I'd brought something to read or at least my knitting. I ventured into his living room to see if he had any books. I'd never been there before, never really had a need.

An old, vinyl brown sofa sat against the right wall in the sparse rectangular room. Thick drapes hung from a picture window above it. Next to the sofa sat a worn wooden rocking chair. Both faced a bank of shelves where a television with a circular knob to change channels rested on the middle shelf.

A few books stood upright above and to the right of the television. I stood on my toes and tilted my head to read the titles. *Phantom of the Opera, Middlemarch, Cyrano de Bergerac,* and *Notre Dame de Paris.* Had Carlton read these? They didn't seem like the type of books he'd read. A theme emerged. These were all books about unrequited love. My thoughts zipped back to Lady S.

Poor Carlton. Darcy had nailed the truth. Sherri had hurt him but good.

A black binder sat on the shelf below the books. Nothing fancy, just an office three-ring type with the word *Pictures* written on a label attached to the cover. Maybe Carlton would like to look through these.

I grabbed the binder and carried it to the kitchen table. Carlton loved a mid-morning cup of coffee, so I made a fresh pot. Another cup would awaken my tired body. I hadn't slept much last night. Stirrings from Chuck's sermon yesterday kept my mind racing way past my bedtime. I couldn't wait to share them with Carlton.

Chuck had preached on the importance of forgiveness. His words worked like a soothing balm to soften the rough edges and showed me I did the best I could with the knowledge I had. Elray would have forgiven me and, because I asked with a repentant heart, I knew God had forgiven me, also.

The scent of fresh coffee permeated throughout the house, and I figured if anything could wake Carlton it would be the lure of a cup of coffee.

I glanced at the clock. Ten. I returned to Carlton's room and listened. Same snoring and raspy breathing. He'd slept longer than usual. I debated waking him so he would sleep tonight but abandoned the idea. His body needed rest when he could get it. So I checked his oxygen levels, returned to the kitchen, and filled my coffee cup.

The binder beckoned.

Should I take a peek? I reached for the cover. Perhaps in a few minutes, I would know the identity of Lady S.

A soft voice inside admonished. *Don't. It's his privacy.*

I pushed the binder to the other side of the table far away from where I sat. Carlton trusted me, and I valued that trust. I had a feeling opening that binder would be like opening Pandora's Box, and I'd lose something valuable in the process.

Dix Huit

Carlton's hacking cough invaded the silence of the kitchen. I rushed to his room. He had removed his oxygen tube and coughed into a handful of tissue. Droplets of blood stained the white paper, and his body jerked from the violent coughs.

I dashed into the bathroom and dampened a facecloth with cool water.

Carlton settled back onto his pillow with his tubing in place.

I wiped his face leaving the cloth to linger over his eyes.

"Mornin'...missed ya," he said, his voice cracking more than usual.

We exchanged the facecloth for a glass of water and his medication. I laid the towel on the nightstand while Carlton took the pills with several small sips of water.

"Better?"

"Yep." He handed the glass to me.

A couple of bloodstains dotted the old blue blanket so I removed it from his bed. He pointed to his closet. "Other blanket in there."

After I placed the new blanket on his bed and started the washer to clean the blue one, I returned to his bedside. "Do you need anything?"

"Yep. Lady S's letters."

The ashen gray of his complexion broke my heart.

The end for him fast approached. Was there nothing I could do to give him peace? Chuck had also preached on missed opportunity. I didn't want Carlton to die without the opportunity to forgive or be forgiven, whatever his case.

I walked toward the dresser where I'd left the letters in the top drawer. "Carlton, would you like to meet with Pastor Chuck again?'

"Did you see him?"

"I did. We had a nice chat. He helped me understand a little about forgiveness. I also attended his church yesterday. He's a good preacher. I'm still thinking about all he said."

"Don't think...do," he said.

Was he avoiding my question? "Would you like to meet with Pastor Chuck again?"

"Don't think so." He pursed his lips and met my gaze when I approached the bed. "I don't care...anymore. Jus' ready to go."

His words splintered my heart. I knew he grew weary, but I didn't think he'd gone this far. Chuck's question loomed in my mind. Did God want to use me to minister to Carlton? If he did, now would be a great time to give me the words because I didn't know how to respond or whether I could get past the tangled knot in my esophagus. *Lord, help me here.*

I lifted his bony hand and let my warmth mingle with the coldness in his fingers. It was as though he'd already left and only an empty shell remained. Until I looked into his eyes. The glistening there reflected his pain and longing.

He wasn't an empty shell.

He still lived, and I became more determined than ever to make his days as content and comfortable as possible.

"Carlton, I can't say I understand how you feel. I don't. But I can only imagine how hard this is for you."

"Past time...should be gone by now."

I wrapped both my hands around his fingers and brought them to my lips where I gently blew on them, hoping to infuse him with warmth and life. "Maybe God has something He needs you to do before you go. A job of some sort."

He snorted. "Me?"

"Yeah, you. He could have taken you yesterday, last night, or two weeks ago, but He hasn't. There's a reason He's kept you around." I continued to blow warmth onto his fingertips.

His lips slowly spread into a grin. The cowboy grin I'd fallen in love with the first time he'd revealed it to me covered his face. I knew he had shaken his mood, if only for a moment. "To keep...you in line," he smarted.

I squeezed his hand and laughed through tears. "Not a chance, Buster. I'm keeping you in line."

His smiled broadened. "How 'bout...a letter?"

"You got it. But first, can you answer a question?"

"Depends...on the question."

I drew in a deep breath and exhaled long and slow. Time slipped away and I needed to be bold. "Why don't you want me to contact Lady S?"

He closed his eyes, and I feared the question would jetty him back into his depression or worse, a raging fit that would further erode his remaining time. Instead, he opened his eyes and spoke between labored breaths. "She don't need...me remindin' her of past mis...takes. Got a good...life with...out me." He paused for a moment, and I debated whether or not to speak.

He continued. "Love her too...much to hurt her...again...or her family."

So he hurt her. I garnered each precious tidbit of information he divulged. "Ever think that she might want to see you?"

"She doesn't." His conviction held, and I knew pushing this would be fruitless.

"OK. But if you change your mind and want me to contact her, please tell me who she is, and I will call her for you."

He nodded.

I turned my attention to the letters on my lap and sensed I'd need extra courage to read today. Were the words of Lady S the only thing keeping Carlton alive? I thumbed through the stack. My chest tightened. Five letters remained.

I unfolded the top letter.

My Dearest Carlton,

I got your last letter. My heart exploded with joy when I saw your handwriting. Yes, I am taking care of myself. I want to be in tiptop shape when you come home. Yes, I am learning as much as possible and yes, I'm reading the books you bought me before you left. Thank you, again. They keep my heart calm at night before I fall asleep. And, just like you with me, you are the last thing I think of at night and the first thing when I awake.

Christmas was wonderful but sad without you. I saw your mama today at Marcel's General Market. She smiled at me and nodded, but she didn't come to me. I wanted so badly to go to her and tell her I understand how she feels, but I didn't. I respect your wishes that we keep our relationship a secret from our parents. My best friend knows. She is actually dating your brother. So we talk about our letters and how anxious we are for this war to be over. My Mama knows, but she hasn't said anything to Papa, and I feel bad that I'm causing her to keep things from her husband. But she knows how angry he'd be, and I think she believes we'll grow tired of one another. I don't think she's ever been truly in love with Papa. I see how they are together, and I can't imagine them ever having what you and I have. I don't see love between them. Only obligation. Sometimes I think they got married as a business deal or because it's who their parents wanted them to marry. I thank God that's not us. Please stay safe. I pray every day morning, noon, and night for your safety. I know God brought us together, and I can't imagine my life without you by my side. I can't imagine life without our kids trampling around my feet. But I can't imagine waking up mornings like now, without your head on the pillow next to mine.

I am waiting so impatiently for your return and our wedding day. It will be the happiest day of my life!

Yours forever,

The future Mrs. Carlton Perlouix - Lady S

The steady drone of Carlton's concentrator yanked me back into the present. Unlike after the other letters, where he stared off into space, this morning he stared at me. A curious, questioning gaze hid behind the moisture pooled in his eyes. "Ever...been in love?" His eyes bored into mine. "Truly in love?"

I stared back and wondered. Had I? I thought I loved Beau deeply, but was what we had in high school true love? And if it was, how could I have so easily walked away from him?

"I'm not sure, Carlton. I know I loved someone in high school, and I regret terribly that I walked away from him. I believe given more time and maturity, it could have been true love."

"Can you...go to him now?"

"Only as a friend."

He nodded. "I see." He flicked his fingers to draw me closer.

I leaned in toward his bed.

"Regrets...are hard. Don't let..." He paused and took several deep breaths. "...them steal your...joy."

I reached for his hand and held it tightly. I'd allow so many things to steal my joy. The more his comment permeated through my brain, the more I came to understand that I'd never really had joy. I'd spent my youth hating a man who didn't deserve it, my early twenties searching for something to fill the bottomless void, and my late twenties with men who didn't really love me. Ones, I never loved. Carlton was right. If I continued at this rate, my life would be one big regret.

He squeezed my hand and our gazes locked. "Understand...me?"

"I do. I do understand." Not able to stand the scrutiny of his glare, I turned toward the window and watched the flittering leaves of the sycamore tree.

Who was I? What had I done that if I died today people would know I existed? How could I find joy when I'd messed up so many opportunities I'd been given?

Carlton cleared his throat and drew my attention back to him. "Forgive your...self yet?"

I smiled and rolled my bottom lip between my teeth. This man had ferried his way into my heart. "Yes, I'm getting there. Still have moments of guilt that attack, but I'm making a conscious effort to let go. What about you?"

"Trying to."

"What's holding you back?"

"Stubborn...I guess."

A small chuckle escaped my lips. "I'd say that is probably true for both of us."

"Sup'ose...Pastor was right."

"About what?"

"For...giveness is freedom."

Funny how harbored guilt and resentment made it so easy to miss the one thing we all searched for—freedom.

"Guess he is right. Question is, do you want to be free of this nagging burden, or do you feel that it's your punishment?" I asked.

Carlton's eyelids closed, and he pushed them open again. He'd waged a battle to stay awake and despite the importance of our conversation, the drugs I'd given him earlier were wining.

He turned his hand in mine and tapped with his index finger. "Freedom," he said and closed his eyes. A few moments later, he nodded off to sleep.

Carlton's steady raspy breaths, the whirr of his concentrator, the *shush-shush* of the wind through the sycamores, and the tweets of the little birds in the branches spoke to me, saying, "He's right. He's right. He's right."

My heart stirred and moved in a way like never before. Praying felt important. Felt right. So I knelt and spoke to a God I had turned away from long before I had gotten a chance to really know Him.

Dix-Neuf

Over the next several days, I read three of the remaining five letters from Lady S to Carlton. In each letter, she poured out her love to him and hinted he had done the same in his letters to her. His condition remained the same. Not worse, but not better. While I expected as much, it broke my heart.

I'd spoken to Debra at our Fourth of July *fais do do* planning session and learned that Annie's condition had worsened. She'd developed pneumonia and was not responding to the treatments.

After the conversation with Carlton about regrets, I didn't want to regret not offering my help to Beau during this time. After a moment, I picked up the phone from my nightstand. As I dialed his number, my pulse quickened. *Please, Lord, let me say the right words.*

"Hello, this is Beau."

"It's Cheryl."

"Cheryl, hi."

I detected a hint of sadness that betrayed his words. "Beau, Debra told me about Annie. I'll be there next Saturday. Is there anything else you need me to do?"

"That's very kind. There is one thing you can do for me. Pray. Pray that, if this is Annie's time, that God would be merciful and relieve her suffering. And please pray that I have wisdom in all this. I feel so helpless."

His words shattered my resolve and the hot sting of tears pressed my eyes. I wanted to be strong for him. I swallowed and sighed. "Sure. I can do that and I will."

"Thanks, Cheryl. That means a lot to me. I know it's not something that's a big part of your life, but it's what has kept me going these past few years."

So that was how Beau managed throughout his horrific ordeal. "I'm thankful your faith has been such a comfort to you."

"It's that peace that passes all understanding."

I didn't quite understand his comment, but I guessed it had something to do with being at peace when your world was in chaos. I would like to have that. "Is that from the Bible?"

"It is, worded a bit differently, in Philippians 4:17."

"I'll look that up. How is Annie today?"

"Not well. I think this might be the beginning of the end. It's been so hard watching her wither away. I've tried to come here every night after work."

I thought of Carlton and his struggle. At least he communicated. Annie had been silent for two years. "Beau, I know this is hard. Please, know I will be praying. And if there is anything more you need me to do, just call."

"Thanks, Cheryl. I will."

After I'd hung up, I retrieved the Bible Chuck gave me from my nightstand and read the passage. Peace. The word itself offered hope for a place I longed to be. A place I had denied myself because of guilt, misunderstandings, and secrets that served no purpose.

I prayed for Beau, Steven, and Annie. Asking God

for his hand over their family came from a place in my heart that wanted nothing but comfort for all of them. I prayed for Carlton, for God's will to prevail, and for me to be open in however God chose to use me. I prayed for God to send Anthony the perfect wife at the perfect time. I prayed Mama would find true happiness. I prayed Mawmaw would continue to be a blessing of strength to all of us.

After I prayed, peace seem to fill a void that had been open for a long time.

~*~

The Fourth of July *fais do do* fast approached and most of the arrangements were in place. The committee members, myself included, assumed Beau's duties and everything was ready for the big day. I needed to find my costume and planned a visit to Mama's attic to rummage through Mawmaw's things.

I rang the doorbell at Mama's house. The unfamiliar cars parked in her driveway kept me from walking in as I usually did.

"Cheryl, hello." Mama opened the door. As usual, she looked elegant. Her loose, classic, up-styled hair highlighted her high cheekbones and perfectly sculpted face. Her lilac blouse turned her eyes deep violet. She sported a rosy glow that suited her well. What could have put that smile on her face?

"I hope I'm not interrupting anything, but I came to find that costume for the *fais do do*."

"Oh, right, yes. The trunks are in the attic. I'll show you where they are and turn the attic fan on for you. It's awfully hot up there. But..." She paused and grabbed my hand. "...before you go up, I want you to meet a few lady friends." She led me into the kitchen.

Aunt Melanie sat at the end of the large farm table with several women flanked around her. Bibles lay open on the table in front of each of them.

Elaine Martin's hesitant smile greeted me. What was she doing here?

Mama swiped her hand across the room. "These are my new Bible study friends. We're starting a new weekly study and they've welcomed me into their group."

I didn't know what to say. I had no idea Mama even considered God, and to learn she was hosting a group of women to study the Bible, fired off many surprise bells. Was this another part of Mama I didn't know? Obviously.

Aunt Melanie blew me a kiss from across the room and winked at me as though she had a secret for me. I walked to her side and kissed her cheek. "Good to see you, Aunt Mel."

"You, too, honey. You'll have to join our little group sometime. When the time is right, of course." She smiled at me and winked again.

Once Mama had introduced me to all six of the women, I couldn't help but feel that I'd been the topic of their conversation at some point. Especially, Elaine Martin. But was I judging too harshly? I had no real reason to believe Mrs. Martin had gossiped about me and Beau's meeting at the diner. Besides, I reminded myself that I wouldn't let what other people thought affect what I knew to be right.

"Hello, ladies. Nice to meet you all and, Mrs. Martin, good to see you again."

"You, too, Cheryl. Last time was at the diner, right?"

I held my head high. "That's right." I squinted my eyes and furrowed my brow. "Let me think...hmm. Was that the morning I had coffee with my old friend, Beau Battice?"

Mrs. Martin's eyes widened. "Ummm...err...why yes, I believe it was." She lowered her head and found something quite interesting in the pages of her opened Bible.

A quick glance toward Aunt Melanie revealed a twitch of a smile with mirth dancing in her eyes. "Cheryl, I have some flowers I picked from my garden for you to bring to Annie. You are still going today?"

I nodded. Leave it to my aunt to know just how to defuse a tense situation.

Mama stood at my side. "Cheryl has been visiting with Beau's wife, Annie, on Saturdays."

Murmurs of "how sweet" floated about the room as each of Mama's friends shared their thoughts about poor Annie.

Mrs. Martin remained silent.

"Well, I don't want to keep you from your studies. Have a good meeting."

"I'll just go and turn that fan on," Mama said.

Once Mama left the room, I leaned in toward Aunt Melanie as I walked out the kitchen to a chorus of good byes and nice to meet you's. "Would you show me where those flowers are?"

"Sure." She stood and followed me into the living room.

Once out of earshot, I turned to her. "What in the world? Mama in Bible study? How? When?"

Melanie beamed. "Prayer. Lots of prayer. I've been praying for this day for years. Your Mama started new meds about a month ago, and it just seemed the right time to invite her to this new study. She said yes. So here we are. She's also coming to church with me. It's a start, and I'm excited. Now if we can only get Mawmaw to come." When she shrugged, her curls bounced on her shoulders. "But, hey, all in God's timing. Right?"

I smiled. "Right." I couldn't help but feel that her comment had been directed toward me more than toward a missing-from-church Mawmaw.

Mama entered the living room carrying a glass of mint infused iced tea.

"So?" she asked. A rosy glow on her cheeks mingled with the sparkle in her eyes and a smile that radiated brilliance into the room. Mama was happy. I could see it, feel it, and knew it. "The fan is on. Feel free to look to your heart's content." She handed me the glass. "You'll need this. It's h-o-t with a capital H up there."

I took a large gulp of the tea. Before I knew what was happening, she hugged me. I held onto her shoulders, iced tea glass and all. This time I held on just a little longer than I ordinarily would. My heart sang for her. I wanted her to be well. Maybe with the new meds and a strong guiding faith, she could overcome the harsh demons that had plagued her life for so long.

A small twitch of jealousy bit just a little. I wanted what Mama had for myself. Would I ever find the kind of peace that conquered the demons of the past?

I'd seen changes in Mama since I came back. Some I had ignored because I was too busy blaming her for all the bad choices I'd made in my life, but some I couldn't help but notice. I suspected those changes had a lot to do with why we stood here hugging one another and not having another classic Broussard brouhaha.

We walked arm-in-arm down the hall. The *whoop, whoop* of the large attic fan filled the room. We opened windows at the end of the hallway and felt the immediate rush of warm air being sucked into the attic.

"I've opened the attic door. The air will take a minute to circulate. You may want to consider doing this later this evening. It's awfully hot."

"I'll be OK."

She nodded and smiled. "Call me if you need anything. I'll be with my group."

With her shiny eyes and happy smile, I maybe saw who she was for the very first time. My mama. And I found that I liked her.

~*~

Even with the large fan sucking air into the attic, the sauna-like heat was stifling. Mawmaw's trunks sat tucked away in the far end of the attic—farthest away from air-conditioned coolness filtering in from below and the large whooping blades.

Mama was right. Later in the evening or early in the morning would be a better time to be up here. I gasped for fresh air. Maybe I'd come back another time when I could breathe. I walked along the walkway in the center of the attic toward the trunks. A fine layer of dust and the low lighting distorted the color of the lids.

I grabbed the handle and slid the first one along the rafter onto the walkway. Perspiration dripped into my eyes as I dragged it back toward the opening. Sweat poured from every pore and drenched my cotton dress. My feet slid in and out of my flip-flops.

I walked back to the other trunk and dragged it toward the opening. Before I reached the door and the sweet cool air, my head started spinning and my vision blurred. I sat on the trunk and took several deep breaths.

Vingt

The thick heated air of the attic felt like breathing in water.

Just then, Mama popped her head up through the opening. "Cheryl, everything OK?"

"Yeah, but I don't think I'll be able to look through these today. Maybe I'll get Anthony to come by and take them down. Could we put them in the guestroom?"

"Sure. Here." She tossed a wet washcloth toward me. It landed on the trunk next to me. "Please come out of there. I don't want you getting overcome by this heat."

I lifted the towel and wiped my sweat-drenched face. The coolness took my breath away. After a few minutes next to my face, the cloth lost its coolness and matched the attic heat.

Revived by the wet towel, I dragged the second trunk next to the first one and climbed down the stairs.

"Thought you might need this." Mama met me at the kitchen counter and handed me another large glass of sweet tea.

Aunt Melanie busied herself with clearing glasses and dessert plates from the table.

The ladies were gone.

"Thanks. Your study over?" I gulped from the glass. Goose bumps rose on my arms in the cool air of Mama's kitchen.

"Yep, we were just about finished when you got here."

Aunt Melanie placed the dishes in the sink. "Did you find anything?"

"No, it's too hot. I'll have to look later when it's cooler. Maybe at night. Or sooner, if Anthony can bring them down."

Mama started running water in the sink while Aunt Melanie reached for dish washing soap. The simple task seemed like something more. They seemed to work as a choreographed dance, something I suspected had not always been the case.

"I can't wait to see what Mama has saved in those dusty ole trunks." Mama turned to her sister and giggled. "Maybe some teenage diaries she kept."

"Oooo, I'd love to know what she was like as a teenaged girl. How often did she accuse us of being, what was it, melodramatic maidens? Maybe she wasn't too different as a young girl."

The sisters laughed and I watched with a grateful heart. They'd been close through the years, but I'd never seen this type of sisterly display of affection.

"Why don't we all go to dinner tonight? I think Angelle is in town. She and Anthony could join us and so could Mawmaw. Wouldn't that be fun?" Mama's excitement was contagious, and I couldn't help accepting her invitation.

As I drove to see Annie, I thought of Mama and all she'd been through. I'd loved seeing the changes in Mama and her interaction with her Bible study friends and especially, with Aunt Melanie. Yet disappointment shrouded me as I left her house. I didn't have a costume and the July Fourth *fais do do* was in five days. If nothing proved suitable in Mawmaw's trunks, I'd have to get real creative. Fast.

~*~

As I walked into Annie's room, the deep resonating tone of Beau's voice filled the room. "Honey, you should have seen his home run. You would have been so proud of him. I love how he's grown into such a good kid. I thank God that we had him. He keeps me from going insane with loneliness. I do miss you so much."

His words bruised my heart. Poor Beau. I tried but couldn't imagine what he must be feeling. Realizing that I'd been standing there for far longer than I should, I turned to leave. Just as I did, Beau came to the door. "Cheryl, I didn't know you were here."

"Just for a few minutes. I walked up and couldn't help but hear you talking to Annie. I didn't want to interrupt." I touched his sleeve. "If she can hear you, I know your words are a great comfort to her."

He hung his head for a moment. "It's probably more of a comfort to me to say them to her." He was truly one of a kind.

And instead of feeling jealous of my friend, my heart swelled with thankfulness that Annie and Beau had been happy together. I loved that Annie had a husband who adored her. And Beau a wife like Annie who, I know, appreciated him.

"How is she?"

"Not doing well today. I was just going to get Steven. He went out to the garden."

"Let me get him. You stay with Annie."

Beau pointed toward the end of the hallway. "Through there." His usually bright eyes had faded to a dull shade of brown and the shadow of a beard spoke of how quickly he'd rushed over this morning.

The garden area had rows of raised boxes where red, white, and salmon-colored geranium blooms spilled from two of the large boxes. Each of the other boxes held foxgloves, pansies, four-o-clocks, and vinca. The explosion of color was highlighted by the bright sunshine.

I slid my sunglasses over my eyes and scanned among the boxes for Steven.

He sat, head down on folded arms atop a cement table.

I swallowed. Poor kid. I'd sat alone on my swing the day my dad died. The overwhelming pain seemed like more than I could ever bear. Aunt Melanie had come to sit with me. While I didn't know exactly how Steven felt, I'm pretty sure I had some idea. I slid onto the bench next to him.

He lifted his head. Redness rimmed his eyes as he squinted to see who sat next to him. "Miss Cheryl, hey."

"Hello, Steven."

He turned toward a bed of roses at the edge of the garden. "Roses are her favorite."

"I know."

We stared at the bushes filled with yellow, white, pink, and red roses. Someone had taken great care of the flowers here.

He continued to look ahead. "She's dying. Isn't she?"

"Yes."

I wanted to hug him and tell him everything would be OK. But he was ten. Would he think of a hug as lame? I had no clue how ten-year-old boys thought.

I ventured a touch on his hand with the tips of my fingers. "My dad died when I was four. I remember thinking my world had ended." I paused and met his gaze as he turned to me. "You'll miss her. A lot."

Tears filled his large brown eyes. "I already do." He swallowed hard.

I swallowed harder. I stood and touched his shoulder. "There's still time to tell her how much you'll miss her."

He stood and I saw the weight of a thousand tomorrows on his small shoulders. The brave little athlete had disappeared, and in his place, stood a scared little boy who had already lost his mama. I wrapped my arm around those tiny shoulders and guided him back inside to Beau and Annie.

"I missed the game today. Dad said I could go, but it didn't seem right to be having fun when Mama wasn't."

"Steven, I may not know a lot, but I know one thing, your Mama would want you to have fun playing the game you love any chance you get. That's just how she was."

"I'll play again. Just not today."

"I understand."

I brought Steven to Beau. It was a time for family and after Beau assured me that there was nothing I could get for either him or Steven, I said good-bye and slipped from the room. As I walked out, the dreadful realization stung that my good-bye to Annie would be my last.

~*~

That evening the dining room of Charlie's Seafood

bustled as usual for a Saturday night. Two smaller tables pushed together formed our table for six, but we had a corner in one of the quieter rooms. Mama and the owner's wife had been best friends since grade school so I suspected the short wait and quiet corner were not coincidences.

Mawmaw sat at the end of the table with Mama and Aunt Melanie flanking each side. We chatted over appetizers of bacon wrapped oysters, cheese stuffed jalapenos, and shrimp cocktails.

My sadness from earlier still hung heavy, but tonight I appreciated more than ever being with my family no matter how dysfunctional. I leaned over toward Angelle who sat across from me. "How are you enjoying spending so much time at home again?"

She smiled. "It's much easier now that I don't live here. How about you?"

"It's not bad. I've had the chance to clear out some of the cobwebs of the past."

She nodded. "I know what you mean. I'm really enjoying my time with your brother. I'm glad to say that's one thing from my past that's good to have around. I'm not letting him get away again."

I laughed. "I'm sure Anthony feels the same."

Anthony returned to the table. As he sat in his chair, he asked, "I feel the same about what?"

Angelle arched her eyebrow and a mischievous grin twitched her lips before she turned to him. "I'll tell you later."

Boiled crabs filled a tray in the middle of the table and individual dishes of fried shrimp, blackened redfish, and for Mama, a broiled flounder.

The waitress brought the check, and Mama stealthily placed her credit card inside the folder.

When Anthony and I protested, she raised her hands. "My treat. I don't get to do this often, so let me enjoy it."

Once the tab was settled, we stood out on the wooden porch of the restaurant and said our good-byes.

"Oh, Anthony, could you stop by Mama's house tomorrow and get Mawmaw's trunks out of the attic for me?"

"Sure. No problem, but it'll have to be very early in the morning. Angelle and I are going fishing tomorrow. Leavin' at the crack of dawn."

Angelle groaned. "I still can't believe I let him talk me into this."

Mawmaw stood from the bench. "Wait a minute. What trunks are you talkin' about?"

"You know, the ones with the clothes you said I could look through for a costume."

Her face contorted into a sea of wrinkles and her brow furrowed. "I never gave my permission for anyone to go browsing through my trunks."

I swallowed and stared. What? Her words pierced. "Mawmaw, don't you remember we talked about going together to the *fais do do*, and I would be dressed as a younger version of you?"

She shook her head—defiance gleamed in her eyes. "Nope. Never said nothin' of the sort."

Mama and I exchanged glances. Her brow furrowed and a frown replaced her brilliant smile from earlier. She placed her hand on Mawmaw's shoulder. "Mama, you told Cheryl she could look through the trunks several weeks ago. Have you changed your mind?"

"Nope, didn't change my mind." Her voice grew

louder and more determined. "Because I never said she could go through my stuff."

I reached for my grandmother's hand. "It's OK. I won't go through the trunks if you don't want me to. No harm done."

She pulled away from my touch and glared with vacant eyes—a stranger's eyes. "Yes, there is harm done. It's not right for people to assume they can invade other people's privacy."

Anthony stepped closer. If anyone could calm her, he could. "C'mon, Mawmaw, you can ride home with me and Angelle."

"Nope, I think I'll walk. My house is jus' around the curve."

Concern flashed in Anthony's eyes. "Your house is five miles from here. You can't walk. Besides the mosquitoes will eat you up." He swatted at a bug hovering around his face.

"I'm about tired of being told what I can and can't do." Mawmaw crossed her arms and sat on the bench. "Now you all go about your business and leave me alone."

Aunt Melanie whispered into Mama's ear and then sat next to Mawmaw. "Mama, we can walk to my house if you want."

"Nope. Honey, I'll be jus' fine." She patted Aunt Melanie's leg, and then crossed her arms and leaned back on the wooden bench.

Mama sat on the other side of Mawmaw. "Mama, I'll sit here with you. My legs are a bit tired."

"OK, baby girl. You rest right here next to me. I think these fine people were leaving, anyway."

"Yes, I think they are."

Anthony guided me and Angelle off the porch and

out of hearing distance. "Have you noticed anything like this before?"

I shook my head. "Never."

"Do you think she's having another stroke?"

My heart raced. *Please, Lord, no.*

We stood at the edge of the parking lot, glancing back to see Mama and Aunt Melanie with heads bowed sitting next to Mawmaw. Were they praying?

Lord, keep her safe and healthy. The prayer flowed through my heart

Anthony touched my arm. "I'll go check on her. Maybe we should bring her to the hospital." He closed the distance to the porch in a few long strides. After a few minutes, Mama, Aunt Melanie, and Mawmaw, with the help of Anthony, walked toward the parking lot.

"Cheryl, are you giving me a ride home?" Mawmaw asked.

I shot a quick glance toward Mama, and then to Anthony. "If you're feeling OK?"

"Why wouldn't I be feeling OK? We had a great meal and good company. Nothin' finer. But it is getting late, and it's past my bedtime."

"It's only eight thirty," Anthony chimed in.

"Yep, thirty minutes past. You young people forget. I go to bed at the same time as the chickens."

"Cheryl, once you get Mama settled in your car, could you come see me?" Mama said.

I raced to my car, started the engine, turned on the air conditioner, and then helped Mawmaw get settled into the front seat. "Mawmaw, I have to talk to Mama for a second. I'll be right back."

"Sure, honey. I'll be right here waitin' for you."

Mama, Aunt Melanie, Anthony, and Angelle stood

a few yards away next to Anthony's car. When I approached, they turned toward me.

"Is she OK to spend the night alone?" I asked.

Mama's face held an unusual shade, much paler than her normal color. "I can't convince her to go to the hospital. She doesn't remember saying those things. Mel will take me home to get my car and clothes. I'll come up with some reason to spend tonight at her house."

"It might be easier for me to do that. I'll stay with her tonight. Don't worry. Mama, Aunt Mel, I'll call you if anything happens."

Anthony reached for my arm. "Me, too. OK?"

I nodded. "That was the strangest thing I've ever seen with her."

"Me, too," Mama said.

Anthony chuckled. "Guess we should not be poking around in those trunks, eh, Sis?"

"I guess not."

We hugged good night and as I walked to my car a small part of me wondered if my very astute grandmother had just put on a show for her family. Had she changed her mind about me going through the trunks and didn't want to admit it? Surely, she wouldn't have gone through such an elaborate display just to keep me from opening those trunks.

Vingt Et Un

Once she'd gone to bed, I'd slipped back to her house and made myself as comfortable as possible on her sofa—an antique torture device I'd renamed the Duncan Phyfe Rack. A few times during the night I sneaked into her bedroom to check on her. Her snoring remained steady. Sunday morning, the incessant *beep, beep* of my phone alarm roused me from my fitful sleep.

I folded the blankets and returned them to her closet. After waking Mawmaw, as I'd done most mornings for the past few weeks, with a fresh cup of her rich coffee, I sat at her kitchen table with a large cup of the aromatic brew. Once she'd finished her cup in bed and joined me in the kitchen, I examined her face. Deeper wrinkles circled her eyes and forehead while the corners of her eyes drooped.

"Mawmaw, are you feeling OK this morning?"

She nodded. "Just a bit tired."

"Do you remember anything unusual last night at the restaurant?"

She shrugged. "No. I don't. Did something happen?"

"Yes, you got pretty upset when I asked Anthony to remove your trunks from Mama's attic. Do you remember anything about that?"

"No. Why do you have to remove them?"

"It's too hot to go through them in the attic."

"Oh, I see." She stared out the kitchen window. I followed her gaze and enjoyed the sunrise breaking over the pasture behind her house. "Don't know why I'd be upset about that. Just a bunch of old dresses and stuff in there."

"Well, you were pretty upset about me going through those trunks."

"Cheryl, I don't remember that." Her eyes widened. "Do you think I may have had another stroke?"

"I don't know Mawmaw, but I think it might be best to let Mama take you in for a checkup."

She pursed her lips and nodded. "OK." Her gaze met mine head-on while tears formed along the corners of her eyes. "Cheryl, it's OK for you to go through those trunks." She patted the top of my hand, but fear continued to steal the softness of her warm blue eyes.

I swallowed hard and paused.

"Mawmaw, I'll come by after church to pick you up, and we'll go through the trunks together. OK?"

"Yes, that would be nice."

I fixed breakfast and lingered a while longer. After our second cup of coffee, I rose to leave.

Mawmaw was back to her old self again. She looped her arm through mine and walked me to the door. "I'm glad to see you're going to church. I've failed in my Christian walk and therefore failed your mother, also."

I patted her hand. "It's never too late, you know. You're welcome to come to church with me today. And I wouldn't worry too much about Mama. I believe answered prayer has guided Mama where she needs to be."

"Really? Whose?"

"Aunt Melanie's."

She smiled for the first time since last night and it warmed my heart to see her eyes sparkle again. "I'm glad to hear that. Glad to hear it. That girl always took after her father more than her mother." She winked at me. "I think I'll pass on church today, but maybe another time. Maybe another time."

"OK, but anytime, you're welcome to come with me."

~*~

I slipped into the back row of Grace Community Church just as the praise band began the morning worship. The lyrics to the popular song stirred my spirit as I followed the rhythm. The time in church flew by, and I became immersed in Chuck's message. He spoke on knowing God so I could know His will for my life. It made sense. What didn't make sense was why I couldn't do it. I wanted to know God more. I wanted to know His will for me.

As I walked out of church after the service, Beau fell in step next to me.

"Cheryl, it's good to see you in church." His voice lacked his usual enthusiastic tone.

"You, too, Beau. I'm glad to be here. Any change with Annie?" We walked toward my car.

He shook his head. "Gerald and his wife are there with Steven. I had to come to church. I needed something to recharge me. I'm heading to be with her now."

His sad eyes pierced a hole through me. What could I possibly say to relieve his pain? Nothing. I knew that. But I could do something. I stopped. He stopped. I placed my hand on his arm and bowed my head. "Heavenly Father, I lift Beau up to You. Place Your hand on his heart, and give him Your peace. Ease his pain Lord with the bounty of Your love. Amen." Warmth spread through my face, not contributed to the high midday temperatures. I had never prayed out loud or in public for anyone before. I didn't understand what had prompted me to do so, but it felt right.

Before he turned to leave, our eyes met.

In them, I saw gratitude. "Cheryl, thanks so much for the prayer. It means a lot. Keep praying will you?"

"I will." I reached for the handle of my car door. "Good-bye, Beau."

"Good-bye, Cheryl." He walked away with slumped shoulders and looked very much like an adult version of how his son had looked yesterday.

I slid into the driver's seat and took a deep breath, pushing back a flood of tears. His grief drilled through me. And when I thought of his Steven, my heart twisted. *Lord, be with them. Be with the whole family. Give them peace.*

~*~

"Mawmaw." I opened the screened door on my grandmother's porch and walked into her kitchen. A teakettle was on the stove with the burner at full flame. "Mawmaw."

As I passed her bedroom, I noticed the bed was unmade. Not at all like my grandmother. She usually made the bed the minute she bounced out of it. I increased my pace as I continued through the house looking for her. While in the living room, the teakettle's high-pitched whistle broke through the uncanny silence. Surely, if she was anywhere in the house, that would bring her out.

In the kitchen, I turned off the flame. Where was she? I dashed out the door and took two steps at a time off the porch. No sign of her in the backyard. Her flowerbed sported many weeds among the brilliant hydrangeas, geraniums, and Shasta daisies. A pang of regret gripped my heart. I should have come here and helped maintain her weed-free garden.

I scanned the side of the house. No sign of her. Where could she have gone? If she went for her walk without me, we'd have to have a long discussion.

A moan and a muffled yell from the other side of the tool shed captured my attention. I ran through the thick grass. "Oh, please, no. Oh, please, no," I repeated. As I turned the corner, my breath caught.

Mawmaw struggled on the ground. A shovel sat on the ground next to her. Her legs were tangled through the netting she'd used to protect her garden from the birds that enjoyed her bounty.

"Mawmaw! Are you hurt?" I knelt next to her. The acrid aroma of the freshly tilled soil filled the air. In a different time, I would have inhaled deeply and enjoyed the scent.

When she turned her head, I saw dirt around her lips. "I'm OK," she blurted out with a puff of dirt.

"Hang in there. I'm getting you out." I tugged gently on the webbing in slow methodical movements. My instincts were to rip the webbing off and get her on her feet, but her paper-thin skin slid under the sharp monofilament.

From her attempts to free herself, she'd created a snarled mess. Untying the knots would take forever.

"Stay put. I'm going back for a pair of scissors."

I ran back into the house, through the kitchen to her sewing cabinet, and rifled through her drawer until I found her red-handled scissors. I dashed out the door, down the porch, and through the backyard.

Mawmaw would be appalled to see me running with scissors.

I wasn't sure if the flip-flopping of my heartbeats were due to the unabashed sprint through the backyard or seeing her on the ground struggling. I knelt at her feet and took several deep, calming breaths. The scissors sliced through the netting. As soon as the netting fell off, freeing her, she tried to stand.

"Hold on." I ran my hands over her legs and arms looking for fractures or abrasions. "Are you hurting anywhere?"

She blew out a breath causing her disheveled hair to rise and then fall back into her face. Dirt smeared her cheeks and covered the tip of her nose. Her eyeglasses lay askew with patches of mud covering the lenses. "Only my pride, dear girl. Only my pride." She attempted to rise, but fell back onto her bottom.

I reached under her arm. "OK, on the count of three, I'll help you stand. One, two, three."

That didn't work. Trying to help her stand from the front in the soft dirt proved too difficult. She didn't budge, and I almost fell on top her.

"Wait. I have a better idea." I bent her knees so both feet were planted in the soil and then got behind her. I slipped my hands beneath her arms. "OK, on three."

At three, she stood with just a little help from me.

"What in the world were you doing? And why

aren't you wearing your alert button?" I asked as we ambled back to the house.

"Oh, the wind had blown the netting off my tomatoes, and the ground needed to be turned. So I got busy." She reached into her blouse. "It's right here. Didn't want to bother the paramedics."

We stepped up onto the back porch. "Sit here." I pointed to her worn oak rocker. "I'll get a washcloth."

Didn't want to bother the paramedics. I shook my head. I'd never known anyone so independent, or was it just plain stubbornness? She worked hard and didn't complain. Many times I'd wished I could be more like her. Even now, at almost eighty, she still had the stamina and motivation of a younger woman. But I had to wonder, could this independent streak of hers be a liability more than an asset at this point in her life?

I ran the water in the sink to warm the temperature and then drenched two washcloths. When I returned to the porch, she swayed gently in the rocker, trying to wipe the mud from her lenses with the edge of her apron. She looked up and smiled. "This is good dirt. Thick and rich. I should have some real nice 'maters this year."

Even though my heart broke for her circumstances, the sight of my mud-drenched grandmother with her gray hair hanging around her face tickled my heart. What a trooper.

I handed her the washcloths. She pointed to the dark splotches on the knees of my white Capri pants and giggled. So I turned around and showed her my backside. At that, she released a full-bellied laugh that touched me to the core of my being.

I sat on the top step and laughed along with her. "I'm so glad you're OK. You don't know how scared I was when I saw you on the ground. Please don't do anything like that again. Use the button. That's what it's for."

Her laughter died and her eyes sharpened. "What? Don't tend to my garden? That's not gonna happen, girl. The day I can't do my own garden and tend to my own house is the day I'm ready to meet my maker. Don't want to go to no ol' folks' home or be a burden to anybody. Especially Melanie, or your mama." She pouted her lower lip. "I'll use the button next time."

"Mawmaw, I meant don't scare me like that again. No more falls. No next time, OK?"

She smiled again. "OK."

"Also, the teakettle was on when I walked into the house."

"Really? I don't remember putting that on."

My gut wrenched for a moment. Was this the after effects of her stroke? Was she getting Alzheimer's? Was there something she wasn't telling us? The questions rambled through my brain intensifying the fear brewing in my heart.

But then again, I forgot things all the time. And, after all, she was seventy-nine. She was entitled to forget things, wasn't she? "Shall we get cleaned up?"

She wiped her face and had to make several passes to get all the dirt off. I helped her wash her elbows and knees.

"Do you still want to look through the trunks this afternoon?" she asked.

I thought she would have forgotten the reason for my return visit, but the fact that she did remember soothed the burn in my gut. "Yes, that would be nice. I'll run home and get cleaned up and pick you up in about thirty minutes. Is that enough time?"

She nodded. "Plenty enough for me."

I sat on the step for a moment after she'd gone into the house. The episode had rankled me. She seemed unfazed. Her inner strength amazed me. The nasty thought of something robbing her of that strength turned my stomach.

~*~

Mama stood at the stove stirring in her favorite bright red, iron pot. "Anthony came by last night after we left the restaurant. The trunks are in the extra bedroom." She dipped a smaller spoon into the pot and sipped the creamy liquid from it. "Mmm. Just right. I'm making crawfish bisque. You two are staying for suppa."

Typical Mama, More command than invitation. But we didn't argue with her. I loved crawfish bisque. So did Mawmaw.

I don't know how Mama cooked the foods she did and kept her amazing figure. I wished I'd inherited her metabolism.

Mawmaw sat at the kitchen table and chatted with Mama. I headed toward the guestroom—the one that resembled the cover of the Easter edition of one of those home magazines. The lilac and pale green of the flowered curtains and bedspread beckoned me in. Although I didn't like the dainty colors or style, I couldn't help but smile. That was Mama, too. She liked frilly and girly. Another thing I had not inherited—her taste in decorating.

The antique trunks lay on the floor next to the bed. Thick leather straps circled the tooled leather covering of the first trunk. It reminded me of a Victorian steamer I saw in a recent movie. The other trunk had leather straps too, but with a plain brown leather covering. No etching. Both were old and had been well cared for. I fumbled with the buckles of the first trunk to loosen the bindings, and then attempted to free the lock. It wouldn't budge. I performed the same procedure for the other trunk, same result.

"Great. I'll never get a costume at this rate." I headed toward the kitchen. "Mawmaw, do you have the keys for these trunks?"

She and Mama sat at the table in deep conversation. Had Mawmaw changed her mind about telling Mama about her little incident this morning? She'd made me promise not to say a word. She looked up. "Keys?"

"Yes, for the trunks."

A deep well appeared above the bridge of her nose. "I don't know. I didn't think they were locked." She looked toward Mama. "Did I give you the keys when I brought them here?"

"Not that I remember, but you did bring a pouch with keys in it. I think you said they were to your house and the tool shed. Maybe the keys to the trunks are in with those."

Mama rummaged through her junk drawer. "Yes, here it is." She produced a small pink leather pouch. Hot pink, no less. Couldn't miss that one.

She unzipped the pouch and peered through. She plunked out several keys and handed them to Mawmaw.

As Mawmaw rifled through the keys, I retrieved a glass from the cupboard and filled it with iced tea. The outside temperatures had climbed to the low nineties. Mama's air conditioning proved a welcome relief. And thank goodness for Anthony. Had he not removed the trunks from the attic, I'd be doomed to find another alternative for a costume.

"Here." She handed four keys to me. "I think the trunk keys might be in these."

"Aren't you coming into the room to look with me?" I asked.

"In a minute." She turned her attention back to Mama. "So Cheryl ran to get the scissors…" Guess she had changed her mind.

I made my way back to the trunks, iced tea glass in hand. Two brass keys and two made of silver. All four were worn and the tops smooth around the curled heads. I slid a brass key with a filigree-curled top into the lock of the first trunk.

Nothing.

I slipped the key into the lock of the other trunk. It turned, loosening the lock. A click resonated through the room and the lock fell open.

Vingt-Deux

The heady scent of cedar mingled with my grandmother's signature perfume floated from the trunk when I lifted the lid. Its fragrance filled the room. Several dresses of pastel blue, pink, and yellow in fabrics of silk, taffeta, and chiffon were folded and stacked to the far right of the cedar-lined trunk. A pair of Mary Jane dress shoes in black patent leather lay next to the dresses along with a pair of elegant silk pumps. I lifted them to the light. The white iridescent of the silk sparkled like the inside of an oyster shell. For what special event had she bought these?

The sound of Mawmaw's shuffling drew my attention. Finally, she joined me. She entered the room and slowly lowered into the chair next to the bed. Her gaze locked onto the shoes. The glint in her eyes matched that of the shoes.

"Your wedding day shoes?" I asked.

She shook her head and remained silent. Her eyes never strayed from the pumps in my hand.

I sensed they held a painful memory. I turned them over. The soles were clean and unmarred. They'd never been worn.

Her gaze followed the shoes as I returned them to the trunk. The earlier glint was gone. Tired, worn eyes etched with sadness greeted me. Guilt gripped. Should I be doing this? Her sadness twisted my heart.

An old Bible with tattered pages rested on the

other side of the trunk. I reached for it.

"My grandmother's Bible." I barely heard her softly spoken words. Her eyes danced again. Was she remembering a happy time? I flipped through the pages. Handwritten words in elegant, faded script framed the typed ones. Many of the printed words were underlined, sometimes with two or three lines.

Mama appeared in the doorway and leaned against it. "What a neat old Bible. Can I see it?"

I handed the Bible to Mama. She turned through the pages as I had. "Wow, so many notes. Mama, do you mind if I read these?"

Mawmaw's gaze remained fixed on me.

I examined an exquisite white chiffon dress trimmed with lace. It had been carefully folded under the Bible. I lifted the dress and let the fabric flow freely. When I stood and held the dress against my torso, tears pooled in Mawmaw's eyes. I dared not ask if this had been her wedding dress but having missed the earlier shoe exchange, Mama's excitement bellowed forth.

"Oh, my. How beautiful. Mama, how come I've never seen this stuff before? Was that your wedding dress?"

Tears spilled from the corners of Mawmaw's eyes.

Suddenly, I felt like a voyeur—like I invaded a part of her heart she'd locked a long time ago.

Her tears flowed against the path of her wrinkles and the luster her eyes usually held was gone. They appeared as dull marbles planted in her skull.

Before I could fold the dress and return it to the trunk, Mama strolled to where I stood and lifted the dress. She walked to the full-length mirror in the corner of the room and held the dress as I'd done while looking into the mirror.

"Oh, Mama, I bet you were the belle of the ball wearing this beautiful dress."

I glanced at Mawmaw. She slumped in the chair with her hand over her mouth, and a steady stream of tears covered her face. I'd never seen her cry before.

I knelt before her. "Mawmaw, are you OK?"

She nodded and took a deep breath. "I'm not feeling well. Would you take me home?"

At her words, Mama placed the dress on the bed and ran to us. "Mama, is something wrong?"

"Just tired." She looked at the dress and with a soft voice said, "Memory lane can be a long, hard road."

Mama apologized while I helped Mawmaw up. Mama tried to send us home with covered bowls of crawfish bisque, but Mawmaw refused.

She leaned on me as we walked out to my car. During the silent drive home, I sensed she needed time with her memories and that opening those trunks had ruptured long sealed hurts.

When I turned into her driveway and stopped the car at her doorstep, she turned to me. "I'm fine. You don't need to worry about me. Go home and enjoy some time with that pooch of yours. And, Cheryl, you can wear anything in that trunk but the white dress." She placed her soft wrinkled hand on mine. "You can go through the other trunk alone. I don't think it's a good idea for me to be there."

"Sure." I swallowed and felt like I'd eaten a handful of sand.

Her eyes, usually full of life, stared at me with veiled sorrow.

"Mawmaw, I don't have to wear anything. It's just a dumb *fais do do*. It's not that important."

"No." She squeezed my hand. "It is important and

I'm honored dat you think I'm someone you admire enough to want to dress like. But, honey, don't put me on a pedestal. I don't belong dere." Her Cajun accent seemed more pronounced tonight.

After helping her get settled for the evening, I drove home. Images jostled through my mind. Mawmaw's pain. The dress. How could a dress bring about such sorrow?

Unless...a flash of words from a Lady S letter seared through my brain. She'd been excited about looking at wedding dress patterns. Had I held the very dress that Lady S had planned to wear to marry Carlton?

Bile rose, burning my throat.

Was Mawmaw Lady S? Millions of other questions scrambled through my brain. One gripped the hardest and the longest—if so, what happened?

~*~

Monday there had been no change in Carlton's condition. When I walked in on Tuesday, Darcy gave me a quick hug. "He's a bit of a firecracker today. Feelin' a little better. Oh, and Cheryl, can you prepare his meds for the week? He got a little restless about three this morning, so I didn't get a chance to do them."

"Sure, I will. Think his friskiness will last a while?"

She shrugged. "Doubtful."

I knew what she thought. I'd seen it many times in terminal patients. A last rally before death consumed them. I hoped that was not the case with Carlton today.

"Missed you," he said when I entered his

bedroom. His eyes twinkled.

"What do you mean, missed me? I've been right here." I walked to the dresser and retrieved the last two letters from Lady S. I figured he'd want me to read them since he hadn't wanted to yesterday.

"Yep, but not the same. Sum...tin' happen?"

I tidied the area around his nightstand, refilled his glass with water, and then turned to him. "What do you mean?"

"You upset. All day yester...day."

How had he become so in tune with my feelings? I shivered as though someone had blown cool air across the back of my neck. No one had ever been able to read me like Carlton had begun to. I wasn't sure I liked it, but at the same time, I did because I'd grown very fond of him. When I thought that his time drew near, a twisted knot tightened my gut.

Should I respond? I couldn't ignore his question, but could I talk about what had happened this weekend? Maybe he would understand about Mawmaw's reaction. After all, his walk down memory lane had left him feeling pretty sad more than a few times. And maybe...maybe he could confirm my suspicions.

I pulled up a chair and began to recount the events of the weekend starting with finding Mawmaw tangled in the garden netting.

He chuckled. "She sounds funny."

"She is. You would like her. She's a feisty old lady with a pretty good sense of humor. She means the world to me."

He nodded and smiled. "Glad you...had her...in your life."

"Yes, Clarice Clement has brought a lot of joy in

my life."

His eyes widened.

I continued with the rest of the story, and I told him about the dress and Mawmaw's reaction.

His eyes glazed over, and he became very still.

My pulse raced. "Carlton?"

He stared right through me as though I was not there. After what seemed an eternity, he finally shook his head. He exhaled long and slow, and then inhaled deeply. "Would you read...my letters from Lady S?"

"Sure." I reached for the letters. A twinge of disappointment gnawed at me. I expected more from him. Confirmation? Acknowledgement? I wanted him to tell me so badly what I wanted to hear. Had he loved my grandmother?

Cheryl, you're getting too close.

As I settled into the bedside chair, Carlton reached out with his hand palm up, and flexed his fingers for me to come closer. I leaned forward and placed my hand in his.

He squeezed. "We all...have a past...that haunts us..." He took several deep breaths. "...better to leave...sleeping dogs..." His gaze locked with mine with as much intensity as his dying eyes could muster. He nodded very slightly knowing he didn't need to finish the sentence. "K?"

I squeezed his hand and nodded. "OK."

"I like you." He released my hand and leaned back onto the pillow. "Don't want...you hurt."

"What do you mean?" Was he telling me what I wanted?

He closed his eyes. "Secrets...from yesterday...hurt...today." He opened his eyes and smiled. "Let's read."

So close. I swallowed my frustration and conceded. He was right. I'd seen it with my patients and their families. So many times buried secrets from the past had a way of bringing in a new wave of pain to the next generations. What could be so bad for me to be hurt by the truth?

I settled back in the chair with the last two letters on my lap and paused. Pressing him would gain nothing. His eyes were closed and his head rested on the propped pillow. When I remained silent, he opened his eyes and turned to me. "Well."

"Well, what?"

"Gonna read?"

"You're not gonna tell me, are you?"

He closed his eyes again. "No need. Please read."

I sighed and fought the tenacious urge to press for answers. Feeling deflated, I began reading.

My Dearest Carlton,

I'm so excited!!!!! I can't wait to see you! Your leave could not have come at a better time. I am counting the days until March first. It will be the best two weeks of the whole last year. Of course, the day at the watering hole is still my special day. I've kept the dress I wore that day, it's tucked away in the hope chest you gave me. It's where my wedding dress will go when it's done. Mrs. Mouton is making it from the pattern I bought at Woolworth's. She keeps asking me who the lucky guy is, but I won't say a word.

I'll be at the train depot when you arrive. Then the whole town will know that you and I are together, including Mama and Papa.

Write me with your exact date and I'll be there! Carlton, I'm still praying for your safety and peace.

All my love,

Lady S

My fingers lingered over the last words. Silence settled the room. Her joy spread from the words and permeated through me. When I braved a glance toward Carlton, his gentle smile told me he had traveled back to when she had sent him this letter. He lowered his eyelids.

I envisioned Mawmaw's dress as the one Mrs. Mouton sewed. What about the dress she'd worn to the water hole? Was it in the other trunk? I blew a long breath. I had no proof that Mawmaw was Lady S. But the fact that she referred to Mrs. Mouton told me that Sylvia Mouton was not Lady S.

I lifted the last letter. Its significance weighed more than the mere ounces of folded paper. Did it contain the words that explained why this man lay here alone as death encroached? Why he had never married? And been unable to forgive? And would he give up this struggle once these last words were read? I draped the afghan from the foot of his bed around my shuddering shoulders.

His labored breathing took on a steady rhythm I recognized. He'd fallen asleep. A sigh of relief escaped my lips. A reprieve of sorts, I wouldn't be burdened with the answers to my haunting questions. I laid the letters on the nightstand and tiptoed out the room and into the kitchen.

As I poured juice into my glass, Carlton's past with all its unanswered questions, whirled through my mind. He seemed like a likeable guy. Why had he not married? The snippet of "Jolie Blonde" sounded from my cellphone. Mama.

"Hello."

"Cheryl we need to talk."

My chest tightened. Her voice was controlled but the underlying nervous tone sent shivers through me.

"Now?"

"No, can you come over...tonight after work?" Her voice quivered.

I sat at the table, juice in hand. "Sure. Mama, are you OK?"

"For now, but I need to talk to you in person. There's something I want you to see."

"What is it?"

"Something I found in Mawmaw's trunk."

My heart sank. "What?"

"I'll show you when you get here."

What was Mama doing snooping in Mawmaw's trunk? "Mama, is Mawmaw with you?"

"No, Melanie is. I called her and she came over about an hour ago. She suggested I call you."

This must be serious. "OK, I'll be over as soon as I can. I'm usually here until five, but sometimes Darcy comes in early so I may be able to head out early. I'll call you when I leave."

After Mama's call, a lead mass settled in my stomach. What could she have discovered that upset her so? While I poured the vegetable soup Darcy cooked for Carlton's lunch, dread filled me. Carlton's words from this morning drifted in the quiet kitchen. Secrets from yesterday hurt today.

Carlton's mood infected the house. The firecracker Darcy had described this morning had disappeared.

He slept most of the day, and when he awakened

shortly after lunchtime, he declined lunch. I didn't argue with him. He would eat when he was ready. He fell back into a deep sleep.

I tidied things around the house and prepared his medications for the coming week. As I dropped pills into the daily slots, I noticed Carlton took the same anti-psychotic that Mama did. Browsing through his chart, I flipped through pages of medication logs to get to his past medical history.

There it was—just as I suspected, schizophrenia. How had I forgotten that? His cancer had captured my attention. Could that be why he and Lady S never married? I thought of how the same diagnosis had affected Mama's life and caused so many problems before she had a proper diagnosis. The same thing could have easily happened to Carlton, especially in his time of growing up. Medicine back then had a long way to go in that area.

"Cheryl." His scratchy voice filtered into the kitchen.

"Coming." I padded down the hallway to his room. "What do you need?"

"Sit wit'...me." He patted the side of his bed.

I glanced toward the nightstand where the last letter sat. Maybe he wanted me to read it. I perched on the edge of the bed and gently placed his hand in mine. The coolness of his skin penetrated through mine. "Carlton, are you in pain?"

He shook his head. "Naw."

My heart sat like a blob in my chest. "What is it?"

His gaze met mine and I glimpsed his hopelessness. It reached into the depths of my heart and soul and twisted like barbed wire. I leaned toward him.

"Forgive...ness."

"What about forgiveness?"

"Al...most there."

I squeezed his hand tenderly, willing my warmth to seep into his fingers. I took a deep breath. I wasn't very good at this, for heaven's sake. I wasn't the model Christian. Not even close. For so many years, I wasn't even a Christian. Who was I to think that I could do this? *Lord, help me.*

I inhaled. My deepening love for this man overwhelmed and guided me to take a chance. To ask the burning question I'd wanted to ask for the past few days.

Strength surged me forward. "Carlton, God's forgiven you. I know He has. He sees your remorse. Do you believe that?"

His Adam's apple slid up and down. His eyes, filled with tears, never left mine. He pursed his lips. "I do...now."

"Forgive yourself. Let it go. It's time."

He simply stared at me. I detected a twinge of doubt in his eyes.

"Carlton, did you do something to Lady S?"

His glare never wavered. He nodded. Tears dropped from the corners of his eyes and rolled down his cheeks.

I brought his fingers to my lips and pressed against them. "I'm sure she has forgiven you."

"I don't...know."

A fit of coughing overtook him. I waited. Helpless.

The episode left him exhausted. I returned to the kitchen to retrieve his glass. After he took a sip, he yielded to the fatigue. His head lolled to the left, and he fell asleep. For the next hour, I sat on the chair next to his bed and watched him sleep. Every now and then I'd glance toward the letter. It drew me. This letter could answer my most burning questions. What had happened? Who was she?

But I resisted. The story was his to tell.

After a while, I walked on legs of gelatin into the kitchen, sat at the table, lowered my head onto my folded arms and sobbed.

Vingt-Trois

With Mr. Bojangles at my feet, I walked into Mama's house.

Mama and Aunt Mel sat at the counter.

Mama met my questioning gaze with red puffy eyes. Her look matched how I felt. Worn.

She stood and reached for my hand. "Come. I want to show you something."

I glanced at my aunt. "Go. I'll entertain my favorite canine friend." She reached for Mr. Bojangles' leash.

Mama led me back to the guest bedroom. Several letters were unfolded on top the flowered bedspread.

I lifted one of the envelopes and read the return address. The letters were from C. Perlouix and addressed to Lady S. My legs quivered, and I plopped onto the bed.

Proof. What I'd wanted to know for so long. What I'd strongly suspected—Mawmaw was Lady S.

One burning question answered.

"Look at these letters. She had a whole life she never said anything about. What do you make of this?" Mama's arched eyebrow and piercing eyes begged for answers. Ones I couldn't give.

"I'm not sure." I rifled through the letters looking at the postmarks. I found the latest and glanced at the signature. It was signed, Carlton. My heart hurt.

Mawmaw had loved my dying patient.

I reached for Mama's hand and guided her to sit next to me. I inhaled deeply and let the words flow. With each part of the story I revealed, her eyes widened, and she squeezed my hand tighter and tighter until I finally had to pry her fingers from around mine. Once I told her all that I knew, her tear-filled eyes met mine. All color had been leached from her face except for the red rimming her eyes.

"You know this man?"

"Yes. I do."

"How?"

"I can't tell you how."

"He's a patient, isn't he?"

I diverted my gaze and picked up one of the letters.

With shaking fingers, she handed me another one of the letters. "Read this one. It's really the one that tells the most."

I found the date in the top right corner in small print: June 23, 1954. It would have been one of the last letters. With trembling hands, I unfolded the pages and then glanced toward Mama. Through the window, rays of late afternoon sun streamed in. The sunshine illuminated the letter in my hand.

All this time, I'd craved the truth. Now that I came so close, it scared me. I didn't want to read the words. Things would be different after this letter. Somehow, I knew this letter would rip open past wounds that should remained scarred. Carlton's words from earlier struck hard. But could I really let sleeping dogs lie?

Mawmaw was Lady S.

I'd never imagined this possibility the day I'd read the first letter. When Carlton had trusted me to share his past, had he known who I was?

Guilt nudged as I scanned the words—a voyeur who traveled back in time. Despite all my doubt and fear, I couldn't *not* read this letter. I had to know.

My Dear Lady S,

I know I don't deserve any forgiveness, but I want you to know how sorry I am. I will obey your wishes and not be part of your life or our child's. I so wish things were different and we could be the family that you deserve. I know your father will never forgive me and would probably kill me if I return to Bijou Bayou. So I'll find a new place to live. Please know that if you or the child ever need anything, don't hesitate to call me. I will be whatever you want or need me to be. Otherwise, I'll stay out of your life. I beg you to forgive me, but I understand if you can't. I don't understand how it happened or why, but I do know I will love you until the day I die. And I'll go to my grave with hurting you as my deepest regret.

Yours always,
Carlton

My gaze met Mama's as I glanced up from the letter. She leaned in next to me and her eyes filled with confusion.

Mawmaw had been pregnant, and Carlton was the father.

"So what do you think?" Mama reached for the letter.

"I don't know what to think." I drummed my fingers on my lips.

"Cheryl, this man could be my father."

Could Carlton be my mother's father? "Wait, Mama we need to talk to Mawmaw. She may have miscarried during the first pregnancy."

Mama nodded. "Maybe you're right. But look at the date of the letter. The timing is right. I don't look anything like Papa or Melanie."

I didn't know what to tell her. She didn't. And when I looked at her now, all that glared back at me were her large, violet-blue eyes. The same eyes I had looked into earlier today. Why had I not seen it before? But I couldn't tell her that. Not now.

"Maybe we should talk to Mawmaw before we jump to any conclusions. I know this is a shock, but she may be able to explain this."

"Cheryl, what's he like?"

I stared at her and saw the uncertainty she didn't bother to hide. Her anxiety level increased in the last half hour, and I didn't want to be responsible for causing an attack that would set her back. "Mama, let's not go there right now." I curled my fingers around hers and stood. "C'mon. Let's get something to drink."

I led her into the kitchen.

Aunt Melanie had already filled three glasses with ice cubes and a freshly brewed pitcher of tea sat on the counter waiting for us.

Mr. Bojangles lapped noisily from a small bowl she'd placed on the kitchen floor.

As we sat at the table, she filled the glasses. She remained silent as she handed the glass to me. I met her gaze. "Thank you."

The coolness of the tea soothed my parched throat. What had Carlton done to make my pregnant grandmother not want to have anything to do with him—the man she loved and intended to marry?

I sat at the kitchen table next to Mama while Aunt Melanie took the chair on the other side and gently placed her hand over Mama's.

"Do you want to go to Mawmaw's tonight? I'll go with you," I said.

We both glanced at the clock on the oven. "It's getting late, and she's probably already in bed."

"How about first thing in the morning? I'll go with you if you want me to."

She glanced toward Aunt Melanie and then back to me. "Maybe we should all go."

Vingt-Quatre

On the drive home unwelcomed thoughts rattled my brain. Surely, there had to be an explanation. Raindrops beat softly on the roof of my car.

Could my mother be Carlton's child?

And if so...

My grandfather?

The steering wheel resisted my possessive grip. As I turned onto my street, a piercing siren invaded the night's quiet. Blurred red lights flashed through my rear window. An ambulance rushed passed me. *Please, Lord, be with whomever they're going to and their family.*

I followed behind until the lights dimmed in the distance. As I approached my driveway, I noticed the flashing disappeared. The ambulance had turned left into a driveway a few blocks from mine.

Mawmaw?

No.

Sweat poured from my palms as I shifted my car into reverse and backed into the street. *Please don't be at her house.*

As I approached Mawmaw's house, my heart battered my chest. Parked in her driveway with its lights flashing—the ambulance. I parked in front of her house, and ventured through the rain, willing my numb legs to carry me to her house. The grass, wet from the rain, sank under my leaden feet.

Her partially opened door seemed miles away. As

I trudged forward, it seemed to move farther and farther away. When I finally climbed the two steps to enter through the side door, voices drifted from the bedroom.

Deep authoritative voices. Command-giving voices.

I froze.

That's when the shivering started. Drenched from the rain, I garnered all the strength I could collect and darted down the small hallway to Mawmaw's bedroom. Two paramedics knelt on the floor next to my grandmother's sprawled body. Her small, still body.

"Mawmaw!" I heard the word but didn't recognize my own voice.

The paramedic farthest away glanced toward me. "Are you a relative?"

"Yes, she's my grandmother. She had a slight CVA a few months ago."

"That's good to know."

"Is she...?"

"She's alive. We're stabilizing her for transport."

"Who called you?" The doorframe supported my weary body as I watched their life-saving measures.

The younger of the paramedics with dark curly hair lifted the alert button Mawmaw wore around her neck. "Can you gather her medications?"

She'd used the button. *Thank you.* I marched to the kitchen. Having a task to perform triggered something inside that made me move, made me forget for an instant my grandmother lay on the floor fighting for her life. This was all I could do to help her. *Lord, help her. Save her.*

I knew my prayer was one He'd heard a million

times, and it was a selfish prayer. I wanted her on this earth for my purposes. I needed her. She was my rock. But, after this evening's revelation, had I really known her? Had her stubborn independence caused years of pain?

Her medications sat in a small basket on her counter. I swept each bottle into a large plastic bag, zipped the top, and found a black marker to label the bag. As I turned, the paramedics rolled her out into the hallway.

"She's stable."

"Are you taking her to St. Martin's?"

"Yes."

The pills in the bottles rattled. My hand shook, causing the noise.

The taller of the two paramedics, a young man with dark hair and even darker eyes, gently retrieved the bag from my white-knuckled grip.

"Miss, is there someone you can call?"

I nodded. My shoulders bore the weight of my head—dense, heavy, and inanimate. I couldn't think. Feel. I watched the scene as though from underwater. Everyone moved in slow robotic motions and the surroundings blurred. On frozen legs, I stood and watched them load her into the ambulance.

The curly haired paramedic approached. "We're taking her now. Is there someone we can call for you?" The red lights highlighted the concern etched on his face.

I shook my head. "No. I'll call."

He nodded and squeezed my shoulder.

Mama. I needed to call Mama.

I picked up my frightened and doused Schnauzer. I hadn't realized he'd slipped from my car and followed me into the house. He licked the side of my face.

As they drove off, sirens blaring, I knew our family would be different after tonight. After today. This would change so much of who we were as a family. As individuals. And I wondered for a brief moment if the truth would or could ever be told. I also wondered if I could continue to nurse a man who had abandoned my pregnant grandmother.

~*~

Mama and I sat in the familiar waiting room chairs. She examined her index finger nail with the intensity of an archaeologist. Her bare face and sunken eyes betrayed her inner turmoil. If what I imagined to be the truth, we would all be laid bare to sins of the past and secrets that had been kept for far too long.

"Cheryl, what's taking so long? We should have heard something by now. It's been almost an hour."

"I'll check." I squeezed her hand as I started for the nurse's station.

A dark-haired lady with sharp features sat behind a computer screen. Her fingers raced over the keyboard. I stood for a few moments to let her finish the sentence she typed. When she glanced toward me, I asked about Mawmaw.

Her tired green eyes radiated compassion. "It has been a while, hasn't it?"

I nodded.

Her lips spread into a gentle smile. "I'll check for you."

I wrapped my arms around my waist and waited. Forever. The second hand of the clock above my head seemed to gong each passing moment. Its chant—taunting and annoying. I knew the longer without any word, the less likelihood of good news.

Mama and Aunt Melanie stepped up beside me.

"Miss Broussard?" A young woman wearing scrubs walked into the waiting area, hand extended. "I'm Dr. Lejeune."

I shook the doctor's hand and introduced Mama and my aunt.

"How is she?" Both Mama and I spoke at the same time.

Dr. Lejeune guided us to a small room off the hallway. She sat on the edge of the desk and pointed toward the chairs. Mama slumped into the farthest chair, followed by Mel, who sat in the one closest to the door. I remained standing in the doorway awaiting her response.

"Mrs. Clement has suffered a major stroke. The bleeding is in the left hemisphere of her brain near what is known as Broca's area. The MRI shows the damage quite clearly. She's a strong fighter. The next twenty-four hours will tell us more. But for now, she's stabilized, and we have been able to administer the necessary medications to help prevent further damage."

The left side. "Will she be able to speak?"

"Her speech may be affected. The odds are not in her favor. We'll know more when she awakens."

Aunt Melanie asked a few questions, none that the doctor could accurately answer. I listened to the words as though through a veil. Everything clouded.

Today's revealed secret and my grandmother's stroke proved to be the earthquake that further crumbled my world. The world I knew and accepted all these years had disappeared.

Despite what I thought about my family at times, I loved them. Even Mama with all her theatrics and past history. I loved her. And seeing her now tore my senses to bits. Her world had surely been shattered as well. The mother she knew. The man she knew as her father. All different than what she'd been led to believe. She sat next to a sister who could be a half-sister. Would they feel the same closeness as before?

Her world now teetered on falsehoods. Would she ever learn the truth? I reached for her hand, gently wrapped my fingers around hers, and squeezed.

"Can we see her?" she asked.

"They're moving her to the intensive care unit. Check upstairs for visiting hours. Once she's settled, they may let you see her for a moment." The doctor rose from the desk.

Mama and Aunt Melanie stood also, and I backed out into the hallway. The doctor returned to the exam room while the three of us headed for the elevators.

"Do you think Mama knew we'd found out?" Mama turned to me.

I shook my head and pushed the floor button for the elevator. "I don't think so."

I knew where Mama was going with this, and I refused to let her go there and take me with her. "Mama, it's not your fault or mine. As you know, secrets have a way of coming out. She couldn't have known we'd read those letters. Besides, maybe she wanted us to know. She didn't have any problem with me going through the trunks."

The ding sounded at the elevator arrival, and we stepped inside. Aunt Melanie pushed the button for the fifth floor. "I think she forgot they were in there."

Could my grandmother have forgotten those letters? After reading her letters to Carlton, I found it hard to believe she would have forgotten him and the letters. Something terrible must have happened to keep them apart. I couldn't image what it was, and now I wondered if I'd ever know.

Poor Mama. Her eyes drooped on the corners and the lines in her forehead deepened. "I can't imagine her forgetting those. She kept them after all these years."

"Yes, I know. This Carlton must have been someone special to her," Mel said.

As the elevator doors opened, I slid my hand around Mama's elbow and guided her into the hallway of the intensive care unit. "Yep, I'd say he was."

Vingt-Cinq

"Here, I brought fresh coffee from home." Aunt Melanie poured steaming brown liquid into designer foam cups. Leave it to Aunt Melanie to make even sitting in an ICU waiting room as comfortable as possible.

"Any word?" Anthony rushed into the waiting room.

He sat next to Mama as she gave him the latest update. Her straight back and calm demeanor belied the thoughts I knew had to be going through her brain. Anthony placed a hand on her knee. Mama looked up at Aunt Melanie who sat in the opposite chair. "The nurses say she's resting. Which they tell me is a good sign."

"Have you seen her yet?" Anthony asked.

"Just briefly. Melanie and I went in for a moment. She didn't know we were in the room. They won't let us see her again until visiting hours later this morning."

I sipped Aunt Melanie's rich coffee and let the warmth blanket my mouth. The bold flavor settled deep, but as much as I willed it to, it didn't warm the parts of me that remained chilled, afraid, and confused. I prayed Mawmaw would have time to talk and Mama would get answers. *Lord, please keep Mawmaw alive until all is forgiven.*

After a few grueling hours, I glanced through the

window on the far side of the waiting room.

Streaks of bright orange, brilliant yellow and riveting red decorated the eastern sky. The large branches of the oak in the adjacent field shadowed the rising sun. Dawn's promise of a glorious new day intruded into the dim lighting. Its presence seemed an injustice with such uncertainty in our family.

~*~

Standing at the entrance to Mawmaw's room, I debated on whether or not to go to her bedside. The features of her face were exaggerated and swollen beyond recognition. Her body formed a tiny lump in the hospital bed. Had it not been for the familiar locks of silver spread out on her pillow, I wouldn't have known she was the same firecracker I knew as Mawmaw. A pillow propped her puffy right hand.

Machines beeped and hissed while LED numbers and graphics filled the spaces behind her bed. My legs had begun a tug of war with my mind on whether they would obey the command to walk toward her.

Move.

Just take a step. I inched my way closer to her bed with Anthony beside me. I was acutely aware he hadn't blazed a trail to her bedside, either.

What was wrong with me? I was a nurse, for heaven's sake. I'd worked in hospitals before. Even in the ICU.

But this was Mawmaw.

This was our family's foundation. I willed my feet to move forward and found myself at her bedside, Anthony on the opposite side. I stroked her enlarged fingers. *What secrets have you harbored? What pain?*

Lord, please watch over her. Keep her aware and able to communicate so all can be forgiven.

~*~

The waiting room at the hospital filled as news of Mawmaw's stroke spread through Bijou Bayou. Many of Mama's friends, as well as Mawmaw's and Aunt Melanie's, arrived with baskets of snacks, books, and magazines. Anthony and I chatted with the visitors until it was time for me to leave for work.

I placed my arms around Mama's shoulders. "Call me if there's any change."

"I will." Her direct gaze tangled with mine. "I want to know about Carlton, Cheryl. Let's talk this afternoon when you get off work."

I nodded. "I'll tell you what I can." I knew Mama wanted as much information about Carlton as possible. He was my patient. The laws required I not share information with her. I would have to ask Carlton today to see what he had to say.

Debra and Chuck entered the waiting room. They hugged Mama and Aunt Melanie, spoke to them briefly, and then came to my side.

Debra wrapped her arms around me and hugged tightly. "Cheryl, I'm so sorry."

Chuck voiced the same sentiments. "Can we pray for you?"

"Sure." We stood in the corner of the waiting room holding hands while Chuck prayed for peace for the family and healing for Mawmaw.

"Cheryl." Debra guided me to the chair next to where we stood while Chuck visited with Anthony and Mama. "We just left Beau's house. Annie died earlier this evening."

"No." Tears welled in my eyes. "How horrible for Beau. For Steven. How's Beau holding up? Steven?"

"It's hard for them both. They've had plenty of time to prepare, and Beau's being strong for Steven. He really loves that boy and has been such a good father."

I nodded and hugged Debra again. "Thanks for coming here. Your presence and your prayers mean a lot. I don't know how much help I'll be this weekend at the *fais do do*."

"Don't worry about it. Two of Chuck's sisters are in town and have volunteered to help where needed. We'll have more than enough help. You concentrate on being here with your family."

"Thanks, Debra." I stood and bid her and everyone else in the waiting room good-bye and then took the elevator down.

While walking to my car, thoughts of our family, Beau, and especially Steven, filled my heart. No child should have to go through what he had for the last two years.

On the drive to Carlton's house, I thought of Beau. My heart swelled with gratitude for him. He'd have the support of his brothers who'd come back to be by his side and all his friends here. While so many people came to Mama's aid this morning, I felt out of the circle. I had been gone so long, no one really knew me anymore. Had it not been for Debra and Chuck, I wouldn't have known anyone personally aside from my family. I started to see what Beau had seen all those years ago. The importance of family and having roots. I understood what that meant.

I dreaded seeing Carlton today. How much should I tell him? But as I thought about my grandmother fighting for her life, I knew today would be the day I would get him to talk. I didn't know how, but some way he would tell me the truth.

~*~

Darcy greeted me in the kitchen. "He's not doing well."

"I was surprised to see your car in the driveway. Didn't the housekeeper come today?"

"Yes, but I didn't want to leave him." She gathered her purse and jacket.

"Oh, Darcy, I'm sorry. I didn't even check in. It's been a long night."

Darcy offered Carlton's chart. "I heard about your grandma. I'm so sorry. How's she doing?"

"It's hard to say. She had a massive stroke." I scanned the entries Darcy made during the night. Carlton's condition had declined.

The gentle pressure of Darcy's hand on my shoulder offered a moment of comfort. "I'll say a prayer for her and your family. I'll also come back early tonight so you can leave early. I only need a couple hours of sleep."

"Thanks, honey." I allowed her to envelop me in her caressing embrace. "You're such a great friend."

She smiled. "You'd do the same for me."

I nodded and realized our friendship had picked up right where we'd left off so many years ago. "I would. Now go home and get some sleep."

After Darcy and the housekeeper left, I ventured into Carlton's room. His sallow complexion and darkened circles under his eyes confirmed Darcy's report. With a wavering hand, I reached for his blanket to cover his arm. This man had hurt my grandmother. The shaking of my hands and tightening in my chest pressed like someone had wrapped me from behind and squeezed. I felt powerless to break free. An overwhelming sadness engulfed. I hated him. And I loved him.

His chest rose and fell in an erratic raspy rhythm. The sound along with the hissing of the concentrator sent more waves of sadness and regret through me. My grandfather. So many missed opportunities. Would my Mama ever get to know the truth? And if so, would she get to meet her father? Should I make it happen?

Carlton's lids fluttered and the blue of his eyes had lost a little more of their luster.

"Hey."

"Hey, back." I squeezed his foot. "Heard you gave Darcy a hard time last night."

He shrugged. "She's...a good..." He turned his head and coughed. When he turned back, he simply stared. Either he'd forgotten what he was about to say or couldn't spend the energy to say it.

I sat on the bed next to him. "Can I get you anything?"

He shook his head. "Read?"

The last letter sat on the nightstand. So innocent, but its presence hovered in the room like the grim reaper. Would Carlton give up the fight after this letter?

"Carlton, are you sure you want me to read this letter?"

His gaze drew me and reflected a sea of calm in the chaos of a tortured soul. "Yes."

I pursed my lips and sighed. I didn't want to read the letter. I knew it contained only words, but those words were powerful enough to change this world. Change what I thought and felt. They had the power to crumble an already teetering foundation of family trust. Could I trust how I would feel about Mawmaw after this? Or about Carlton? Would this truth really set anyone free? Nausea rolled my stomach as though a thousand hummingbirds fluttered inside.

Once rearranged, the recliner faced Carlton on the side of his good ear. I descended slowly into its lushness but refused its comfort. Throbbing indecision snaked its way through me. When I lifted the letter, the weight of years of secrets and pain rested in mere ounces in my fingers. Secrets that held hearts captive for decades. The source for long-term lack of forgiveness and missed opportunities for happiness and freedom would be defined in the words on this one page. It was a twenty-ton chain attached to a tanker's anchor.

With trembling fingers, I opened the envelope and removed the letter. No comforting scent of lavender wafted forth as I unfolded the single page.

Carlton's lackluster gaze never left me.

I exhaled and began reading.

Carlton,

This will be the last letter you will ever receive from me. While it's been three months since we met during your leave, it's taken me this long to decide whether you deserved a letter.

I decided to write to you simply because I do not want to see you when you return. Please do not try to contact me. The man who forced himself on me was not the Carlton I knew and loved. While the bruises on my arms and legs have disappeared, the ones on my heart remain. I don't know what

happened to you there, but you've turned into a monster. One I don't want any part of.
Clarice

No Lady S. No Dear Carlton. Images in my mind formed with no coherent basis. Carlton physically attacking my sweet little Mawmaw who loved him? How was that possible? He loved her, too.

I lifted my gaze to Carlton, whose closed eyes streamed tears through the corners. His gut-wrenching torment hammered me, and I didn't know what to think or feel. I clenched my fists and pressed them into my thighs. Compassion for his pain flowed through me, but I didn't want to feel it. I wanted to hate him. Why shouldn't I after what he'd done?

Sobs racked his body as he allowed the grief to engulf him. I reached for his arm, but hovered inches from its surface. Why should I comfort him? He didn't deserve my pity.

His sobs subsided and he lay quietly. When he finally met my gaze, guilt poured from his soul. All I saw was an emaciated body and a tortured soul who had spent a lifetime regretting his crime. But I still wanted to hate him. I wanted to grab his skinny arms and shake him. I wanted to rip the oxygen tubes from his face.

Raw emotion gushed from a long-dormant depth. A cavern of hurt I'd carefully tucked away to avoid the pain of reality. I slumped back into the recliner and surrendered to the onslaught.

Vingt-Six

"Cheryl." Carlton's raspy voice replaced the deathly silence of the room.

Tears saturated my cheeks. I allowed my gaze to meet his.

"It was a...long time ago." He inhaled deeply. "But it still...pains me."

"Carlton, why? Why did you hurt her? She loved you."

His eyes filled, and when he closed them, a fresh stream flowed onto his cheeks. "The illness. Pills have...helped."

I remembered the pills he took. His mental illness. It's what had pushed him then. Made him lose control. It's what had driven Mama all those years ago. The truths came crashing around me like debris from a blown up aircraft. My world had been that aircraft, and now I struggled to understand what or how to feel about what I'd just learned. I struggled to put the pieces together.

"Have you spoken to Clarice since?"

He shook his head and then his eyes flashed wide. "How…?"

"I read your letters to her."

"Oh." He rested his head further back on his pillow. "Did you tell her?"

I shook my head. "Nope." Now was not the time to discuss Mawmaw's stroke. "Do you know what she's been doing all these years?"

He shook his head. "Tried to...but couldn't do it. Just know she...had a baby girl..." He took a deep breath. "Mine."

I swallowed through the constricting blob in my throat. The thought slammed through me like a sledgehammer. He knew who I was when I told him about Mawmaw and the netting. I don't think he realized his daughter was my mother. He didn't know who I was.

When Darcy had spoken to me about the job, she'd told him I was an old friend from high school. She hadn't given him any particulars about me. But surely he'd seen the resemblance to Mawmaw. Had that been why he'd asked me to read the letters? Had he made the connection? And if he had, why not tell me?

Carlton's gaze never left me. His pleading eyes begged for understanding.

Something I didn't want to give, but I knew he had suffered all these years.

He hadn't understood the severity of his illness, and it had condemned him to a life of pain and torment. One without joy or happiness. He'd paid an enormous price. He hadn't hurt her intentionally. He'd suffered all these years and been denied the necessary help to make him better. His illness then was no different than what he suffered now. But the consequences had been severe. Lives had been ruined. Changed. It was no different than what Mama had done.

As the warmth of understanding washed through me, forgiveness bathed my heart. For him and for Mama.

Thank You, Lord.

I lifted my shaking fingers and tenderly laid them on the top of his liver-spotted hand. When I braved a glance toward his face, the corners of his mouth lifted slightly and a trail of tears ran along the creases of his eyes. I caressed the wrinkles of his hand.

At that moment, I knew. He needed the truth. All of it. So did my mother.

"Carlton, Clarice, your Sherri, is..." His doorbell rang.

Both Carlton and I started from the intrusion. No one ever visited.

I patted his hand and stood. "I'll be right back."

When I peered out the window of the living room to see who stood at the front door, my breath caught.

Mama stood on the front porch, her violet-blue eyes, eerily similar to Carlton's, were set in a determined stare at the letters on the doorframe. Her five-foot-seven-inch frame seemed to be made of steel as she held her head erect with her arms folded across her chest. How had she found this place?

For the second time today, I dreaded doing something I knew was the right thing to do.

She would never forgive me for not telling her about Carlton. I trudged to the door, knowing the encounter would be difficult at best.

My hand rested on the doorknob. *Help Lord, I need Your words.* I turned the knob and opened the door about four inches. I braced myself for the coming attack.

Mama's eyes widened. "Cheryl, I want to see him."

I pursed my lips then exhaled. "How did you find this place?"

"I followed you."

"You what?"

"He's your patient. No wonder you wouldn't tell me who he was." She tried to push the door open fully. "I want to see him."

I held my ground. "Mama, I'm not sure that's a good idea. First, let me check with him to see if he wants to see you. He's not doing very well."

"I don't care. I want to know if he's my father. Mawmaw can't answer my questions, and I need answers. Now." She glared, her laser-like gaze searing right through me. She would not give up. The mighty Vivian was on a mission, and she wouldn't leave until she got what she came for.

Unfortunately, Carlton had control over whether she got answers or not.

"Wait here." I closed and locked the door. As I approached Carlton's bed, my chest tightened. I didn't want to wake him, but hadn't I been determined just minutes ago that the truth be known? I laid my hand on his shoulder and shook gently. "Carlton."

He awoke. "Whaa..."

"Carlton, there's someone here to see you. It's Vivian Broussard. Clarice's oldest daughter."

I knew the moment he made the connection. His pupils dilated slightly, and his brows lifted. "Here?" He pointed to the floor next to his bed.

"She's out on the porch. Should I let her in?"

His gaze searched mine as though he wanted me to answer for him.

"Carlton, there's something else you should know." I paused. I hated dumping this on him so abruptly. "She's my mother."

His brows lifted higher. "Your mother?" He ran his tongue along his chapped lower lip. "Hmmm. I see."

"I didn't know she was coming here."

He smiled and reached for the damp washcloth I'd left on his nightstand. "Need to clean...up first."

I took a step closer and reached for the towel. With gentle swipes, I wiped his eyes and mouth. I ran the wet washcloth over his hair and then a dry one. He allowed me to wrap my arms around his shoulders and tilt him forward. I held him up and propped a couple of pillows behind him. The effort took a lot from him, but he inhaled as deeply as he could and smiled.

Once we'd completed his grooming, he held tightly to my hand. "Thank you," he whispered and then nodded.

As I walked back to the door, the incessant ringing of the doorbell charged through the house. I couldn't help but smile. Vivian.

Once again, I opened the door to meet the glare of my incensed mother.

"How dare you keep me waiting like this." Her voice pierced. How dare I? Warmth spread through my scalp.

I pointed to kitchen. "In there. Now."

She brushed past me and headed toward the table.

"Sit." I pointed to the chair at the far end. My anger brewed dangerously close to erupting. "We need to talk before you see him. Or you don't see him." I crossed my arms. "Understand?"

Her brows furrowed, and then she exhaled while she reluctantly descended into the chrome and vinyl chair.

I sat opposite her. "Mama, Carlton is very ill. He wants to see you, but you cannot upset him. If at any time in your visit, I feel you are upsetting him, I will ask you to leave. He is my patient, and I am responsible for his well-being right now. Agreed?"

She nodded and slumped into the back of the chair. She seemed to deflate like a blown-up doll that lost its air. "Cheryl, I just want answers." Tears misted her eyes.

I caressed her hand. "I know you do. Give Carlton, time. I'm sure he'll give them to you." I stood and linked her fingers through mine. She followed me to his bedroom.

Mama stood at the doorway a moment before allowing me to guide her toward Carlton's bed. Once we were next to him, his beautiful eyes glistened as he met Mama's. He lifted his hand to her. "Vivian."

I stepped back and placed her hand in his. "Mama, meet Carlton."

"It's n-n-nice to meet you." Her voice wavered. I edged the side chair behind her and encouraged her to sit. Then I walked around to the other side of his bed and sat in the lounge chair. She stared at him in silence.

He shifted in the bed and sat a bit higher. Carlton removed his hand from Vivian's grip and tenderly traced the side of her face. His Adam's apple bobbed as he swallowed. "You have...my eyes."

She glanced toward me and then back at Carlton. "I do."

He smiled. "I dreamed of...this day." He turned to me, winked, and tilted his head toward Mama. "She's beauti...ful. My daughter."

I locked gazes with Mama. "She is, Carlton. She is beautiful."

Mama returned my gaze with tear-filled eyes. "Why?"

He reached once again for Mama's hand and then closed his eyes and opened them again. His head lolled to the right, and I saw the effect of the emotional turbulence from this morning. He parted his lips but no words bellowed forth. I knew how much the effort cost him. He wanted to answer Mama, but fatigue conquered.

"Carlton, secrets have been kept for a long time. Do you mind if I share them and your medical history with Mama?"

"Share." He lifted his left hand, reached for mine, closed his eyes again, and then lowered his head onto the pillow behind him. I removed one of the pillows and lowered the head of his bed. Once I arranged his bedding and ensured he was comfortable, Mama eased her hand out of his, stood, and headed toward the door. I followed with the ribbon-tied bundles of Mawmaw's letters.

Mama sat in the same kitchen chair as earlier, staring out the window. Her rosy cheeks were now a lighter shade of pink. I sat next to her again and handed her the bundles. "You've read the letters from Carlton to Mawmaw. These are Mawmaw's letters to Carlton."

With shaking hands, she reached for the letters. "He's my father, Cheryl. I can see so clearly that he is."

"I think he is. You have the same features and, of course, the eyes." I placed both my hands on hers and looked into her eyes. "Mama, there's something you should know. He takes the same type of medication you do."

As the words sank in and realization dawned, her eyes softened, and she pressed her lips together. I reached across the table and hugged her neck. "I'll come over tonight after my shift. I'll tell you what I know. But it won't be much more than you'll know after you read the letters. Will you be at the hospital?"

She continued to stare out the window. "All this time, Mama kept him from me. Why would she do that?"

"Read the letters. Some of the answers are there."

She simply nodded and stood as though she were a marionette controlled by invisible strings.

"Will you be all right to drive or should I call Anthony?"

As though a hand pulled her strings, she straightened to her tallest, pushed her shoulders back, and smiled. "Cheryl, I'll be fine. Maybe for the first time in my life. I'll be just fine." She reached for my hand. "I want to come back and visit him. Would you ask him if that's OK?"

"Sure, Mama. I'll ask, but I'm pretty sure he'll be fine with you visiting. I believe he would like that very much."

She strolled to the door and turned back toward me. "Cheryl, thank you for taking such good care of my father." She smiled. "Your grandfather."

I nodded and pushed back the tide of emotion threatening to take over.

Her car kicked up dust plumes as she drove down the long driveway.

Oh Mama, will you still feel the same once you read that last letter?

Vingt-Sept

Darcy arrived early for her shift. We spent a few minutes exchanging information. I shared the events of the day with her and told her the truth about my relationship with Carlton. She'd been as surprised as all of us, but responded differently than I expected. As I drove home, her words lolled through my brain.

"Cheryl, there is a reason for everything. God has a way of putting us just where we need to be." With that, she'd given me a hug and ushered me out the door.

Carlton had not awakened after Mama left, and I didn't want to wake him to tell him good night.

Had God placed me in Carlton's care so the truth could be revealed? The chain of events that happened with me in the middle brought us to where we were today. It began with Jarrod and coming back home. When I thought of all that'd been revealed and how I understood so much more than when I arrived, I had to thank God.

I thought of Beau and remembered Annie passed away yesterday. My heavy heart sagged when I thought of his loss. And Steven's.

Chuck's church loomed ahead, and I took the exit. Hopefully, he'd be in his office. I sat in the parking lot staring at the large cross affixed to the front of the building. That cross symbolized so much. It represented the ultimate sacrifice and redemption.

Lord, thank You for what You've shown me. Guide me through all that's happened. Let me be strong for Carlton, for Mama, and for Mawmaw.

The silence in the car allowed me to focus on thoughts of Christian love and forgiveness. I felt, for the first time, that I had let go of the resentment and anger toward Mama and toward Carlton. Would I have been as charitable had he not had his illness? Had Mama not had hers? Guess that didn't matter. What mattered was the freedom from the burden I'd carried for so many years. When I remembered the brief light that sparkled in Carlton's eyes when he saw Mama, I suspected he'd been released from the prison he'd condemned himself to all those years.

I leaned back onto the headrest and closed my eyes. The air conditioner blew cold air on my face. *Lord, please don't take Mawmaw or Carlton until they've had an opportunity to forgive each other.* A calming serenity replaced the jittery nervousness I harbored since Mama knocked on Carlton's door.

I drove to the hospital enveloped in peace. One that I couldn't understand until I remembered the verse Beau had told me about. The hospital parking lot sported fewer cars tonight than last night, which meant a closer parking space.

When I entered the intensive care waiting room, Mama and Aunt Melanie sat next to one another in the far corner of the room.

Aunt Melanie knitted the turquoise afghan she'd been working on, and Mama thumbed through a magazine. There was little resemblance between them. They shared the shape of Mawmaw's nose, but that was it. The more I looked at Mama as Carlton's daughter, the more I saw the similarities they shared.

They both looked up as I approached.

"How is she? Any change?" I slid into an opposite chair.

Mama rested the magazine on her lap. "She woke up this afternoon and went right back to sleep."

I glanced at the clock on the wall near the nurse's station. A few more minutes before visiting hours. A leather satchel rested at Mama's feet. The ribbon previously tied around the bundle of letters stuck out the top.

I didn't know if Mama had shared this afternoon's events with Aunt Melanie, so I didn't say anything. Mama's stoic posture and graceful stance seemed dreadfully off kilter. Last time we were here she was a mess. Today her demeanor exuded strength and poise.

I didn't understand the changes. Yet, maybe I did. This time she'd been consistent with taking her medication and her new faith sustained her.

"Cheryl, would you like to see Mawmaw first this evening?" Aunt Melanie asked.

"No. You and Mama go, I'll see her after."

Mama turned toward me and smiled. "Honey, you and Aunt Melanie can visit with her. I'll wait for Anthony. He should be here in a bit, and we'll visit her together."

"Sure, Mama." I sat next to her. "Would you like to go out for coffee after visiting hours?"

Her lips spread into a smile that reached her beautiful eyes. "Yes, I would like that. We have some things to discuss. Don't we?"

"Only if you want to."

"I do. I need to."

"Very well." I rose and extended my hand to my sweet Aunt Melanie. "Shall we?"

She placed her hand in mine, and we walked together toward Mawmaw's room. "Cheryl, I'm a little concerned about your Mama. She seems a little too calm. Is she all right?"

"I think so. I'm hoping to talk to her when we go out for coffee. Maybe, thanks to you, her newfound faith is responsible for her behavior."

"I bet you're right. She has been reading her Bible a lot."

We reached the door to Mawmaw's room.

Aunt Melanie glanced toward me and inhaled deeply. "Here we go. It's so hard to see her like this."

I squeezed her hand gently. "I know. And worse, she would hate for us to see her this way." *Lord, have mercy.*

We walked through the glass door and passed the curtain surrounding the foot of her bed.

To my surprise, Mawmaw lay in bed with eyes wide open. She smiled when we came into her view. A lopsided grin. Joy bubbled inside me. *Thank You, Lord.*

"Mama, you're awake. How are you?" Aunt Melanie released my hand and reached for Mawmaw's.

An incoherent guttural reply gushed from her lips. Her gentle eyes, marred with frustration, focused on Aunt Melanie as though begging to be understood. I placed my hand on the foot of the bed to steady myself. Watching her struggle so hard to speak felt like claws ripping my heart to shreds. That she would lose her ability to speak seemed so unfair. Mawmaw's words had always blessed.

Aunt Melanie brought Mawmaw's hand to her lips and showered tender kisses on her knuckles. "It's all right, Mama. I can see you're feeling better. Give it time. The words will come."

Mawmaw's gaze softened and the earlier fear drifted away. A settled calm was apparent in her tender eyes. She nodded and a small asymmetrical smile appeared, causing her eyes to twinkle. I swallowed the lump in my throat. Mawmaw was still there. Behind the paralysis and aphasia her spirit burst through. *Thank You, Lord.*

Her eyes met mine, and I languished in its bathing warmth.

Aunt Melanie stepped back and ushered me in the spot she'd occupied.

"Hello, Mawmaw. You had us all worried. I'm glad to see you're getting better. Hang in there. Aunt Melanie is right. Give it time, the words will come."

She nodded and her lids slowly lowered. I kissed her cheek causing her to awaken. "Mama and Anthony are waiting to see you, so I'll step out."

Aunt Melanie kissed her, too. "Sleep well, Mama. I'll be here in the morning for the next visiting hours."

Mawmaw's garbled reply drifted toward us as we left the room. The muscles in my shoulder and neck tightened. I turned and blew her a kiss. Much to my surprise she mimicked the action. A good sign. I smiled and waved good-bye.

~*~

As I drove to the coffee shop to meet with Mama, I stopped at the local florist.

"Cheryl, it's good to see you. I heard you were back in town." Angie Boudreaux stood behind the counter. While we hadn't been best friends, we had been together for all twelve years of school.

"Hello, Angie. This your place?"

"Yeah, bought it from Mrs. Waguespack about four years ago. Can I help you?"

I smiled. "Yes, I'd like to send something for Annie Battice."

Angie nodded and wrote on the order pad on the counter. Once we'd settled on what type of spray and price, I paid the total and signed the card. In a strong hand, I simply wrote: Praying, Cheryl.

Angie looked up at me. "Ya know, Cheryl, I thought for sure you and Beau would've gotten married."

"Yeah, so did everyone." *Including me.* I thanked her and headed for the door.

I dialed Beau's number, expecting to leave a message just to give him my condolences.

"Hello. This is Beau."

"Uh...uh...Beau?" His voice made me pause. I stopped on the sidewalk outside the florist. "It's Cheryl. I just wanted to say how sorry I am about Annie. How's Steven holding up?"

"He's upset, I know, but trying so hard to be brave and not show it. Continue to pray for us. We feel all the prayers and love."

"I will." I got the details on the funeral time and told him I'd see him there. "Hang in there, Beau. I know this is hard."

"We've expected this for a long time, but the reality still comes crashing in. I heard about your grandma. I'm so sorry. How is she doing?" Just like Beau to think of my grandmother in the midst of his grief.

"She's awake and trying to communicate. Her speech has been affected."

"Well, if I know Clarice, she'll figure out a way to overcome, or for sure, compensate."

I smiled. "Yeah, I'm sure she will. Take care of yourself and Steven."

"You bet."

~*~

Mama sat across the tiny bistro table sipping on an espresso as I slid into the opposite chair. I clasped the latté she'd ordered me.

"How was Mawmaw when you saw her?"

"She was awake and trying to speak." Mama's clipped tone lacked her usual emotion.

I paused. Should I be bold enough to ask her what was going on? But how would we ever get past our family's issue if we didn't change how we approached things?

"Mama." I reached across the table and brushed my fingertips along the top of her hand. "What's going on?"

She met my gaze. "What do you mean?"

"You haven't been your usual self, and I'm just curious."

She sighed. "First, my new medication is working really well. And second..." She flipped her hand over and grasped my fingers and squeezed. "...I'm finding peace in my faith. Trusting God is giving me strength to continue taking the meds and to rest in His hands through this craziness. Also, meeting Carlton seemed to free something inside of me. It was so nice to just be...accepted. He looked at me as just his daughter and was proud of me."

When I looked at her, I saw newfound

confidence—in her erect posture, in her direct gaze, and in her words. A long bound part of my heart released, and a love I have never known for her burst forth. I gently squeezed her hand to encourage her.

"All my life, Mama treated me like a porcelain doll that would break at the slightest bump. I always felt when she looked at me, she didn't really see me." She pointed her index finger to her chest. "Now I know why. I'm sure I served as a constant reminder of Carlton. She couldn't accept me as just me. Carlton, did that today, and it felt good."

"How do you feel about her keeping this from you?"

"I'm upset with her, but for now, I can't vent that anger. She needs my support, not my condemnation. I refuse to let my feelings get in the way of her progress. When the time is right, I'll talk with her about this."

"Mama, you do understand why I didn't say anything about Carlton, right?"

"I understand your patient confidentiality, but I'm also a little upset you didn't tell me."

"I know. When you called me over is when I found out for sure. I've been reading those letters to him, but never knew Lady S was Mawmaw. Speaking of letters, have you read them yet?"

"Some of them. I'll read the remainder later tonight."

A sliver of fear pierced. Would Mama feel the same after she read the last letter?

"Mama, there is something I'm concerned about. I'm afraid that Carlton will pass away before he and Mawmaw can reconcile and she can forgive him. He needs her forgiveness so he can forgive himself. No one knew he was ill."

Mama's gaze blanketed me with warmth and tender understanding. She patted my hand. "Wow, that's a tall order. You know there would have been a time not too long ago when I would have gone marching into her room demanding answers. Even gone so far as to drag her over to Carlton's. But this, I'm afraid, is something we can't orchestrate. Death is in God's hands. I'm starting to accept that all we can do is pray on this one and be there for them as best we can."

This lady who sat across from me was a new Vivian. One I liked. A lot. Loved, even.

It was the Mama I craved all my life. One who gave uncritical advice, was calm and peaceful, and who offered to walk the journey beside me. This was the Mama I dreamed about and once when I was a little girl, had asked God to send me. Gratitude, strong and bold, washed over me. For the first time, I felt that our roles were right. I didn't feel the need to reassure and comfort her. She had comforted me.

I reached across the table and hugged her, spilling my latté in the process. Laughter erupted between us. "Hey, laughter laced with tears, that's my trademark." She wiped her fingertips gingerly across my cheek then mopped up the spilled coffee. Some things were the same, and I found great comfort in that. They were the things we loved.

The new things would make us even better. In that, I found greater comfort.

Vingt-Huit

A week flew by. I'd arrange for Anthony to meet his grandfather. He and Carlton had much in common and told fishing stories. Well, Anthony told most of the stories, and Carlton nodded and laughed.

Mama spent as much time with Carlton as possible.

I spent as much time at the hospital with Mawmaw as I could. My time was certainly not my own. Poor Mr. Bojangles began to think I'd abandoned him. I hired a student to care for him in the afternoons and take him out for his daily walks. At least he was getting exercise. I wished I could say the same for me. Aside from an occasional stroll down Carlton's driveway, I stayed sedentary.

Mawmaw made steady, but slow, progress. This stroke had been more severe than the last one. Her speech continued to be impaired, but with the help of physical, occupational, and speech therapy she improved and learned wonderful compensation techniques.

The Fourth of July *fais do do* had been a hit, according to Debra, a small part of me regretted missing it and honoring Mawmaw. I'm not sure the truth would have come to light had I not foraged in those trunks for a costume. Guess I could thank the *fais do do* for finding my grandfather.

A week of Mama's daily visits gave Carlton a

stronger will to live; he laughed more and the etchings on his face seemed to lose their depth. I walked into his room on Wednesday at noon to find Mama sitting at his bedside reading the letters to him.

"Hey, my lil...lady."

I tugged at his toe—our morning ritual. "Hey, yourself."

There it was, that special smile he dealt out more often these last few days than I'd seen in the whole time I'd cared for him. I leaned over and kissed Mama's cheek. "How goes it?"

"Quite well. We're reading the letters from Lady S," she said.

I glanced toward Carlton.

His smile faded just a bit, and if I hadn't been watching him closely, I'd have missed it.

"Feelin'...all right...today," he said.

"Really?"

He nodded but a shift in his gaze told me otherwise. His breathing came in short raspy gulps and seemed more erratic than normal.

He held Mama's hand and reached for mine. "My...girls."

The gesture warmed my heart, but a pang of guilt bridled the edges. What would Mawmaw think about our betrayal? For it wasn't anything but a betrayal. She had not wanted Carlton in her life, Mama's, or mine. And while she struggled in a rehab hospital a mere fifty miles away, here we were comforting the very person who had caused her a lifetime of pain. I battled the demon tossing me back and forth with what and how to feel about this unusual circumstance. *Lord, show me what You want me to see from this.*

With my left hand, I patted his bony, wrinkled

hand clenched to my right. "Carlton, let me review your chart and see what medication you may need. I'm glad you're enjoying your time with Mama."

"I am." He turned toward her. "She's...so...kind."

I glanced toward Mama. Her cheeks blossomed into a rosy shade of pink and her eyes twinkled. "I'm just glad I can be here with you." She tucked a loose corner of his blanket. I absorbed the scene and etched it in my mind. Mama in the role of caregiver again, but this time, she reveled in it. Flourished from it.

On my way to the kitchen, I placed my hand on her shoulder. "Can you help me in the kitchen for a second?"

"Sure." She arranged the letters on the nightstand and followed me down the hall. "What's wrong?" she whispered.

I refrained from answering until we were away from Carlton's hearing.

Once there, I turned toward her. "How long have you been here?"

"Since seven."

"So you haven't gone to see Mawmaw this morning?"

"No." She pursed her lips. "I can't see her right now. And besides I like getting to know *my* father."

I sighed. "You're having a hard time holding your anger, aren't you?"

She slumped into the red vinyl chair at the kitchen table. "Yes."

I sat next to her. "Mama, you have to decide how you're going to deal with this. But you will have to deal with it. Avoiding her is not the answer. Remember, you told me about this all being in God's hands."

She exhaled, long and low. "I know." Mama lowered her head and traced the curly-cue patterns on the Formica tabletop. "Cheryl, I feel cheated, and I'm having a hard time overcoming that I've missed out on knowing my father. I can't help but blame Mama for it."

"You haven't read the last letter have you?"

She lifted her gaze. "No. Why?"

"Because I think it will help you understand. Wait here." Standing next to her, I placed my hand on her shoulder and silently prayed. *Lord, work in her heart.*

I entered Carlton's room to find him asleep. Relieved that I didn't have to explain my actions, I retrieved the last of Mawmaw's letters and brought it to Mama. "Here. Read this now."

While she read the letter, I scanned Carlton's chart and noticed he hadn't received as much pain medication last night as he had on previous nights. Darcy had written a note that he'd denied pain and refused the medication.

I suspected he knew Mama was coming today and wanted to be coherent and awake for her.

Darcy had prepared the syringe, knowing he would need it. I slipped it into my pocket and turned toward Mama.

"He raped her?" Her incredulous tone carried throughout the stark kitchen.

I nodded. "Mama, remember his mental illness and the fact he'd just returned from the front lines." I lifted my finger. "Wait, here. I'll give him this medication, and I'll be right back."

Upon my return to the bedroom, I found Carlton awake wincing in pain as he tried to move in his bed. I helped him get comfortable and lowered the head of the bed. "I've got something for the pain."

"Where's...Viv?"

"She's in the kitchen and will have to leave soon."

"Will...she...come...back later?"

"She'll probably come back tomorrow. For now, you need to rest."

He nodded, and I slipped the medication into the IV line.

"How is he?" Mama asked when I returned to the kitchen.

"Tired and hurting. I gave him something for pain. He should be able to rest now. He asked if you were coming back to see him."

"Of course, I'm coming. But I do need to talk to Mama." She held the letter out in front of her and waved it gently up and down. "So many secrets. So much unnecessary pain. I wonder if my diagnosis would have taken so long had we known about this family history."

Her words struck me. I found it interesting Mama would think about all that happened to our family as a result of an undiagnosed illness.

I shrugged my shoulders. "It's hard to say, maybe. But who knows."

"Cheryl, I know how Carlton feels. I know the regret for doing something so horrible that the remorse eats you alive. And all the time you're doing it, you know it's wrong, but are powerless to stop yourself."

Had Mama's crawling into herself and allowing everyone around her to help her been her way of dealing with the remorse? Seemed strange to me. I never saw anything resembling regret from her. As my mind sifted through the drawers of memories I had locked many years ago, I remembered moments where

Mama tried to reconcile her actions. Small gestures where she tried to help me. All of which I had considered methods of manipulation.

While Mama understood how Carlton felt, I could sympathize with how Mawmaw felt. Regardless of why the pain is inflicted, it's hard to ignore the scars it wields.

My scars were finally softening but still remained, and I suspected I held on to them like a badge of honor. A bit of the stubbornness I recognized in Mama and Carlton. Maybe facing myself could be the worse demon of all to conquer.

Letting go of the entitlement of pity for having been wronged would be a good place to start. While I'd forgiven, I still had a long way to go. *Lord, help my unbelief.*

Mama stood and gathered her purse. "I'm going to see Mama. I think she's doing well enough that I can let her know we know the truth."

"Do you think that's a good idea? Can you do this without letting the anger erupt?"

She lifted the letter. "She didn't know about his illness. She just thought he was a bad person she needed to protect me from. Knowing that eases the pain and the anger."

"Would you like us to go with you?"

"Honey, I'd love for you and Anthony to be there, but it's not something you have to do. I can do this alone. I think Mawmaw would feel more comfortable if you and Anthony were there. How about y'all meet me at the rehab center after you get off work?"

"Sure. I'll call Anthony. He'll come."

With that, she nodded, pecked a kiss on my cheek, and was out the door.

Mama never ceased to astonish me. She could switch from being so independent to dependent in an instance. And my problem had been thinking she was one or the other.

I returned to check on Carlton whose loud rhythmic rasps told me he was sound asleep. As I watched him, I recognized the personality similarities between him and my mother. I'd been perfectly fine accepting those character flaws in Carlton, so why had I not been able to accept them in Mama?

~*~

Beau sat across from me at the diner, steam rising from the hot cup of coffee on the table before him. It had been almost five weeks since Annie's death. He and Steven had left town for a couple of weeks after the funeral. I'd agreed to meet him for a quick cup after work before I headed to the hospital to see Mawmaw.

"So how's your grandma?" He stirred the steaming liquid.

"She's getting better. They've transferred her to a rehab hospital and she's able to push her wheelchair. She is doing standing transfers on her good leg. Her speech improvement has been really slow. She can say a few words, but conversations are impossible. The good thing is, she can write. It's hard to read because it's with her left hand, but it's how we communicate."

"Well, at least she can write. That has to alleviate some of her frustration."

"Some. She can't write or figure out the words as fast as she wants to convey them. Mostly all she writes is, 'I want to go home.'" I smiled. "That's how I know Mawmaw is still in there."

He laughed. "Yep, that would be Clarice."

"How are you and Steven doing?"

"We're doing fine. Thank you for coming to the funeral. I know we didn't get a chance to talk much, but you being there meant a lot to Steven and me. The flowers were beautiful. I know Annie would have loved them. Roses were her favorite."

I smiled. "I know."

"We miss the visits to the nursing home. At least there, we could talk to her, brush her hair, touch her. Now there's nothing but a cold headstone. Regardless of how everyone else in my family pays homage to graves, I can't talk to a marble slab. Neither can Steven. When I asked if he wanted to go to the cemetery, he politely refused. Guess we would both rather remember her when she lived. Sorry, I know that was a long answer."

"No, don't apologize. I agree. I'd rather remember my loved ones by the kind of people they were and not the kind of coffin or tombstone they had." I thought of Elray and the time I'd spent at his graveside. I wished I'd had good things to remember him by. "That's how I'd want to be remembered."

He nodded and took a sip. "Did you ever solve your romantic couple mystery?"

I lowered my cup and debated on whether or not I should share our family's secret. At one time, I had trusted Beau with my life, but so much had changed. I hesitated.

He arched one brow. The left one. At one time, that move would send me into peals of laughter. Mostly, because I'd tried to mimic him and never could.

I took a deep breath and in a flash, decided I

would tell him. He would keep this secret if I asked him to and maybe he could offer some well-needed advice.

The family secret of a lifetime took all of ten minutes to share with Beau. Ten minutes. I marveled at the insignificance in time to relay a secret that had brought about all the hurt and deceit that encompassed a lifetime and had shaped the lives of those affected in irreversible ways. As I reflected on the time, a part of me wondered, had Mawmaw been honest years ago about her past would Mama's disease have been diagnosed sooner? Would my feelings about leaving Bijou Bayou been different and could the man sitting across from me be my husband?

"Wow." Beau leaned back onto the diner seat. "That's a pretty wild revelation. How did you find this out?"

I told him about the letters and all that had transpired.

"How can you be sure he's your Mama's daddy?"

"We're waiting on the results of the DNA testing. We should get those today. We're fairly certain he's my grandfather."

Beau shook his head. "That's so hard to believe. All this time..."

"Yeah, can you believe it? I guess the thing that blows me away more than anything, is I thought I really knew Mawmaw. Now I question if I really knew her at all. How could she have kept such an enormous secret all these years?" My coffee had cooled, and I let the lukewarm liquid flow down my throat.

Beau leaned back onto the red vinyl seat. "Yeah, that's pretty heavy duty. But think about it, Cheryl. Can you imagine the burden she carried with keeping that secret? She must have thought Carlton a real threat to her and Vivian. She had to believe she was protecting Viv and keeping the secret was the lesser burden than subjecting Viv to someone she thought dangerous. That had to be difficult for her. Especially in the fifties. Times were a lot different back then."

Bonnie, our waitress strolled by and filled our cups with fresh coffee. Steam trails once again drifted from our cups. Beau was right. Things were quite different then.

"I see what you mean about her thinking he was a threat. But it breaks my heart because they really loved each other so much. Those letters were so poignant and honest."

"Sometimes there are monsters that steal love. Carlton's illness did that."

Had Annie's accident been the monster that stole his love? As I stared into those milk-chocolate eyes, I knew that Beau and Annie were meant to be. He and I would have never had the kind of love he'd had with Annie. I needed to leave town to be the person I am now and that meant leaving Beau. I would have never appreciated him like I knew Annie did. Beau needed a wife who could do that. The revelation brought freedom. The last bit of freedom my heart needed.

"Maybe it's not too late for reconciliation," he said.

It took a moment to realize he meant between Mawmaw and Carlton. "Maybe. Mawmaw doesn't know that we know. Mama was going to tell her that first week, but Aunt Melanie talked her out of it. I'm glad she did. I'm not sure Mawmaw's recovery would be going as well. Speaking of Mawmaw" —I glanced at my watch—"I need to get to the hospital. Tonight Mama is going to tell her the truth. Oh, and for now, can you keep this between us?"

"Sure. No problem."

I left enough money on the table to cover our tab and skittered out before Beau had a chance to slip the bills back into my purse. When I glanced toward him from the door, he shook his index finger at me. His brilliant smile warmed my heart and spurred me on.

Vingt-Neuf

I walked into the lobby of the newly built rehabilitation facility near Lafayette. The ten acres in the country had been donated, and an endowment had paid for the state of the art building.

Mama and Anthony planned to meet me here at seven, and I was a few minutes early. On my way to Mawmaw's room, I spied her wheeling her chair down the hallway toward me, her right leg and arm doing all the work. The hospital had provided a one-arm drive chair, and it gave her some degree of freedom—not nearly enough for Mawmaw.

When we met, I bent over and kissed her cheek. "Hello. Have you seen Mama and Anthony?"

She shook her head.

"I'm sure they'll be here soon."

She lifted the small dry erase board tucked between the side of her chair and her thigh. She scribbled with a fuchsia colored pen on its white surface and then held it for me to see. *What's up?*

"We'll fill you in when they get here. Have you had dinner yet?"

She nodded. "Yeeesss."

Her verbal answer brought a snippet of joy. Something I needed. "Good. Let's go to the library. We can sit there and wait for them."

"OooK." She wheeled her chair around, and when I reached to push her, she shook her head. "Noo."

"Very well. You're right. You need to do this yourself."

I walked while she wheeled next to me toward the elegantly decorated library. In the middle of the room, a set of leather couches flanked a mahogany coffee table. I slid into one end of the couch on the right and Mawmaw parked her wheelchair next to me.

After a few minutes, Mama's singsong voice flittered down the hallway as she addressed Mrs. Nelson, another resident who'd suffered a stroke at the same time as Mawmaw.

I glanced at Mawmaw. She lifted her eyes in a rolling motion and, for a moment, reminded me of myself as a teenager when I'd run to complain to her about some unfair punishment Mama had inflicted upon me. A smile settled on my lips and in my heart. She still had her sense of humor.

Mama and Anthony walked in. Mama caressed Mawmaw's shoulder and pecked a kiss on her cheek. "Mama, how are you?"

Mawmaw nodded.

Mama kissed me, too.

Anthony knelt in front of the wheelchair and wrapped his arms around Mawmaw's petite shoulders. "Hello, Honey Bunches, what's new? You been shakin' up this place?"

Mawmaw's laughter filled the room. Anthony could work magic. From the time he was a kid, he could elicit a deep belly laugh from her. She kissed his cheek and then ran her fingers through his disheveled hair.

Anthony managed to pull off a just-out-of-bed look. Surprisingly, he wore it well. He leaned over and kissed the top of my head. "Hey, *Te.*"

I squeezed his hand. "Hey, bro. How's Angelle?"

"Very well. She's coming to town this weekend. Maybe we can get together for dinner."

"I'd like that."

Mama sat on the opposite couch at the end closest to Mawmaw.

Anthony sat at her side.

Mama took a deep breath and began. "Mama, there's something that we've discovered that we need to discuss with you."

Mawmaw nodded. Her lips pouted and brows attempted to meet, but with her affected facial muscles only one brow moved inward while the other remained still.

Mama reached into her purse and retrieved the letters she'd found in Mawmaw's trunk. "We found these letters."

Mawmaw eyes widened. One brow shot up while the other remained in place giving her face an asymmetrical cartoonish look. As realization settled, she hung her head for a moment. When she looked back at Mama, a proud determination filled her eyes. She reached for her board. She wiped away her previous message with the sleeve of her blouse and wrote frantically. *I did what I had to.*

Mama nodded. "We know you did. Mama. I'm not faulting you for that. I've talked with Carlton."

Again, Mawmaw's eyes widened, and she exhaled loudly. "Whaa?" She attempted to speak but frustration overtook. She wiped the board and wrote: *He's here?*

"Yes. Once I read these letters." She lifted the letters from her lap. "I had to know if Carlton was my father."

Mawmaw scrambled to erase her message and add a new one. *Harold was your father.*

"Mama, Papa was a good father to me, and I'm not denying that. We did DNA testing, and I got the results this afternoon. Carlton is my biological father, and I have a right to know him."

Mawmaw's eyes misted. When she tried to speak, guttural incoherent sounds escaped her lips. I slid off the couch and sat on the floor next to her chair. I reached for her limp hand and pressed it against my cheek.

Mama nodded in my direction.

My cue. "Mawmaw, Carlton has a mental illness—the same as Mama. The stress from the war brought out the worst in him, and you suffered his loss of control. There's not been a day that's gone by he hasn't regretted what happened."

Mawmaw looked down at me, and when she did, tears spilled from her eyes onto her cheeks. "I loved..." She searched for her next word. "...him."

"I know you loved him. I read the letters. He loved you, too. Very much. He still does."

She closed her eyes and more tears trickled out the corners, running along the valley of wrinkles.

Now came the part I dreaded. I inhaled deeply. "Mawmaw, Carlton is dying. And he can't forgive himself for what happened. It would mean a lot to him if you would visit him." I paused. Held my breath and watched her face.

She opened her eyes and stared directly at me. Her red-rimmed eyes, now devoid of tears, took on a sharpness that seared right through me.

I let out the breath I'd been holding and inhaled again to prepare for her response.

"Nooo." She retrieved her weak hand with her strong one and slipped it out of my grasp and then wheeled herself backward out of the library. She stared at Mama. "No, no, no, no." She repeated the word over and over as she turned into the hallway. Those emotion-filled words echoed through the halls as she wheeled toward her room.

Mama stood, but Anthony reached for her hand. "Let her be. We've just dropped a bomb on her. She needs time to process this. Remember, her brain has been damaged. It doesn't work like it did before. Give her time."

A blade of guilt slashed, causing my stomach to sting as though it had been sliced open with a scalpel. While I expected her to be reluctant, I didn't expect the adamant refusal. Remorse washed through me. What had we done to her?

After a moment, Anthony stood next to me and extended his hand. I reached for it and allowed him to help me up.

I glanced toward Mama and met her caring gaze. "She'll change her mind, Cheryl. She will." Mama's confidence surprised me. While I admired her positive attitude, I couldn't agree with her.

"I'm afraid if she doesn't change her mind soon, it will be too late."

Mama placed her arm around my shoulder. "I know, honey. There's nothing I'd like to do more than drag her to him, but it's not the right thing to do. We let her know. Now it's up to her."

Lord, guide her.

I struggled with an overwhelming need to intervene again.

Lord, guide me.

"I'll check on her and meet you in the parking lot," Anthony said.

"Shouldn't we at least tell her good night?" Mama asked.

"I think it would be best if we let this rest for tonight. I'll tell her you'll see her tomorrow."

Mama sighed. "I'll see you at the car."

As Mama and I walked out into the hot August night, a sonata from cicadas serenaded and sparks of light from fireflies twinkled in the empty field next to the parking lot.

"Cheryl." Mama laced her arm through mine. "I'm glad you came back to live here. I've missed you."

Her words sliced through the old scars that blocked out warmth and kept my heart rigid. My heart was free to move and flow in caring directions I'd resisted before. "Mama, I'm glad I moved back, too. It's been nice getting to know you." It really had.

She squeezed my arm. "I believe Mawmaw will come around. I'm praying for both she and Carlton to have the blessing of forgiveness from each other."

"The blessing of forgiveness. That's a good way to say it." And as I headed to my car, I realized Mama and I had given each other the blessing of forgiveness. Peace cradled me like gentle hands. More than ever, I wanted the same peace for Carlton and Mawmaw. I lifted my eyes to the starry night. *Lord, bring them together. Let her forgive him. Let him forgive himself.*

~*~

"G'mornin'." Carlton sat in the recliner next to his bed and greeted me as I walked into his room.

"Well, good morning to you, too. Look at you

sitting up. Darcy tells me you had a decent night last night."

He nodded. "Did."

I sat on the side of his bed next to the recliner and patted his hand. "Glad to hear it. You needed a good night."

"Yep. No bad dreams."

"Good. Mama sends her love and says she'll come by this afternoon to see you."

His lips spread and his dreary eyes sparkled for an instance. "I like that."

"I knew you would."

He rubbed my hand with his other hand. "I like you."

I smiled with my lips. I smiled with my soul. "I like you, too."

The desire to discuss Mawmaw burned like acid in my throat. I couldn't tell him she refused to see him, but the need to reassure him he was forgiven burned just as strong. *Lord, if I should tell him, command my words.*

"Carlton, did you know I was Clarice's granddaughter?"

"Nope. But..." He took several deep breaths. "...you reminded...me of her."

"Is that why you let me read the letters?"

He nodded. "I had her again...when you did."

So that had been his motivation. It was as though she were reading those letters to him. A sigh from deep within escaped, capturing Carlton's attention. He rubbed the top of my hand with his thumb. "You OK?"

"Yes." I thought of Beau's description of a love-stealing monster, and my heart filled with sorrow. So much loss and a flourishing love that never had a chance to blossom into what it could have been. The desire to discuss Mawmaw with Carlton dissolved with each stroke of his thumb on my hand. Gratitude filled my heart and tears stung my eyes. I had, at least, been a comfort to him for those few moments.

Why had things turned out the way they did?

My thoughts drifted back to the grandfather I knew all my life. He had been a grounding force in our family. Mawmaw had been his world, and he had looked out for Mama as though she had been his daughter. Maybe, we needed to be part of his life as much as he had needed to be part of ours. Instead of asking why things had not gone a different way, I began to see things had gone the way they had for many reasons. Some of which I would never know, but for some, I couldn't contain the mushrooming gratitude building in my heart.

Mawmaw had felt safe. Pawpaw had showered us with unconditional love. We had been blessed despite all the bad we'd experienced.

I knew being here today was no accident. Carlton and I were meant to cross paths. Plain and simple. But it had to be now. Not before, when we weren't ready to understand or accept the truth. I'd been given the awesome privilege of being a friend to Beau and Steven when they needed one most. I'd been blessed. *Thank You, Lord. Thank You, for Your perfect timing.*

During my reflections, the gentle stroking of Carlton's thumb ceased. He had fallen asleep. I tilted the chair back, tucked his blanket around his shoulders and knees, and planted a tender kiss on his forehead. "Rest, Grandpa. Rest."

After lunch I helped Carlton return to bed. His fatigue returned, and his breathing grew more difficult than in the morning. When Mama arrived, he had been napping for about an hour.

"How is he?" she asked as she entered the kitchen bearing bags of groceries.

"He's struggling."

Her gaze darted toward me. Fear flashed and lit the blue in her eyes. "Is it...?

"The doctors say he may have a month at the most. But they also said the same thing last month. So I don't know. And really, only God knows."

"Cheryl, would it be all right for me to see him?"

"Oh sure. He's had a good nap this morning. I'm sure he would love a visit from you."

"There's something else." Mama lowered her lashes and avoided eye contact. "Would it be OK if I sat with him this afternoon, that is, if it's OK with Carlton, while you visit Mawmaw? She's asking for you."

"Do you think she's ready to change her mind?"

Mama shrugged her shoulders. "I don't know. She wouldn't talk to me about it. Clammed up tighter than Norene Nesbitt's spandex shorts."

I shook my head and laughed as I envisioned Norene Nesbitt, Mama's friend from high school and her neon green spandex shorts. Some things, no matter how absurd, were a comfort. "I'll check with Carlton."

~*~

I tapped on the doorframe to Mawmaw's room. Her single bed was pushed against the far wall under her window. I gazed around the sparse room. Despite Mama's insistence, Mawmaw had refused her attempts at decorating the room to make it homey. She didn't plan to stay here long.

I walked across the room to where she sat in her wheelchair next to the bed reading the letters from Carlton. "Hello, Mawmaw." I bent down and kissed her cheek and then sat on her bed. "How are you?"

She nodded. "OK."

"I see you're reading the letters Carlton sent you."

She nodded again and looked up to meet my gaze. Her shining eyes told me this trip down memory lane was a painful one. She slid the dry erase board onto her lap and scribbled, *He was so kind before the war*. She wiped the words away after I'd read them and then added more. *I miss that Carlton.*

Trente

"I'm sure you do, Mawmaw." I gingerly touched her knee. "I believe I have met *that* Carlton."

The intensity of her glare pierced me. "How?"

I told her how he had asked me to read the letters to him because I reminded him of her. I shared how emotional he had become while the letters were read and that he'd told me how much he had loved his Lady S.

"Lady...S." She smiled the crooked smile of a stroke victim, but on her it was endearing. Intriguing. The name seemed to put her in a different place and time very similar to how Carlton became when I'd read her letters to him.

"Yes. He still thinks of you as his Lady S. Care to share what that means?"

She wiped the board with her sleeve and then wrote *He called me his Lady Sheri.* She wiped the board. *He meant the French Chéri.* She wiped again. *I didn't have the heart to tell him it started with a C not S.* She pouted and looked years younger.

I smiled. "Mawmaw, he's never forgiven himself. Have you thought anymore about coming to see him?"

She wiped her board clean and held her fuchsia pen above the surface. She paused as though she had a change of heart. After a long exhale she wrote, *I have. Can't in this wheelchair.*

I pressed my bottom lip between my teeth. How

could I stress the importance of her coming as soon as possible? Carlton may not have the time she needed.

"I understand, but you know it won't matter to Carlton. He would love to see you. You do remember, he has lung cancer and may not be around much longer?"

She nodded. And lifted the board with the same words as before.

"Sure. Should I tell him?"

"No."

"If he knew you were coming to see him, he'd be very excited."

"Noo tellin'."

I sighed. At least she'd agreed to see him. I'd expected another adamant refusal. *Thank You, Lord.* I'd learn to appreciate the small daily blessings.

"Very well. I won't say a word to Carlton. Can I tell Mama?"

She nodded and scribbled. *But she can't tell either.*

"I'll make that clear. How's your therapy coming?"

"Good."

I picked up the stack of letters and laid them on my lap. "You know, Mawmaw, what happened between you and Carlton was horrible. I hate that your love was torn apart by that awful act. As hard as it's been, I'm beginning to see how God takes the horrible and molds something good from it. He's molding me, us. I know all of this has been hard for you." I patted her hand.

Her eyes bored into mine and softened before she nodded. She scribbled on her board. *I loved him. Now love God more. I have you.*

My grateful heart swelled as I bent toward her and

kissed her cheek. "I love you so much."

She smiled—a lopsided smile that warmed the whole room.

I lifted the letters. "Would you like me to read these to you?"

Her eyes met mine and crinkled at the corners when she smiled again. "Yes."

So I helped her transfer to bed, elevated her feet, and propped her head up. Once she was comfortable, I sat in her wheelchair next to the head of her bed and spent the remainder of the afternoon reading the letters her first love wrote to her over sixty years ago.

She rested with her eyes closed and, every so often, a tear flowed out of the corners.

"Cheryl, wake up." Mama's soft voice whispered close to my ear.

I had fallen asleep in Mawmaw's wheelchair with Carlton's letters in my lap.

Mawmaw snored gently next to me. The late afternoon sun sinking low in the western sky cast evening shadows on the burgundy bedspread.

I shook my head to awaken. "What time is it?"

"It's almost 6:00 PM. Mama has to go to the dining room for supper in a few minutes. But first, did she talk to you about seeing Carlton?"

"She did. She'll see him when she's not in the wheelchair. And she doesn't want us to say anything to Carlton."

Mama lowered her head. "Tsk tsk. Carlton will be disappointed. Does she realize he may not have much time?"

"We discussed it, but she's adamant about no wheelchair and no telling him."

Mama exhaled long and hard. "Well, that's Mama

for you."

I chuckled. "Yep, seems her strong stubborn streak is still there."

"Yep, wonder what she'll have to say when she finds out I'm installing an elevator in my house. I'm sure she won't be too happy about that."

I had to agree.

"Whaaa?" Mawmaw awakened from her nap.

"It's time for supper."

Once transferred back into her wheelchair, she crooked her finger in a come-here motion. I leaned toward her. She pecked my cheek. "Love...you."

Tender strokes of love caressed my heart. "I love you, too. And don't worry. We'll work hard to get you walking so you can see Carlton again."

"Yes, Mama. He'll be so excited." Mama added.

My grandma flashed her crooked smile to Mama and me and wheeled herself down the hallway to the dining room. We followed and said our good-byes once we helped her get settled at the dining table.

"Wow, that was a change of heart. What did you tell her?"

"Not much. Only that the Carlton I knew was very much like the one she'd fallen in love with and that he still loved her."

"Amazing. Wouldn't it be awesome if they were re-united somehow before he died?"

I smiled and reached into my purse for my keys. "Yes, that would be awesome." *Lord, it's in Your hands.*

~*~

The following two weeks flew by and Carlton's condition slowly deteriorated. I feared the month prediction made by his doctors would actually be true this time. *Lord, keep him here until all is forgiven.* Daily, I prayed for him to be left on this earth until he and Mawmaw had shared the blessing of forgiveness. His tormented life had been punishment enough for a horrible mistake made so many years ago.

My heart grieved knowing he'd never had the peace he so needed to forgive himself. He'd missed out on living a life of peace.

While Carlton's condition dwindled, Mawmaw grew stronger. I exchanged Wednesday mornings with Beau, for time with Mawmaw. Beau and I spoke often, and we met for coffee whenever we could.

No guilt and no worries about what the town gossips thought.

Mrs. Martin had mentioned something to Mama about whether my relationship with Beau was appropriate. Mama had instantly put her in her place and did so with a quote from Ephesians. Go Mama.

I attended Mawmaw's therapy sessions and encouraged her to keep fighting. I also reminded her how good it would feel to walk into Carlton's bedroom and say hello.

"C'mon, Miz Clement, you can do this." Mawmaw's physical therapist, Lark LeRoux, provided excellent motivation and got Mawmaw to do so much. This morning they stood in the parallel bars. Mawmaw held on with one hand while Lark helped move her weakened leg forward.

"That's five steps! Great job!" Tears filled my eyes when Mawmaw lifted her hand in triumph.

"Yes!" Her eyes glistened, and her smile beamed from across the room.

"Miz Clement, that was awesome. I don't think

I've ever seen anyone walk like that on a first try. You are amazing." Lark high-fived her and helped wheel her out from between the bars. "You'll be using the walker in no time."

Lord, make it so. It meant a lot to Mawmaw to walk into Carlton's room, but what would happen to her determination if he passed away before she could accomplish that feat? Once again, I reminded myself God had this situation in His mighty hands and I had to trust. That seemed to be the hardest part. I realized, for the first time in my life, I did trust. I wasn't trying to push things in the direction I thought would produce the end result I wanted. Things would work out for the best and, while I continued to have moments of doubt, my weekly attendance at church and in Chuck's Bible study gave me the strength to turn my focus to God's presence instead of my fears.

Mawmaw propelled her wheelchair next to me. "How 'bout dat?"

I lifted my hand for her to high-five me, too. "That, my dear, was phenomenal."

Lark, in navy blue scrubs, released her long brown hair from its ponytail and came to stand beside me. "She is doing great. I love the progress I'm seeing. She's very motivated and that makes a huge difference."

"Yeah, she is a toughie. I'm proud of her."

"See you tomorrow, Miz Clement." Lark turned and walked toward her office at the corner of the gym.

"See ya." Mawmaw grinned her crooked little grin. "Coffee?"

I liked her new mischievous smile. "Sounds good, I'll follow you to the dining room."

~*~

Carlton refused to sit in the recliner. He slept most of the afternoon. I sat next to his bedside, knitting a teal shawl for Mawmaw with yarn Aunt Melanie had given me.

"Hey." His gravelly voice filled the quiet bedroom when he awakened.

"Hey, yourself. How ya feelin'?"

"Like...been hit...by a bus."

"That bad, huh?" I straightened his blanket.

"Yep."

"Lady S?" He asked about Mawmaw every day since I'd told him about her stroke.

"She walked in the parallel bars today. It was great."

He smiled. Actually showed his teeth. "Good."

"She's a fighter."

He nodded. "That is true." He grimaced.

"Do you need something for pain?"

Another nod.

I headed to the kitchen for his medicine. This was not good. I'd given him pain meds less than four hours ago. His pain grew in intensity and required increased doses of medication. Before long, he would be incoherent from the large dosage of drugs, and even if Mawmaw could make it here before he passed, he wouldn't even know she was here. I sighed.

After I administered the medication, his gaze met mine. His tired eyes lacked the usual sparkle. "Won't...be...long." He lifted his hand for mine.

I slid my hand into his. "Hang in there, Carlton. It's all in God's timing."

"I'm ready." He took deep breaths. "So tired."

"I know you are." Should I ask again? I sensed time running out and doubt crept in where I'd been confident only this morning. *Lord, give me the words.*

"Grandpa."

He smiled with weakened lips that quivered slightly from the effort.

"You know..." I inhaled deeply. "...it's time to forgive yourself. God has already forgiven you."

He stared at me with blank eyes. "It was...wrong."

"I know, but your sickness controlled you. It's the past. Let it go."

"Still wrong."

Would he feel the same if he knew Mawmaw had forgiven him? The unspoken words scorched my lips. All I had to tell him was Mawmaw had forgiven him. It would make such a big difference to him. But as much as the words begged to be spoken, they dissolved before I voiced them. She hadn't told me she'd forgiven him. And I couldn't lie to him. He deserved more. Even if my lie would ease his troubled soul, it would serve to be based on something less than what he needed. He needed truth. I needed truth. We all did.

He reached for my hand, squeezed, and allowed his eyes to slowly close. "You...good." With that, he leaned his head to the side and allowed the medication to take him to the only place he could find rest for now.

Trente Et Un

Labor Day weekend loomed, and Mama invited the whole family to her house. It seemed she had a special announcement. Usually I have a sense for what Mama was up to, but, on this, I hadn't a clue.

Carlton's condition continued to slowly deteriorate. Darcy and I worked hard to keep him alert. Managing his pain required higher doses of drugs, rendering him unaware of his surroundings. Yesterday, in a moment of acute awareness, he asked if I would suffocate him with his pillow. Before I could answer, he'd fallen back into his drug-induced sleep.

I prayed for his release from the pain. At that point, I wasn't sure if I wanted him freed of his physical or mental pain, unsure which one hurt him the most. A part of me regretted ever learning the truth about this man and for growing to love him as much as I did. Seeing him suffer like this jabbed shards of glass through my breaking heart. The bigger part of me thanked God for allowing me to know my grandfather in this special way. Once again, another example of God turning bad into good and using His perfect timing.

Hopefully, Mama's announcement would offer some respite of good news during this hard time. So much bad had happened in the past few months, maybe it was time for a bit of good news.

Sunday morning, we arrived at Mama's house to

decorations on the doorframe.

I sat next to Anthony and Angelle on Mama's couch watching Mama and Aunt Melanie standing next to the fireplace. My aunt had her arm around my Mama's waist.

Mawmaw, whom I'd picked up from the rehab facility, sat in her wheelchair next to the couch.

Mama's friends from her Bible study group filled every sitting surface in the room.

"Everyone." Aunt Melanie lifted her glass of sweet tea and turned toward Mama. "My beautiful sister has an announcement to make."

It seemed such a formal presentation. What were these two up to?

"Today." Mama cleared her throat. "Pastor Chuck from Grace Community Church has agreed to baptize me right here behind my house in Bijou Bayou."

Wow, I hadn't expected that one. At that moment Chuck and Debra appeared from the kitchen. Mama getting baptized? I guess I never thought that she'd never been. Mama's electric smile and twinkling gaze scanned the room. Her violet eyes burst with happiness. My heart smiled with her. I jumped from my seat and ran to her. "Mama, I'm happy for you." She embraced me, and I returned the hug.

"Thank you, Cheryl. It means the world to me you're here. I love you."

Our gazes met. I saw years of emotion she hadn't shared, and I hoped she saw the same in mine. I really loved her and wanted more than anything to be part of her life.

Anthony and Angelle rushed to her also. "Let's get this going!"

The family and Mama's friends from her Bible

study group made their way out the back door and down the stairway to the bank of the glistening Bijou Bayou. I pushed Mawmaw in her wheelchair toward the outside elevator Mama had installed.

Pushing Mawmaw through the thick St. Augustine grass required Anthony's help, but we made it to the small dock of the shallow cut in area where Mama and Chuck walked into the bayou.

Chuck spoke about how it was never too late to dedicate our lives to Christ and that no matter what we'd done in the past, it was just that—the past. He prayed for Mama's faith, that it would grow strong, and she would be a reflection of Jesus in all she encountered. He spoke of the importance of the rite of baptism and its symbol of faith in the crucified, buried, and risen Savior. After her immersion, Mama was officially baptized in Bijou Bayou.

Later that afternoon, after we'd all feasted in true South Louisiana tradition on as many possible Cajun dishes as the kitchen could hold, we sat around the living room visiting, also in true South Louisiana tradition.

I slipped away from the group and out the back door to retrieve the prop needed for my own exciting announcement. I walked back into the house and toward Mawmaw, who stayed in her spot. "We have another surprise for everyone."

Our guests turned as I produced a walker with front wheels and a right arm platform attached. When I placed it in front of Mawmaw's wheelchair, silence as thick as the evening fog filled the room.

"Mawmaw has something she wants to share with all of you."

Mawmaw stood from her chair. I helped slide her

weak arm under the Velcro straps of the arm platform and guided her fingers to form around the handle. She held tight with her left hand and pushed the walker across the carpet while taking slow methodical steps toward a shocked Mama and Aunt Melanie, who stood twenty feet away.

I pushed the wheelchair behind Mawmaw loving the joy in Mama's eyes as she waited with both hands steepled around her mouth.

Silence filled the room while Mawmaw trudged across the carpet to where her daughters stood. Once, Mama tried to run toward her, but Mawmaw backed her off with a guttural "No."

Aunt Melanie, with eyes glistening, linked her arm through Mama's to keep her still.

With each step closer to Mama and Aunt Melanie, Mawmaw stood taller and braved longer steps.

Anthony broke the silence with rhythmic claps. Angelle followed with Chuck and Debra. Before long everyone in the room joined in.

The applause fueled Mawmaw. She smiled and stood even taller. When she reached her daughters, she stopped and tested her balance. Once certain of her stance, she reached to Mama with her left hand and hugged her neck. "Congrats."

When she released Mama's neck, I rolled the chair behind her and released her right arm from the straps. "You can sit now, Mawmaw."

She reached for the chair with her left hand and descended onto the cushioned seat.

Mama and Aunt Melanie stared at Mawmaw through tears. They stood in awe not sure what to say or do.

Finally, Mama spoke. "This is awesome, Mama.

You are amazing, and I love you." Mama held onto Mawmaw's hand. Aunt Melanie hugged her neck. "You are such an inspiration to me. I love you."

"Love you." Mawmaw whispered to Melanie and Mama. She turned to Anthony and then to me. "All you."

As I glanced around the room, my throat cinched with emotion. Our family, dysfunctional and struggling, was together and supporting one another. I'd never heard Mawmaw tell Mama she loved her before.

The words resonated through the room and floated around us like God's embrace, infusing us with hope. Hope that the truths revealed would make us stronger and free us from the bonds keeping us from being all we could to each other. It offered hope that she would be around a while longer and our family would be whole. A family who knew each other's ugliness, but still stood firm in support.

Mawmaw pushed her chair back into her spot and looked directly into my eyes. "I'm ready to see Carlton."

Trente-Deux

Beau's lips lingered on the edge of his soft drink straw while he waited for my answer. We sat in the diner Wednesday afternoon and reflected on all that had happened since my return to Bijou Bayou. He had lost a wife.

I'd gained a grandfather and a newfound relationship with my mother.

The events changed both of us.

He lifted his eyebrows and met my gaze head on. "Well? Stayin' or leavin'?"

I hadn't given much thought to whether I would stay in Bijou Bayou once my job with Carlton was over. Something I didn't want to think about. Finally, I blurted out my first thought. "I think I'll stick around." The reasons I left all those years ago seemed pointless now. I enjoyed having family and trusted old friends around. "It's comforting to be here now. Something I never thought I'd feel and certainly not anything I'd ever say out loud."

I smiled when he shot me his all-knowing look. He laughed. "It's taken a long time for you, *Te*. But you're here now and that's what's important."

"I suppose so." A quick glance at my watch confirmed what I'd suspected. Time to go. I promised I'd meet Mama, Anthony, and Aunt Melanie for dinner at Charlie's. "I gotta run. See you next week?"

He lifted his drink in a mock toast. "I'll be here."

I flipped a few dollars on the table to cover my sweet tea and apple pie.

"Whoa, no way. This is my treat." He stuffed the dollars into the side pocket of my purse as I tried to slip by him.

I abandoned any argument, knowing it was futile. We met on Wednesdays after work because I'd started working Wednesday mornings since Carlton's condition had worsened. Our conversations offered new insights into each of our lives, and I loved getting to know Beau again.

While he hadn't changed a whole lot, he had changed immensely. Beau's gentle kindness continued to permeate his worldview and contributed to his very essence. He had matured into a leader and wise counselor. I loved his ideas and listened when he shared spiritual knowledge with me. Most of all, he kept his sense of humor and made me laugh until my sides ached.

I headed toward the door and on my way out, Mrs. Martin walked in. "Cheryl, honey, it's good to see you." She embraced me in a hug that I thought I would never break free from. No judgmental looks, she seemed genuinely happy to see me. She waved at Beau on her way to her table.

"My turn next time." I called to Beau from near the door.

"We'll see." His response followed me. I shook my head. That was my dear friend, Beau. A true southern gentleman.

A gentle breeze brushed across my face. It gave the promise of autumn and cooler temperatures. And maybe the promise of a happy future here in Podunk Bayou Dullsville. The thought brought a smile.

~*~

Carlton's steady whizzing greeted me as I entered his room.

Anthony sat in the recliner next to his bed holding his hand. He'd gotten here early. "Hey, Sis." He stood when I approached and pecked a kiss on my cheek.

Today would be the day Mawmaw would see him.

Mama chatted nonstop last night at dinner about the upcoming meeting.

I wasn't sure who in our family was more excited. But seeing Carlton's condition this morning tempered some of the joy.

Darcy stood at his bedside adjusting the drip on his IV.

"How was last night?" I placed my handbag and knitting bag on the floor next to the antique dresser.

She tilted her head toward the kitchen.

Anthony moved to the recliner and returned Carlton's hand into his own while Darcy and I walked to the kitchen.

"He's fading, Cheryl. His pain has increased, and he needs higher dosages of the medication to keep it barely under control. I can't see how he can take much more of this."

Steel prongs tightened around my heart. I hated his suffering. *Lord, be merciful.*

"Mama will bring Mawmaw today. Maybe that will help him." I tried to sound hopeful, but with the progression of his cancer, he probably wouldn't know she was in the room. Tears burned my eyes.

"Oh, Cheryl. I'm so sorry things have turned out the way they have. I wished they'd gotten together sooner." She placed her arms around my shoulders and hugged me.

"Me, too. Me, too," I said and leaned my head onto her shoulder. "Thanks, Darcy." I stepped away and helped her gather her belongings.

When she walked out the door, she said, "Call me if you need me today. I'm good on three to four hours of sleep."

I nodded but knew I wouldn't disturb her sleep.

Once Darcy left, an eerie quiet settled in the kitchen.

I headed back to Carlton's room. As I stood next to his bed and gazed upon his elderly, frail body, I saw less of the man who needed forgiveness and more of the soul who needed comfort. He'd been forgiven by his Creator and that was the most important thing. I learned from Chuck, he'd accepted Christ as his savior a few weeks back when he realized the end drew near. But while Carlton withered away, he still lived. No matter how close death loomed, Carlton wasn't a dying man, but God's creation who still lived and needed comfort.

The Lord showed me a different perspective and was telling me in a gentle firm voice. *Do your job, and let Me do Mine.*

My job wasn't to get Mawmaw to forgive him. It was to comfort this man as best as I could as he accepted the inevitable. Death drew near. But until his last breath, he lived.

The cinch around my heart loosened and the freedom to be his nurse, his granddaughter, and his friend rushed in like a raging wave to propel me forward. That's when my heart exploded with bountiful love, and that's when I saw him as my grandfather, this tiny man who battled so bravely a horrible, unseen monster that stole his life bit by bit.

I couldn't grieve the lost years. Only bask in gratitude for the gift of getting to know him. I wanted to treasure his remaining days and show him love and kindness. I wanted so much to show him something good from that evil act so long ago. And that something good from Carlton would live on. I knelt at his bedside.

Anthony followed and knelt with me, as well. He grasped my hand while holding onto Carlton with the other.

I cleared my throat. "Lord, You've forgiven him and that's all that matters. It's my selfish desire that he have Mawmaw's forgiveness before You take him. Lord, he's Yours. Give us the strength to go on without him."

"Amen." Anthony's emotion-filled response nearly broke my resolve and sent me sobbing uncontrollably.

Mama's voice beckoned from the kitchen. "Cheryl, we're here."

The squeak from the wheel of Mawmaw's walker followed Mama's voice. She'd come.

Anthony helped me stand. We stood next to Carlton's bed and waited for Mama and Mawmaw to enter.

"Come in. He's sleeping."

Aunt Melanie walked in, too. "I hope it's OK for me to be here."

I hugged her tightly. "Of course. I'm glad you are."

"How is he?" Mama and Aunt Mel slid off to the side to allow Mawmaw to enter the room.

I shook my head and lowered my eyes. My tongue refused to form the words. When I met Mama's gaze, her eyes glistened.

Anthony circled the bed and kissed Mawmaw's cheek. He walked next to her as her careful steps brought her closer to Carlton's bed and the chair I had placed next to his bed for her. The same chair where I had sat and read her letters to him — a lifetime ago. His Lady S had come to see him, and he didn't know it. I squelched the rush of emotion threatening to erupt. I couldn't fall apart now. Someone needed to be strong for them.

Anthony guided Mama to the recliner on the other side of Carlton's bed.

Mawmaw lowered herself into the leather armchair and stared at Carlton. Her stoic features remained void of emotion. Slowly, she leaned forward and placed her hand on top of his right hand. Her touch or the fading medication, I'm not sure which, awakened him. He groaned, but didn't open his eyes.

I leaned close to his left ear and whispered. "Carlton, it's Cheryl. Someone is here to see you. Your Lady S."

His lips moved but no sound emerged.

"She's on the other side of your bed."

He tilted his head toward the right.

The fingers on his right hand twitched, and he slid his hand over hers.

Mawmaw laughed in her guttural voice.

The corners of Carlton's lips tilted slightly. He'd heard her.

Suddenly, I felt as though we were invaders in this intimate moment of reunion. I straightened, glanced toward Mama, and then toward Anthony and Aunt

Mel. They must have been feeling the same because Anthony nodded toward the kitchen and Mama stood and reached for my hand. "I'll fix us a cup of tea."

"Sounds wonderful." I blinked back the sting in my eyes. A love smothered so long ago had been rekindled, if only for a brief moment. The amazing thing—no words had exchanged.

That was the power of love. I reveled in that. For Mawmaw. For Carlton. For all of us. It gave me hope for all of us lost souls struggling to survive in a world that would rather we stay lost. I was so blessed to see it was never too late to forgive and receive forgiveness.

Mama dabbed at her eyes while she stood at the sink filling the kettle. "Wow, I believe we just witnessed a miracle."

I smiled, my heart bursting with bittersweet joy. "Yes, I believe we did."

Thank You, Lord.

Epilogue

One Year Later at the Bijou Bayou Fais do do

"Cheryl, dance with me." Beau stood next to our table his hand outstretched. The sounds of the lively accordion, fiddle, washboard, steel guitar, and a bevy of other instruments belted through the hot humid Saturday afternoon. A Cajun tune blared from the stage, one Pawpaw would have called, *chancky, chanck* music.

I wasn't sure if my two-step skills were still intact, but I was willing to give it a try. It was nice to reflect on my history and know that I'd gotten so much from so many. A rich heritage, one that I grew more proud of with each passing day. I stood and placed my hand in Beau's. "I would love to."

We reached the dance floor, a portable platform, under the lighted limbs of several mighty live oaks. The trees framed the parish property where the *fais do do* was held each year. As I began to move around the floor steered by Beau's expert guidance, I couldn't help but smile. Life was good.

"What's so funny?" Beau met my gaze and smiled also.

"I was just thinking how nice it was out here in Podunck Bayou Dullsville."

He laughed. A tilt-your-head-back, from-the-belly laugh. And I joined him as he twirled me around the floor until the end of the song. The pink chiffon dress I wore bellowed out with each swirl. Mawmaw's pink chiffon dress. The idea from last year had been such a hit the committee decided to repeat it this year. The dress still had the subtle scent of her perfume and reminded me of a young Clarice in love with a young Carlton.

At the table, Mawmaw beamed in an amazing white dress made by the one and only Mrs. Mouton, Beau's great-grandmother. The dress she'd intended to marry Carlton in. This was the second time she'd worn it. The first was at his funeral. A week after they'd reunited, he'd died while holding the hand of his beloved Lady S. From the first day of their reunion, she'd never left his bedside.

Her walking improved with the help of her steady companion—her Quad cane. She was still the feisty independent grandmother I adored. Her speech had improved also, but she continued to communicate mostly with her board. Mama and Aunt Mel have gotten her to attend church on Sundays.

She regretted all the years of not being with Carlton. And the years of secrets that caused the family so much pain. She writes often about the day they were reunited. But she's quick to assure us that she lived a good life with Pawpaw and loved him very much. She says she can't wait to see them both in heaven.

Mama has been faithful to church and Bible study. The change in her has been remarkable. No violent mood swings. She's happy. That makes me happy. As I see the smile on her face and the twinkle in her eye, I know she's in a good place.

She danced with Dr. James Scarfield, the new dentist who moved to town from a small town in

Colorado. She'd met him last week at church. She proudly wore Mawmaw's lilac dress. So there we were Mawmaw, Mama, Aunt Melanie, and me. All dressed in one of Mawmaw's old dresses. Surprisingly, they fit with only a few alterations.

Anthony twirled Angelle around the dance floor. He had proposed at Christmas with a wedding scheduled in September when the weather would, hopefully, be a bit cooler. Anthony's brilliant smile reminded me of Mama's. His eyes lit up when he looked at his fiancé, and my heart swelled with happiness for him.

Aunt Melanie, dressed in the more subtle of Mawmaw's dresses, had started her own business. A bakery called Lagniappe. She had the whole town coming by for the star of the menu—her red velvet cake. I'm one of her best customers. What can I say?

"Miss Cheryl, would you take a picture of me and Christy?" Steven handed me his cellphone. He'd brought a girl to the party, much to Beau's chagrin. He didn't want to admit his boy was getting older. I snapped the photo and returned the phone. "It's a great picture. Send me a copy."

"I will. Thank you." His cool, athletic grin didn't fool me. I saw the mirth dancing in his eyes as he escorted Christy to the dance floor. It was fun to see the younger generation embracing the Cajun heritage. I knew that so much stood to be lost as the older generations died. But change was inevitable, and I looked around and saw my family and friends gathered around. All different people than what we'd been. And that's a good thing.

Beau sat next to me and handed me a red snoball. "Anthony said you've been dying for one of these."

Tante Lulu's anisette snoball. Life was good. I kissed Beau's cheek. "You are a life saver."

As I delved into the sweet crushed ice, I thought of Carlton and how much I missed him. My short time with him had given me such joy, and I'd learned so much about my family and myself. And about God. How He can use the most unlikely people to show Himself. And by yielding to God's will, we can do so much. Even forgive.

I'd been truly blessed by getting to know Carlton. A sweet gift.

Darcy and I have moved on to other assignments and share our compassion and care to new patients. She's become a true and trusted friend. So has Debra. The three of us meet often for coffee.

Somehow, Carlton had touched all of us in a way that made us better. Better as individuals and better as a family. And, as I look around and forge through this earthly life, I know that's all any of us could hope for.

Thank you for purchasing this Harbourlight title. For other inspirational stories, please visit our on-line bookstore at www.pelicanbookgroup.com.

For questions or more information, contact us at customer@pelicanbookgroup.com.

Harbourlight Books
The Beacon in Christian Fiction™
an imprint of Pelican Ventures Book Group
www.pelicanbookgroup.com

Connect with Us
www.facebook.com/Pelicanbookgroup
www.twitter.com/pelicanbookgrp

To receive news and specials, subscribe to our bulletin
http://pelink.us/bulletin

May God's glory shine through
this inspirational work of fiction.

AMDG

CPSIA information can be obtained
at www.ICGtesting.com
Printed in the USA
FSOW01n2127130215
5179FS